CROSS̶██
BETWE███

"Don't let fo███████████████ ̶ay of saving your br█████

The vein in his neck started to throb. The woman had a way of exasperating him to the boiling point, making him lose whatever tenuous hold he had on his emotions. Without thinking, he grabbed hold of her, startling them both.

"If you've come here to find out if I still want you, Hannah, then here's your answer." Drawing her to his chest, he kissed her passionately. All the hurt, longing, and resentment he'd experienced in the past five years was communicated in that one kiss. But there was something else too. Something Travis hadn't counted on. Feelings he thought dead and buried were still very much alive and fighting to reach the surface.

APPLAUSE FOR MILLIE CRISWELL AND "ADVENTURE THAT DOESN'T QUIT."*

"Nobody does a better Western romance with style and panache than Millie Criswell. As the bard would have said: 'All's well with a Criswell.'"
—**Harriet Klausner**, *Affaire de Coeur*

*Joan Johnston, author of *After the Kiss*, on *Dangerous*

*Please turn this page for praise for
Millie Criswell's previous outstanding romance . . .*

CROSSING THE FINE LINE
BETWEEN LOVE AND HATE . . .

"No one blends home-spun humor, multidimensional characters, and sensuous fantasy like Millie Criswell! Her pen is skillful and sure, proving she's one of the best in the Western romance genre!"

—Literary Times

"Millie Criswell proves once again what a master storyteller she is."

—Rendezvous

"Millie spins an absolutely delightful yarn."

—Janelle Taylor, author of Destiny Mine

. . . AND HER WONDERFUL PREVIOUS NOVEL
DANGEROUS

"4 1/2 stars! *Dangerous* is a delight. Ms. Criswell's charming characters work their way into your heart along with a story that propels you forward with wild adventure and smoldering sensuality."

—Romantic Times

"I don't think I've ever had so much fun reading a 'serious' romance. . . . I can't wait to see what she has in store for Travis and how the Bodine family comes out in the end."
—**Gayle Fine, *Under the Covers***

"Fantastic! 5 bells! An adventure you won't soon forget. . . . Ms. Criswell is just superb. . . . Don't miss this one!"
—***Bell, Book, & Candle***

"Superb characterizations and unique and intriguing plot kept this reviewer up until the wee hours to finish the book! Enjoy!"
—***Calico Trails***

"Uniquely Criswellian! As always, Millie Criswell delights, captivates, and totally entertains her readers."
—**Romance Communications**
(Web site review)

BOOKS BY MILLIE CRISWELL

Wild Heather

Sweet Laurel

Prim Rose

Desperate

Dangerous

Published by
WARNER BOOKS

ATTENTION: SCHOOLS AND CORPORATIONS
WARNER books are available at quantity discounts with bulk purchase for educational, business, or sales promotional use. For information, please write to: SPECIAL SALES DEPARTMENT, WARNER BOOKS, 1271 AVENUE OF THE AMERICAS, NEW YORK, N.Y. 10020.

DEFIANT

MILLIE CRISWELL

DEFIANT

WARNER BOOKS

A Time Warner Company

If you purchase this book without a cover you should be aware that this book may have been stolen property and reported as "unsold and destroyed" to the publisher. In such case neither the author nor the publisher has received any payment for this "stripped book."

WARNER BOOKS EDITION

Copyright © 1998 by Millie Criswell
All rights reserved.

Cover design by Diane Luger
Cover art by Ron Broda

Warner Books, Inc.
1271 Avenue of the Americas
New York, NY 10020

Visit our Web site at
http://warnerbooks.com

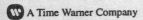 A Time Warner Company

Printed in the United States of America

First Printing: August, 1998

10 9 8 7 6 5 4 3 2 1

To Jen and Matt, my two legal eagles.
Congratulations on achieving your goals.
I'm so proud of you!

Chapter One

Misery, Texas, Spring 1880

HANNAH LOUISE BARKLEY HEAVED A DISCON-
tented sigh as she gazed down Misery's dusty main
street toward the small white Methodist church where
Easter Sunday service would be held the following day.
She'd been gone five years, and five years hadn't been
nearly long enough.

Everything looked the same. Across the street the
front window of Robinson's General Store still bore the
crack of Tommy Mullins's baseball, the dress displayed
in the milliner's shop looked at least two years out of
date, and Doc Leahy's office was still located upstairs
from the druggist. The wooden sidewalk she strolled
upon was as splintered, rotted, and neglected as it had
been the day she'd left.

Though she had missed her father and Maude in
the years she'd been gone, there wasn't much about the
town she'd pined for.

Misery would never change. And neither would the folks residing in it. They were small-minded, unsophisticated, nosy, and prone to gossip. In New York, no one knew your business unless you wanted them to. Here, everything a person said or did was held up to public scrutiny, pulled apart, dissected, and commented on, oftentimes in the morning edition of the *Sentinel*. She hadn't missed that quality of small-town life in the years she'd been gone.

And it was the main reason that she had decided to come home unannounced. She didn't intend to give the gossipmongers any fodder to chew on until it was absolutely necessary.

She had returned to Misery for one reason and one reason only: her father's illness. The judge wasn't a man given easily to complaints or self-pity, so when she'd received his letters relating how poorly he'd been feeling of late, she hadn't hesitated to come home and care for him.

He'd given so much of himself to her over the years—his vast legal knowledge and passion for the law, his unwavering support and love when she'd finally made her decision to leave. It was only fitting now that she gave something back.

She'd vowed once never to return. Well now she had, and she hoped that it wouldn't prove to be the second biggest mistake of her life. The first had been falling in love with Travis Bodine.

Judge Thaddeus James Barkley glared intently at his housekeeper, who was fussing over him like a mother hen with a newborn chick. Her efforts were proving downright irritating to a man used to doing for himself. Normally he would have made his displeasure known by shouting his disapproval, but he'd been feeling poorly today and couldn't muster up the energy to bark.

Doc Leahy couldn't find any medical reason why the judge had been so tired and irritable lately and had told Thaddeus in no uncertain terms that his malady was all in his head. The judge, who'd always thought that Doc was a few slices short of a loaf, had told him in very colorful and distinct terms what he'd thought of his diagnosis.

"Imagine Doc telling you that you was making things up, like you was one of them hypochondriacs or something," Maude Fogarty stated, clearly annoyed and snorting her disdain as she fluffed down bed pillows and adjusted the red crocheted shawl over his shoulders. "I think you should see someone more knowledgeable than that quack Doc Leahy. In my opinion, he's no better than a snake-oil salesman."

"Be that as it may, Mrs. Fogarty, he's the only doctor we have at the moment, and I don't intend to go traipsing off to Denver or San Francisco to consult a specialist. I'm pretty much stuck here in Misery until the new judge arrives." And that wouldn't be anytime soon, according to what he'd heard. Maude gave his shoulder a comforting pat, and his lips pinched tightly. He might very well be sick, but Thaddeus James Barkley wouldn't tolerate being treated like a child.

"You'll be feeling like your old self again when Hannah Louise arrives, Judge," the housekeeper assured him. "The sight of that gal's face is sure to put a smile on yours and perk your spirits right up."

"When did the letter say she'd be arriving?"

Retrieving the missive from her apron pocket, Maude smoothed it out, as she had the ten previous times she'd read it. Maude Fogarty's baby girl was coming home, and no one was more pleased about that fact than Maude.

"Says here she'll be arriving this coming Monday. I can hardly believe we'll be setting eyes on our Hannah Louise again after five long years. I sure have missed my darling girl." The older woman's eyes misted, and anyone who knew Maude well knew that her tears were a rare occurrence. The woman had a hide as tough as the bark on a cottonwood, a spine as stiff as the steely color of her hair, and a heart as tender as young asparagus.

"It'll be good to see her again," Thaddeus concurred, tugging the shawl more securely around him. He'd written to Hannah of his extreme tiredness, the twinges in his chest, but never dreamed that she'd drop everything and come running home to care for him. But he was pleased that she had, nonetheless.

It wasn't fair that her mother'd had the privilege of being with Hannah Louise all these years, while he and Maude had been deprived of her company. But then, Fiona Barkley wasn't what he considered a fair woman. Far from it, in fact. He and Fiona had been separated for nearly ten years for what she insisted were irreconcilable differences.

His wife was a woman who never gave an inch without taking a yard in return, who was never satisfied unless she had the last word in any conversation. Marriage to Fiona had been a mixture of heaven and hell, love and hate. But never boring.

Maude's lips puckered in distaste. "That gal would never have left for New York City if it hadn't been for that Bodine boy." She shook her head, and the graying knot at the nape of her neck threatened to spring loose. "Imagine him breaking our gal's heart like he did. I'll never forgive Travis Bodine for that."

The judge heaved a sigh at the painful memory, and the stubbornness of women in general. Hannah Louise was too much like her mother for her own good—stubborn, opinionated, and put on this earth to make a man suffer.

"Now, Maude, you know I chose not to take sides in the matter. What's done is done. I'm just happy our girl is coming home where she belongs." For how long, no one knew.

"Travis has a tough road ahead of him with the upcoming trial and all. I bear the boy no ill will for what's happened, and neither should you. Let bygones by bygones, I say."

Maude crossed her arms over her ample chest, not the least bit swayed by her employer's generosity of spirit. "*Hmph!* I ain't as forgiving as you seem to be,

Judge, and I doubt very much that Hannah Louise will be either."

"Your brother's going to hang. You've got my word on that, Bodine."

Travis stared at the cocky smirk on the prosecutor's face, and his lips flattened into a thin line. He and Will McGrath had developed a hostile, competitive relationship in grade school and nothing much had changed since then. His brother's murder trial would likely stretch their animosity to the breaking point. Travis intended to get Rafe acquitted, no matter what he had to do.

"Don't count on it, McGrath. Your conviction rate here in Taylor County stinks. It's likely you won't even be reelected the next time."

As his greatest fear was voiced, the prosecutor's face crimsoned, nearly matching the color of his russet hair. He hated the Bodine brothers with a passion, and he didn't bother to disguise that fact. "You're out of your league, Travis. You haven't got the experience to handle a trial like this one. And if you think I won't be reelected, then you're just fooling yourself. I've worked too hard to get where I am. And I'm not going to let you or those murdering brothers of yours ever get the best of me again." He turned on his heel and stomped out, slamming the door behind him.

Releasing the breath he'd been holding, Travis seated himself behind the battered oak desk and reached for the bag of gumdrops he always kept close by, popping a sugar-coated candy into his mouth.

If bluster and arrogance could win this case, then he hadn't a care in the world. Unfortunately it was going to take a lot more than gall to get his brother Rafe acquitted of the murder of Bobby Slaughter. Slaughter had been one of the men his brother held responsible for the brutal murder of his first wife after Rafe had quit the Texas Rangers. But Rafe claimed he had shot Bobby Slaughter in self-defense.

Travis knew his limitations in a court of law. He was a damn good civil attorney, but criminal law wasn't his area of expertise. With evidence and witnesses piling up against Rafe, he was going to need excellent representation. No mistakes, no errors in judgment could be made.

McGrath had been right about one thing: he was out of his league.

Though he'd done his best to convince his family, especially his bullheaded father, that Rafe would be better off with an experienced Eastern lawyer, Ben Bodine would hear none of it, insisting in his blustering manner that "Bodines took care of their own." Even his eldest brother, Ethan, the Texas Ranger who'd brought Rafe back to Misery to stand trial, had chosen to take their father's side. Considering Ben and Ethan's long-standing antagonistic relationship, that was nothing short of miraculous.

Three short raps on the door interrupted Travis's

disquieting thoughts, and he looked up to find Enos Richards poking his head through the doorway.

"Got an empty chair downstairs, if you're still looking to get your hair cut today, Travis. Looks like you could stand to lose an inch or so. I reckon your family's going to expect you to attend Easter service tomorrow."

Travis tugged absently at the dark hair brushing the collar of his shirt and wondered if there was anything that went on in town that the affable barber wasn't privy to. "I'll be down directly, Enos. Thanks." The barber disappeared, and Travis heard heavy footfalls on the stairway leading to the barbershop directly below his law office.

Misery wasn't so different from many other towns of its size. Everyone knew everyone else's business. As irritating as that could be on occasion, Travis also found it to be an endearing quality. Folks cared about each other, helped each other out in times of trouble, and Travis found he liked the feeling of being part of one big extended family.

He had attended law school in Boston and found it to be a cold, unfriendly city. Maybe that's because his thick Texas drawl had proclaimed him a stranger from the beginning, and he'd never warmed up to those clipped-speaking Northerners. The exception to that was his brother Rafe's wife. Emmaline was a woman with a warm heart, a hot temper, and a quick smile, despite her New England heritage.

Thinking of Emma brought Rafe to mind. Who would have thought all those years ago when he was trailing after Rafe and Ethan, worshiping the ground they walked on, as only a younger brother can do, that Rafe would one day be in jail and on trial for murder? And that Travis would bear the responsibility for getting the former Texas Ranger freed?

He hadn't done a good job so far of reaching that goal. Judge Barkley, now retired but still presiding until the new judge arrived, had denied Rafe bail, and his brother was presently biding his time in the Misery jail.

Travis had pleaded Rafe's case as eloquently as he could in an attempt to reassure the judge that a married man with five adopted children and another on the way wasn't likely to run. But the judge had denied the bail request based on Rafe's past history of having been a fugitive from the law.

Travis admired Judge Barkley despite their difference of opinion on the matter, and despite everything that had gone on in the past regarding Travis's failed relationship with his daughter, Hannah Louise.

A frown crossed his lips as it always did whenever he was reminded of Hannah. But he couldn't help wondering what she was doing now, how she looked, if she ever thought about him, about what they'd once shared.

"Give it up, Bodine," he chided himself with a shake of his head. Hannah was gone. It wasn't likely that he was ever going to see her again. And he was well rid of the headstrong woman who had brought so much heartache into his life.

"I declare, Travis Bodine! We had no idea you were so talented with your hands. Did we, Margaret?"

The faint buzzing of women's voices had Travis glancing up from the nail he was pounding in place as he secured the floor joists to the porch frame later that afternoon. He groaned inwardly at the sight of Olive Fasbinder and Margaret Willoughby standing on the street in front of his half-finished house. With everything he had to contend with at the moment, he sure as heck didn't need two husband-hunting spinsters breathing down his neck. And Olive and Margaret had made it quite clear by their overly solicitous behavior that they were interested in pursuing him.

Setting the hammer aside, he pasted on an affable smile, wishing he could turn himself into smoke and disappear into thin air. He had no interest in them, or any woman for that matter. "Good afternoon, ladies. What brings you to this end of town today?"

A soft blush crossed Margaret's freckled cheeks, and her voice trembled slightly when she spoke. "Olive and I are here to invite you to sit with us at church tomorrow, Travis. That is, if you don't already have other plans."

He opened his mouth to refuse the invitation, but Olive was quicker, adding, "We checked with your brother, and Ethan assured us that you didn't."

Gritting his teeth, he replied, "Really?", thinking that the only recourse he had left was to kill that damn interfering brother of his when he got the chance. Rafe wouldn't be the only Bodine standing trial for murder. "That's very kind of you, ladies. But I hadn't really—"

"We won't take no for an answer," Olive said, devouring him with her eyes, until Travis felt the need to fasten the two top buttons on his shirt and roll down his sleeves in self-protection. He was starting to feel down-right naked in front of the two women.

"We understand your stepmother is holding her annual Easter celebration after church, Travis. Olive and I have already received invitations to attend. We're really looking forward to it."

"Well, isn't that just . . ." *the worst possible news I've ever received.* ". . . terribly kind of Lavinia. She's so thoughtful."

"How come you're not at your office working on your brother's case? Margaret and I were surprised when Mr. Richards told us you were here at the new house." She stared wistfully at the structure.

The house was two-storied with a wide wrap-around porch, the kind of porch where a handsome young attorney and his wife could sit in the evening and enjoy the cool night air. When it was completed, there would be many windows to allow in lots of sunlight, and two fireplaces to snuggle before on a brisk winter's evening.

Olive released a sigh. "It's certainly going to be splendid when it's finished. Isn't it, Margaret?"

Margaret's faint blush turned into a full-fledged crimson hue. "Oh yes! Why, any woman would be proud to live in such a fine house. Are you building it for any special reason?"

Realizing that he had no more stomach for construction today, he retrieved his coat from the nail where he'd left it hanging and shrugged it on. The pleasure and solace he normally found while working on the new house had disappeared the moment the two women had made their presence known.

"I'm building it to live in. That's all. Nothing more. I want to be closer to my office, and I'm tired of living at a boardinghouse." And he wanted something of his own, something permanent. Something that would last.

"Mama always says that a man should have a proper roof over his head and a proper wife to go under it," Olive stated, obviously applying for the position.

"I'm content to live under my roof . . . *alone* as a bachelor." He'd made his feelings on the subject clear, but could see by Margaret's determined expression that she wasn't buying his explanation for a second.

"Maybe you've already met the woman you're going to marry, have known her all your life, and just haven't realized it yet," the carrot-topped spinster insisted. "When you do, you'll jump at the chance to enjoy matrimonial bliss. Why look at your brothers. They're both married now and happy as larks, from what I hear."

It was true: Rafe and Ethan were content with their new brides and impending fatherhood, but that didn't mean for an instant that Travis had any intention of joining them in their matrimonial bliss. He'd nearly gone down that road once before with disastrous results, and he had no intention of traveling it again.

Hannah Louise Barkley had made the journey far more aggravating than he'd ever thought possible. He'd learned his lesson the hard way about the contrariness of women, about headstrong females who relished a career over home and family life, about promises made but never kept.

Never again, he vowed. Never again.

"You have been sorely missed, Hannah Louise," Judge Barkley confessed to his only daughter as they made their way to church Sunday morning, his eyes bright with love and happiness, a tender smile curving his lips. "Five years is too long. Much too long to have stayed away."

"I've missed you too, Papa." Hannah patted his hand, worried that he had aged so dramatically in the last few years, but relieved he'd been well enough to accompany her to service this morning. "But I doubt everyone shares your sentiments."

"You mustn't hold on to your bitterness, child. What happened is in the past. You've made a new life for yourself, and others have gone on to do the same."

"If you're speaking of Travis, Papa, then you needn't worry that I'm going to fall apart at the mere mention of his name. I don't ever think about Travis Bodine anymore. I was a child then, immature in my thinking, with unrealistic expectations about life and love. I'm a grown woman of twenty-eight now." A true spinster, if prevailing notions still held. "Why do I need a man in my life when I have you?"

He shook his head. "At least you still have a sense of humor about you, Hannah Louise. I'm glad of that."

"I've grown a tough hide over these last five years, Papa. I've had to, to survive in the male-dominated world I've chosen for myself. What happened with Travis was hurtful, but I got over it. And him."

There was something about his daughter's too vehement protests that didn't strike a truthful chord with Thaddeus. What was it Shakespeare had said about protesting too much? Hannah Louise was protesting that everything was hunky-dory, that she didn't give a damn about Travis, the town, or anything else. And that worried him. That worried him a great deal.

The church was packed by the time Travis arrived. His family's pew was filled to overflowing with his father, Ben, and his wife, Lavinia, his sisters-in-law, assorted nieces and nephews, and that traitor brother of his, Ethan, who didn't bother to hide his self-satisfied smirk as his gaze roamed over the two spinsters now motioning to Travis.

"*Psst!* Travis, come sit with us. We saved you a seat." Olive and Margaret scooted over to make room for him in their pew, looking pleased as preening felines that they'd managed to snare him for the next hour or so.

The Reverend Potter was long-winded and known for his boring, officious sermons. This being Easter Sunday the service would probably extend beyond the sixty-minute norm.

Shooting his brother a dagger-filled look that promised retribution before the day was through, Travis nodded his acceptance to the two women and took the seat they proffered, fighting the urge to groan.

The organist began to play "Amazing Grace," one of Travis's favorite hymns, saving him from engaging the two spinsters in conversation. Just as he was about to give thanks to the Almighty for sparing him that much, the doors at the back of the church opened, admitting a shaft of brilliant sunlight down the aisle.

A collective gasp went up. Choking sounds from Olive and Margaret had him turning his head to see what, or who, had caused such a reaction in the normally staid congregation. His mouth unhinged, even as his eyes widened in disbelief.

If he'd been a drinking man, he would have thought himself hungover and his eyes playing tricks on him.

If he'd been a superstitious man, he would have thought that a voodoo curse had been laid at his doorstep.

If he'd been a cowardly man, he would have jumped over the backs of the pews, broken through one of the stained-glass windows, and hightailed it out of town.

For God in all His wisdom couldn't have been so unjust as to bring Hannah Louise Barkley back into his life.

But He had.

Chapter Two

WALKING DOWN THE AISLE, HANNAH LOUISE clutched her father's arm like a lifeline, ignored the hushed whispers and some not so quiet comments about her arrival, and stared straight ahead at the ancient cleric standing at the podium. She thought surely the Reverend Potter would have gone to meet his Maker by now. The man had to be nearly eighty-five and looked as if a stiff wind could topple him from the pulpit.

Out of the corner of her eye she spotted Travis Bodine seated next to Olive Fasbinder and Margaret Willoughby, her childhood nemeses. Her heart accelerated, and her palms started sweating inside the pristine white-cotton gloves she wore.

It was as if the last five years had never happened. Travis looked just as handsome as she'd remembered— startling blue eyes, thick dark hair—damn him! And damn herself for noticing how the sunlight glinted off of it, how the dimple in his chin made him look boyish, and for being affected by the mere sight of him.

Damn! Damn! Damn!

Sliding into the pew her father indicated, she tried not to feel Travis's heated stare boring into her back like an auger, refused to recognize the tight knot that now centered in the pit of her stomach, and prayed with all her heart that she would survive this day and the many others to follow.

As the good reverend droned on about the resurrection and the light, about finding forgiveness in one's soul and loving our fellow man, Travis had the distinct feeling that the aging man's sermon was directed at him. Of course, he knew that notion was ridiculous. But even so, his palms itched and his forehead dripped sweat with more force than a leaky well pump. Reaching for his gumdrops, he found his coat pocket empty.

Why had Hannah Louise come back? Why now? And why did she have to look so damn desirable?

His life had been in total disarray after she'd left and was finally getting back on an even keel. Except for the turmoil caused by Rafe's trial, he was now content for the most part, and he didn't need anything or *anyone* to disrupt that serenity or divert his concentration from the matter at hand.

And Hannah Louise Barkley was definitely a diversion.

He'd never thought to lay eyes on her again, but she looked just as beautiful as the last time he'd seen her five years before. Her flaxen hair shone like wheat ripening in the field, her complexion unmarred by time or circumstance was as smooth and creamy as newly churned buttermilk. He remembered how soft her cheek felt beneath his hand, how her eyes clouded with passion whenever he kissed her, how her lips parted ever so slightly and tasted sweet and tender, like ripe strawberries off the vine.

He could hear the sweet clear sound of her voice over everyone else's as she sang out the hymn, and he wondered if that was because he had been so attuned to her at one time.

He had loved her more than life itself once, had planned to marry her, have children with her, spend his life growing old with her. But that had all changed. And the old hurt and fierce rage of what could have been but was not because of Hannah's unreasonable quest for a career had his temper simmering all over again.

Hannah shifted uncomfortably in her seat and wondered what Travis was thinking. Nothing kind, she'd venture. At one time their thoughts had mirrored each other's. At one time they had loved and laughed and been inseparable. At one time Travis had been unselfish and sensitive to her needs.

And she had loved him with all her heart and soul.

He'd been her very best friend while they were growing up. Along the way that friendship had blossomed into love, with plans to marry and start a family. But now that friendship, that undying devotion they'd once shared, had dissolved into loathing. And all because she had wanted to pursue a law career.

It had taken Travis four years to complete his studies to obtain a law degree. The burden of working before and after classes and the difficulty of the curriculum had added an additional year to his schooling.

While he'd been gone, Hannah had rediscovered the law. It had always been part of her life. Because of her father's position as a judge, she had lived and breathed legal matters on a daily basis. But she had never considered a law career for herself until Travis had gone off to the university, leaving her alone with time on her hands and an insatiable thirst for knowledge.

And so Hannah had begun studying her father's law books. The more she read the more fascinated she became with complex legal issues. Debating the finer points of law with the judge over dinner each evening whetted her appetite even further, until she finally decided to pursue her own degree.

Travis had been opposed to the idea from the first. His letters were full of admonishment about the unsuitability of a woman pursuing such a career. But she had gone ahead anyway, believing that once he returned, once she had her degree, he would see things in a different light.

But instead of being pleased at her accomplishment, at the notion that the two of them could work together, share common goals and ideals, he had been enraged upon returning home. Even now the memory of his bitter words tormented her.

"You said you wanted to marry me, Hannah, bear my children, be my wife. Now you're telling me that you've defied my wishes and secured a law degree anyway? That having children will have to wait?" Travis's anguished expression turned cold and congested. "I don't want a competitor for a wife. I want someone who's going to love and support me."

Stunned by his reaction, Hannah's face paled, her voice reflecting the hurt she felt. "I can't believe you're saying this, Travis. Not after I've worked so hard these past three years to obtain my degree and fulfill my dream of becoming a lawyer. Do you know how difficult it is to be a woman and still manage to achieve what I have?"

"You should have waited until I returned. We should have discussed this, made the decision together. For chrissake, Hannah! We're supposed to be getting married."

"But I thought you'd be thrilled that we'd be able to work together. And I didn't set out to undermine your accomplishment. I know how difficult it was for you. And I'm very proud of what you've done. But I wanted to achieve something on my own. And I have. What's wrong with that?"

He looked at her as if she'd lost her mind. "What's wrong? A woman shouldn't aspire to the same career goals as a man. That's what's wrong. It's not fitting. And it makes me look weak and incompetent. The law is a man's domain. Women should beget children, not torts."

"I intend to have children eventually, just not right now. We've got plenty of time—"

He shook his head, his expression unyielding. "You either drop this ridiculous plan of yours to practice law, or the engagement is off. I love you, Hannah. But I'll not be made the laughingstock of Misery—a man who has to compete with his very own wife."

He had plunged a knife straight into her heart, killing all her hopes and dreams, and the love she felt for him.

"If that's how you feel . . ."

"It is."

There were more bitter words and cruel accusations. In the end, she had returned his ring, packed her bags, and left for New York to live with her mother.

That was five years ago. And in all that time nothing had changed. Certainly not her feelings. She still had that same burning resentment toward Travis that she'd had the day he'd broken their engagement.

And the sorrow of losing the only man she had ever loved.

Church service was over, but not the ordeal of facing Travis again. And though the sun glittered brightly, warming the April day to a comfortable degree, Hannah Louise felt chilled to the bone.

It was customary for parishioners to shake hands with the reverend, then mingle in front of the church to exchange small talk, recipes, invitations, and gossip. And Hannah Louise feared that gossip would be uppermost on everyone's mind today because of her unexpected arrival.

Hannah's heart gave a funny little lurch as she spotted Travis's commanding presence immediately. It was hard not to. Travis Bodine was the kind of man women noticed.

Striking in a black superfine suit and string tie, he was escorting a group of women she didn't recognize, save for his stepmother Lavinia, down the front steps of the church. Both of the younger ladies were pregnant, and she wondered if Travis had finally found the malleable woman of his dreams and gotten married. The thought disconcerted her, if only momentarily.

His brother Ethan sidled up next to the group, putting a very proprietary hand around the dark-haired woman's middle, so Hannah supposed she belonged to him. That left the redhead, who was patting Travis's cheek in a very tender fashion.

"Hannah Louise Barkley!" Lavinia Bodine broke away from the group and stepped forward to give Hannah an affectionate hug, her eyes moist with tears of happiness. "It's just wonderful to see you again. Why didn't you let someone know you were coming home?"

She turned to the judge and cast him a censorious look. "Shame on you, Thaddeus! Why didn't you let us know Hannah was coming home?"

"Hannah arrived early, Lavinia. It was a surprise to me as well. Quite a pleasant surprise I might add." He chucked his daughter's cheek. "My girl's always been full of surprises."

Lavinia Bodine was a kind, caring woman who'd always put the welfare of others before her own. A quality sadly lacking in her stepson, Hannah thought, smiling warmly at the woman who'd almost been her mother-in-law. "You're looking very well, Lavinia. How are Mr. Bodine and the rest of the family?"

"Why don't you find out for yourself? I'd love to have you and the judge join us at the ranch this afternoon for our annual Easter celebration. It'll be just like old times. Do say you'll come."

Unprepared for the invitation, Hannah hesitated, but not her father, who was nodding enthusiastically, much to her dismay. "Sounds wonderful to me, Lavinia. I've been cooped up at home for weeks, but I feel well enough to socialize a bit." He turned to his daughter. "What do you say, child? Shall we join the Bodines for Easter dinner? You know what a wonderful cook Mrs. Bodine is."

Though it was on the tip of her tongue to refuse, Hannah didn't have the heart to deny her father's wishes since he looked so taken by the idea of visiting old friends and eating someone else's cooking besides Maude's.

The possessive housekeeper would be furious if she knew. Maude Fogarty believed no one was capable of cooking the judge's meals or taking care of him as well as she did. And there weren't many, except for the judge himself, who had the temerity to contradict her.

"Are you sure you're feeling up to it, Papa? I don't want you overdoing."

"At the moment I feel fit as a fiddle. Look"—he pointed across the yard—"there's Ben and Ethan. I'll just go over and say hello." Departing before she could make any further protestations, he left Hannah alone with Lavinia.

"Are you sure this won't be an imposition, Lavinia?" she asked. "It looks like your family has grown considerably since I've been gone." It was going to be terribly awkward facing everyone again, acting as if nothing had happened. And the idea of confronting Travis made her throat dry.

Her gaze following Hannah's to the brood of children now surrounding Travis and Emmaline, Lavinia smiled contentedly, patting the young woman's hand. "I'll always consider you part of our family, dear. And it's no imposition at all. I'm sure my new daughters-in-law would love to meet you."

"Then Travis has married?" Hannah's stomach fisted as her gaze zeroed in on the auburn-haired woman once again. She was pretty in an impish sort of way.

The older woman laughed. "Mercy no! But Ethan and Rafe have, if you can believe that. Those two bachelors have finally met their match in Wilhemina and Emmaline."

Hannah Louise didn't bother to acknowledge the relief she suddenly felt. "I hadn't heard. But then, Papa and I have spent most of our time catching up on mundane things since my arrival."

"Then you don't know about Rafe?" Lavinia's eyes clouded with sorrow.

"No. I—"

"Rafe's been arrested for murder. He's in jail awaiting trial."

Hannah gasped, unable to believe such a thing. Rafe Bodine was the last man she would have ever thought capable of murder. She hadn't known him well—he and Ethan had been gone Rangering much of the time she'd been growing up—but still she knew him to be a man who held great respect for the law and an even greater affection for his family. It just didn't seem possible that such a dedicated lawman would end up in jail.

Before she could question Lavinia further Travis stepped forward, holding out his hand to her, and all thoughts of Rafe Bodine fled.

"Hello, Hannah."

The deep timbre of his voice, the warmth of his hand, sent unwelcome sparks of awareness darting through her. She pulled her hand back quickly. "Travis," she replied politely, hating the fact that he still had the power to affect her while she didn't seem to faze him one little bit.

"You're looking well." It was the understatement of the year, and Travis knew it. Hannah looked breath-takingly lovely, and it was all he could do not to step forward and take her in his arms, as he'd done a hundred times before.

But that was then. Before . . . His ardor cooled quickly.

"As are you," she said.

Lavinia grew annoyed at the couple's forced politeness. She had never stopped believing that Travis and Hannah Louise belonged together, even if they didn't think so. They'd been too impulsive and immature when they'd gotten engaged, and their immaturity had nothing to do with their age, but rather with their unrealistic expectations of what sharing a life with someone else would entail.

Marriage was a give-and-take proposition. It was making concessions, communicating when you didn't feel like talking, sharing yourself when you wanted to be alone. And accepting the flaws along with the good.

Hannah and Travis hadn't had time to learn that before they'd broken up. Maybe with a little push in the right direction, they would this time.

"Hannah Louise and her father are going to join us for Easter supper, Travis," Lavinia said, deciding to put an end to their foolishness. "Isn't that wonderful? It'll be just like old times."

Unwilling to be reminded of "old times," Travis remarked, "I may be late, Lavinia. I have some work left to do on the house," and Hannah's sigh of relief was audible.

"Travis is building himself a fine new house," his stepmother explained. Unable to mask the pride in her voice, she added for his benefit, "Although Travis has been busy with the house, I'm sure he can set aside his work for one day to make time for family and old friends." Her reproach was not lost on the young lawyer, who nodded reluctantly.

Lavinia might be as sweet as molasses most of the time, but Travis knew his stepmother had a spine of steel when the situation warranted. He decided to let her have her way, though he found her interference annoying and unwelcome.

The day was shaping up to be a rotten one as far as he was concerned. Hannah Louise was back and looking like she'd just stepped out of the pages of a fashion book. Her expensive blue-silk gown brought out the deep color of her eyes; the matching lace-trimmed bonnet emphasized the perfection of her oval face.

Sighing, Travis wondered how he was going to spend all day in her company pretending not to notice what had taken him five years to forget.

From across the yard, Will McGrath stared at Travis and Hannah together, and all the past jealousy and anger he felt came rushing to the forefront. She could have chosen him, married him, but instead she had chosen Bodine. It was just one more reason to hate the bastard. Though he had many.

The Bodine brothers had always overshadowed him, whether in school or at the various riding and shooting competitions they'd entered over the years. They were a close-knit bunch, and he had always resented that closeness, that camaraderie they seemed to share.

Growing up an only child, Will had missed the sibling rivalry, the pranks, and the fun that brothers experienced. Growing up poor, he'd worn the Bodines' faded, secondhand clothing, watched his parents kowtow to them, like they were somehow better because they had a productive ranch and the money that resulted from it.

He hadn't sought the glory or been treated like a hero by the townsfolk, like Rafe and Ethan, hadn't been given a legal education on a silver platter, like Travis, but had worked hard for everything he'd gotten.

He had succeeded on his own terms. By currying favors, taking bribes, using powerful men when necessary as a means to an end, he had achieved his present stature. And he had no intention of allowing Bodine to defeat him in court, to ruin his exalted standing in the community. He was finally somebody—the prosecutor of Taylor County, Texas—and no one was going to take that away from him, certainly not Travis.

Bodine had defeated him once with Hannah Louise. But this time it was Will who would win. No matter what he had to do. The law could be manipulated, even bought. He'd found that out over the years and used the knowledge with much success.

"Mercy me, Will McGrath, you look as angry as a bear with a thorn stuck in his hide."

Turning to find Olive Fasbinder sidling up next to him, Will pasted on an engaging smile, knowing that the spinster liked to carry tales, and he didn't want anyone to know how upset he felt. "I was just lost in thought, Olive."

Following his gaze, she shook her head in disbelief. "I can't believe that woman actually had the gall to show her face around here again. And that Travis is actually talking to her."

Will's eyes darkened and narrowed. "Some folks

are slow to learn their lessons, my dear." Travis still hadn't learned his. But he would. And soon.

Bracing herself against the rough bark of the tree, Hannah inhaled deeply of the scent of apple blossoms. It had been ages since she'd breathed the heavenly smell, and she realized it was one of the things she had missed while living in the city.

There were a great many things she enjoyed about New York—the convenience of shopping and variety of merchandise, the vast selection of restaurants, and the wonderful cultural offerings of its many museums and theaters. But the one thing it sadly lacked was clean country air.

City smells of garbage and smoke rising from the many industrial stacks clouding the skyline a murky gray, contrasted greatly with the fragrance of spring wildflowers, the cerulean blue sky, and the blossoms of fruit trees lining the orchards of Misery's many farms and ranches.

The Bodines had always had an abundance of fruit trees in their orchard. She and Travis used to climb this very apple tree when they were children. And when they were older they had spent many evenings sitting beneath it making plans for their future.

A complete waste of time, as it had turned out, she realized, frowning.

The sound of voices alerted Hannah that she was no longer alone. Shielding her eyes from the glaring sun, she watched Lavinia's daughters-in-law approach.

They were both charming women and had been very gracious in their welcome of her. She hoped they could all be friends, despite her past relationship with Travis.

"There you are, Hannah Louise," Emma said, holding out her hands and looking lovely in a green-sprigged muslin dress. Willy wore lavender and looked just as pretty. "We've been searching all over for you."

Hannah smiled warmly. "I was just enjoying the solitude, but I welcome your company. There isn't much quiet in the city."

"We know," Willy said. "Emma's from Boston. And I spent a great deal of time working at the Horticultural Society there after completing college."

Hannah's eyes widened at the unexpected revelation that Willy was a kindred spirit. "So you're a career woman?"

"Was. I'm married to Ethan now, and we're expecting our first child." She patted her abdomen so proudly Hannah felt an unexpected stab of envy deep in her breast.

Hannah had never cared much for Ethan Bodine. The arrogant Texas Ranger had been vocal in his belief that she and Travis had been ill suited from the first. But she was happy for Wilhemina just the same. The young woman seemed a good match for the intractable Ranger. Maybe her influence would serve to soften his unflattering, unfaltering opinions of others.

The three women continued chatting and getting better acquainted, unaware that they were being observed from a distance.

Travis watched his sisters-in-law laughing at something his former fiancée said, and his lips thinned in anger. He wasn't pleased by the fact that Emma and Willy found Hannah Louise such good company and had taken it upon themselves to welcome her with open arms. He'd have much preferred if they'd kept their distance and minded their own business.

Hannah might be a guest of his father and stepmother, but he didn't have to pretend to like that she'd been invited to his home.

Perhaps everyone had forgotten what was truly important at the moment. And it wasn't Hannah Louise's return to Misery. He had his brother's life in his hands. Rafe's trial would begin soon, and he had more pressing matters to deal with than Hannah Louise Barkley. As soon as the barbecue came to an end, he intended to remind his family, especially his stepmother, of that fact.

Travis questioned his brother at the jail the following day, hoping to discover some small piece of evidence that could be used to exonerate him.

"Tell me again, Rafe, the circumstances surrounding the shooting of Bobby Slaughter. And don't leave anything out. Even the smallest detail may be important."

"For chrissake, Travis! You've asked Rafe to tell that story ten times over. How many more times are you gonna need to hear it? I can practically recite it by rote."

Travis's blue eyes narrowed, and he shot his eldest brother an annoyed look. "You might be a damn good

Texas Ranger, Ethan, but you know nothing about preparing a defense case, so I suggest you keep your big mouth shut, your opinions to yourself, and let me interrogate Rafe as I see fit."

"Travis is right," Rafe said, leaning back against the cold wall of his jail cell, the narrow bunk he'd been forced to sit and sleep on a painful reminder of how quickly his circumstances had changed for the worse. "Let Travis do his job."

Ethan hated losing an argument to anyone, especially his brothers, but by the stubborn set of both men's jaws it was plain that this was one he wasn't likely to win. "Oh, all right! But it seems to me we should be doing something a lot more useful than asking a bunch of questions we already know the answers to." Removing a cigar from his vest pocket, he lit it, prompting Rafe to raise an eyebrow in question.

"I thought you'd quit smoking because of Willy's pregnancy." If anyone had told Rafe eight months ago that his confirmed-bachelor, woman-hating brother Ethan would be married and expecting a first child, Rafe would have told them they were nuts. But newly married Ethan was head-over-heels in love with his bride, horticulturist turned bounty hunter Wilhemina Granville, a spirited woman he'd met while looking for Rafe after the murder of Bobby Slaughter.

"I did. But Willy's not here, and I feel the need for a smoke. Unless you and Travis want to object to that, too."

Used to Ethan's irascible ways, Travis let the comment pass. Leaning forward in his chair, he directed his next words to Rafe. "Tell me again what happened."

"I returned to the ranch house to find Ellie gone. I discovered her body in the barn. She was dead, as was our unborn child. I knew in my gut that it was Hank Slaughter's gang that had done the murders. The bastard had threatened to get even with me after I'd put him in prison."

"It was you and Ethan who had arrested him, right?" Travis asked, and Rafe nodded.

"I took out after them. It wasn't hard to pick up their tracks, and I soon discovered that they had split up. I followed a set of the horse tracks to Justiceburg, and that's where I found Bobby Slaughter, Hank's younger brother."

"At Madam DeBerry's bordello, correct?"

"That's right. Bobby was screwing his brains out with Judy when I walked in on them. Bobby was terrified when he saw me. I never saw a guiltier-looking son of a bitch. And even though I went there with the intention of killing him, I didn't shoot him in cold blood."

"Judy DeBerry claims you did."

"That's right," Ethan concurred. "When I interviewed her she said you pulled your gun and shot Bobby down in cold blood. Of course, I knew she was lying straight off, but there was no way I could get her to change her story."

"She was in love with the bastard. What did you expect her to say? But it didn't happen the way she claims. Bobby's gun was beneath his pillow. He reached for it, aimed it at me, and fired. He had every intention of killing me, but my draw was quicker, truer, and I shot him dead."

"The whore claims you threatened her life."

Rafe gazed at his younger brother, who was writing fast and furiously, and taking notes of everything he said, his expression filled with regret. "I won't deny that I tried to intimidate her in an attempt to get her to talk. I needed to know where the Slaughters were headed, and she was the only one who could help me find them."

"So you might have threatened her with bodily harm?"

"I think I told her that if she didn't stop screaming she was going to get some of what Bobby got."

"Shit, Rafe! You told her that?" Ethan paced back and forth across the narrow jail cell and puffed his cigar agitatedly, creating a smoky haze about him.

"She was screaming at the top of her lungs that I'd killed Bobby. What the hell else was I supposed to do?"

"Is there anything else you can remember?" Travis's voice remained much calmer than his brother's. "Anything at all?"

"I remember thinking that I had to get out of there before the sheriff showed up. And that I had to find the Slaughters."

"You sure as hell are in a shitload of trouble, little brother. But I guess you already know that."

"Yeah. But thanks for telling me anyway, Ethan. It was something I was just dying to hear."

Ethan winced at the disheartenment in Rafe's voice. "Jesus! I'm sorry. I—"

"Forget it. Just find some evidence that's going to get me out of this place. I want to go home to my wife and kids. With Emma expecting our baby, I'm worried that this is all going to be too much for her, that something's going to happen, and that I'm going to lose her, too, just like I lost Ellie."

"That's not going to happen, Rafe. Travis here is going to get you off. You and me didn't spend all that money on that fancy Eastern law school for nothing. Ain't that right, Travis?" Ethan prodded.

Wanting to give Rafe the reassurance he needed, Travis smiled confidently and nodded in agreement, but he wished now that he'd never thought of becoming a lawyer, never allowed Rafe and Ethan to pay for his expenses for Harvard.

A formal legal education was a rarity out West. Many lawyers were self-taught and apprenticed themselves to experienced practicing attorneys to learn the ropes. For Travis to have been given the opportunity to study law at one of the most prestigious law schools in the East had been nothing short of a miracle. And a dream come true. A dream paid for by Rafe and Ethan.

Travis knew early on that he wanted to do something with his life besides ranching. Unlike his brothers, Travis had always preferred reading to roping and using his wits, not his brawn, to defeat an opponent.

Despite his father's strenuous insistence that he stay on the ranch and follow in his footsteps, because his brothers had chosen not to, Travis was determined to succeed in his goal to study law and live life as he saw fit.

Rafe and Ethan had taken his side in the matter, and his father had finally come to terms with Travis's decision, grudgingly accepting it. He owed them for that, and for so much more, and he couldn't let them down now that they needed his help.

But as much as he wanted to believe that he'd be able to get Rafe acquitted, he just wasn't sure. The prosecutor was out for blood—the DeBerry woman, too—and Travis was facing the biggest battle of his life with very little ammunition.

Chapter Three

Hannah was bored. She'd only been home a few days and was already discovering that she didn't have enough to keep her busy. Flipping through the pages of the *Ladies' Home Journal*, she heaved a dispirited sigh and wondered how she would rectify that.

Hannah was used to being active and involved back home in New York City. Whether assisting the poor with their legal problems, or volunteering once a week at the Christian Ladies' Relief Society—her mother's pet project—she was never without something worthwhile to do.

She thrived on challenge, on keeping her mind active and her wits sharp.

Nursing her father back to health was not going to take up as much of her time as she'd originally thought. Maude was there every day to see to the judge's comfort, meals, and such, and to scrutinize everything Hannah attempted to do on her own, relegating Hannah to the position of companion.

Though she enjoyed spending time with the judge, chatting with him about the day's events, or reading the newspaper to him when his eyes grew too weary to perform the chore himself, it just wasn't enough to keep her occupied.

After speaking to his doctor, and making her own observations, Hannah had formed the opinion that her father's illness had more to do with loneliness than any specific physical ailment. According to the doctor, the judge was in excellent health for a man of his age. And she had noticed that his spirits and color had improved one hundred percent since her arrival home. Perhaps her father's illness was all in his head, just as the doctor had claimed.

With that in mind, she had been giving a great deal of thought as to what she could do to keep herself busy. She wanted to do something worthwhile and productive, not just fill her time with embroidery, sewing, or reading magazines, hobbies she felt little passion for. She set the *Ladies' Home Journal* aside. Law journals were more to her taste anyway.

The law was her greatest love, her greatest challenge, and that's where she wanted to devote her energy. So far, the only solution to her problem was one that would no doubt create bigger problems in the end.

After telling herself a thousand reasons why she shouldn't, why her idea was totally ridiculous and out of the question, Hannah had decided to offer her expertise and services to Travis as cocounsel on his brother's defense case.

She knew that she'd be asking for trouble if she went ahead with her plan. It would be extremely difficult for both of them dealing together on a daily basis. They had spent most of the time at the barbecue last Sunday avoiding each other like the plague. They wouldn't have that luxury if they were thrust together day and night to plan a criminal defense case.

Hannah knew firsthand how laborious and difficult it was to prepare for a trial such as this one. Hours of painstaking research were involved, not to mention interrogation of witnesses, sifting through mounds of evidence, preparing briefs and arguments, and a multitude of other tasks that were necessary to ensure success.

It was an investment of time, and of oneself. And mutual respect would be necessary if they were to work successfully together.

Travis would no doubt refuse any and all assistance from her, because of his views on women and the law, and because of what had happened between them in the past. But they were older now. More mature. And perhaps they'd be able to put past animosities aside.

She decided that it was worth a try. There were far more pros than cons: Rafe Bodine would no doubt benefit from her legal expertise, she had a lot more experience in criminal matters than Travis, she would keep herself occupied with something she enjoyed doing immensely, and this trial would offer a bigger challenge than any she'd previously been given. It would also serve to give Travis the confidence and support that he needed to win by having her on his team.

From what Emma had confided the day of the barbecue, Travis was not used to handling criminal cases, his area of expertise being civil law. His sister-in-law had expressed concern that the prosecuting attorney's case against her husband was a strong one. McGrath had an eyewitness who was willing to testify that Rafe shot the victim, Bobby Slaughter, in cold blood.

Emma was worried that Travis might not have enough experience to deal with McGrath, though she was fearful of expressing those concerns, lest she injure her brother-in-law's pride.

Better to injure Travis's pride, than to see Rafe Bodine hang.

Hannah's instincts told her three things: First, the prosecutor would stop at nothing to get a conviction against Rafe. Will McGrath was an ambitious man. And she knew from past association with him that there was no love lost between him and the Bodine family; second: they could win this case if they worked together; and third: Travis needed her help, whether he wanted to admit it or not.

It was well past midnight, but Travis felt compelled to pore over his law books one more time in the hope of finding something, anything, that might aid him in preparing Rafe's defense. And he also needed something to block the image of Lavinia's shattered expression when he'd taken her to task yesterday at the barbecue.

He felt ashamed about the way he'd spoken to his

stepmother. Lavinia had showed him nothing but kind-
ness over the years, taking his side more times than not
against his father, and he feared that he'd hurt her terribly by his harsh condemnation. And all because she had
invited Hannah Louise to the family's Easter celebration.

Heaving a disgusted sigh that he'd allowed his former fiancée to come between him and his stepmother,
he vowed to make it up to Lavinia the next time he saw
her. If she allowed him back into her house and her good
graces!

A knock sounded on the door. Travis looked up and
was surprised to find Ethan entering. Since his marriage
to Wilhemina his formerly footloose brother had stayed
pretty close to home in the evenings, and Travis wondered what prompted the late night call.

"You're working mighty late tonight, little brother."
Ethan pulled out the chair in front of Travis's desk and
straddled it, not bothering to wait for an invitation. "And
you look like you lost your last friend.

"*Tsk. Tsk.* Couldn't be that you're feeling bad about
the way you spoke to poor Lavinia, could it? Willy said
she was mighty upset after you lit into her like you did."

"Did you come here to cheer me up, Ethan, or just
to make me feel dirtier than pond scum?"

His brother grinned. "Actually, I came into town to
check on Rafe and saw your light on. Knowing that you
usually keep banker's hours, I thought maybe someone
might have broken in here." He cast a disparaging eye
about the sparsely furnished office, noting the old desk

and chair, a leather sofa that had seen better days, and the bookshelves filled with Travis's prized law books. "Not that you've got much to steal, mind you."

"Thievery is the least of my problems." Frustrated, Travis pounded his fist on the open law book. "I think I'm in way over my head on this one, Ethan. It's going to take a lot more late nights to figure out the best strategy for defending Rafe."

Of the three brothers Travis was the most eventempered and levelheaded. His uncharacteristically anxious behavior toward Rafe's upcoming trial worried Ethan. "What can I do to help? No one expects you to do this all on your own, Travis. We're all willing to lend a hand."

"I appreciate that. But this is something that I'm going to have to do on my own. I can't rely on my big brother to bail me out this time.

"Judy DeBerry is going to be the prosecution's biggest ally and the Achilles' heel of our defense. If I can't shake her testimony, I'm going to have a far more difficult time winning this case."

"Judy DeBerry's a whore, the madam of a bordello. How credible a witness can she be?"

"Will McGrath says she's willing to testify that she saw Rafe shoot Bobby Slaughter in cold blood. Her eyewitness testimony is going to be very compelling to a jury. There are going to be men on that jury who have frequented whorehouses, maybe hers, at one time or another. I've got to try to either shake her testimony or find a way to discredit it."

They might have had a better chance if women had been allowed to serve on juries. But to that date Wyoming was the only state to allow women the vote and the privilege of serving on a jury.

Ethan whistled shrilly. "I can see now why you're so worried, little brother. I didn't put much store by the whore's statement when I first heard it. But listening to you tell it, I can understand your concern.

"As I've said many times before, Rafe is in a shit-load of trouble."

"Yeah. And it's up to me to get him out of it. It's ironic, isn't it, Ethan, that after all the times you and Rafe pulled me out of scrapes, stood up for me with Pa, now I'm the one who everyone's depending on? I don't mind saying that it scares the hell out of me."

"I don't think our faith in you has been misplaced, Travis. You're going to work much harder to get Rafe acquitted of this murder charge than any fancy Eastern lawyer we could have hired. You've got more at stake and much more to lose than some silk-suited nabob from Boston or New York."

"There you go trying to cheer me up again."

Flashing a grin, Ethan stood. "It's the least I can do. After all, that's what brothers are for, right?"

As Travis watched Ethan depart into the cold night air, he thought of the many storms the Bodine brothers had weathered. Their mother's death of pneumonia eight years ago had been the hardest ordeal. Devastated by the loss of his wife, their father had withdrawn into himself for a time, leaving his sons to grieve for a mother they cherished and to seek solace from each other.

Through the years, no matter the trials or tribulations, they had each other to look to for comfort, support, and friendship.

The bond that tied the three of them together was forged by blood, tempered by tears, and strengthened by their devotion to one another. It wouldn't be severed by anything. Not even something as coldly intimidating as a murder trial.

"Well, look what the cat drug in. If it ain't Travis Bodine. There's just no accounting for some folks' gall, is there?"

Travis nearly winced at the venom in Maude Fogarty's voice. Though five years had passed since his breakup with Hannah Louise, the housekeeper still blamed him for Hannah's abrupt decision to leave Misery for New York City. Apparently she had yet to forgive him.

"Miss Hannah's not here. Though I suspect you already know that." The door started to close, and he put his foot out to block it.

"I do." Travis had observed Hannah leave the house not ten minutes before, which was why he'd decided to pay a call on the judge to seek assistance with Rafe's trial. "I've come to see Judge Barkley, not his daughter."

"*Hmph!* Don't know why anyone in this house would want to talk to you after all the misery you caused, but it ain't my place to make that decision. Wait here. I'll see if the judge wants to see you."

He stepped into the foyer, and she glanced back over her shoulder, a warning look in her eyes. "Don't be touching nothing while I'm gone, you hear?"

"Yes, ma'am." He hid a grin as she harrumphed again and stalked away, for her admonition served as a reminder of how many times she'd told him that very thing over the years.

As a youth he'd spent many hours visiting at the Barkley home. Back then, the judge had been newly appointed to the bench, his wife, occupied with civic duties and charity functions, was often gone, and Hannah Louise had been left mostly to her own devices, accounting, no doubt, for her independence and stubbornness.

Mrs. Fogarty had been there to supervise, but she'd turned a blind eye to many of the escapades children were wont to get into. Hannah Louise could do no wrong in the housekeeper's opinion. And even when she'd blackened his eye during a particularly vicious argument, the woman had taken Hannah's side, insisting that Travis had no business fighting with a girl who was several years younger than he and far more delicate.

A few minutes later, the housekeeper ushered him into the judge's walnut-paneled study, muttering invectives under her breath, then slamming the leaded-glass door so hard as she walked out that Travis feared it would break.

"Don't mind the old hag, boy." The judge smiled

apologetically. "She's in one of her moods today. I told her the oatmeal was lumpy this morning, and she took offense. Hell and damnation! I could have papered the walls with it."

Seating himself in one of the red-brocade wing chairs by the fireplace, Travis noticed how much better the judge's appearance was and felt relieved. "Are you feeling better, Judge Barkley? I'd heard you'd been ill."

"I have good days and bad. That fool Doc Leahy can't find anything wrong with me. Says it's all in my head. Guess when I'm buried six feet under he'll finally admit to being wrong."

Noting that the judge's wit was still razor sharp despite his age, Travis smiled. "Rumor has it that Doc started out to be a vet, but no one would let 'im touch their livestock, so he became a physician instead."

Chuckling, Thaddeus slapped his knee, which resulted in a fit of coughing. "Damn! Hand me that decanter of whiskey, boy," he choked out. "It's the only thing that quiets this damn cough."

Reaching for the crystal decanter, Travis suddenly paused, a look of uncertainty on his face. "Are you sure you're supposed to have this, Judge? I don't want Mrs. Fogarty accusing me of trying to poison you." Or worse: Hannah Louise.

"Ha! If I haven't died from eating the old bat's cooking, I doubt I will from drinking good old Texas redeye."

Unable to dispute that point, Travis filled the glass half-full, handing it to him.

"What's on your mind, Travis? I appreciate the visit, but I doubt you'd risk encountering my daughter unless it was something important."

"I've come about Rafe's case. I've not had much experience in criminal law, and I wondered if you might be able to point me in the direction you think would be the wisest to take."

The judge leaned back, studying the earnestness on the young lawyer's face, flattered that Travis had thought enough of him to seek out his advice. He was surely sorry that things hadn't worked out between him and Hannah Louise. With their good looks and brains, they would have given him a fine bunch of grandbabies.

Thaddeus had never stopped wondering if maybe he was to blame for the way things had turned out. Hannah Louise had been brought up to be independent and a freethinker. And he and Fiona had certainly set a poor example by their own failed marriage.

Heaving a sigh, he finally said, "The law's a lot like gambling, son. You've got to play your hunches, go with your gut before you make your bet."

"But how will I know if I've made the right decision? My brother's life is on the line. I can't afford to make any mistakes."

"You'll know. We lawyers have instinct. Pay heed to that inner voice deep inside you. It won't steer you wrong."

Travis had been hoping for more than platitudes and was unable to mask his disappointment. "That's it? That's all the advice you can give me?"

"I'm still the presiding judge until the new one shows up, Travis. It wouldn't be proper for me to assist you in any way, give you preferential treatment, so to speak. But I will give you one bit of advice: go with your strengths, the facts that are likely to sway a jury to your way of thinking.

"Ask yourself: If I was on the jury, what would make me acquit? What evidence would I find the most compelling? Whose testimony would carry the most weight?"

The clock on the mantel chimed one, and the judge motioned toward it. "Unless you want to be here when my daughter returns, I suggest you hightail it back to your office."

Travis rose to his feet. "I'm much obliged to you for hearing me out, Judge, and for offering what advice you could."

"Sometimes young lawyers think all the answers are in books and in their heads, but I think more problems can be solved by looking at what's in your heart and in the hearts of the jurors."

Travis was to ponder those words many times over in the difficult days ahead.

Trying to decide between the red or green grosgrain ribbon, Hannah held the ribbons up to her hair and gazed at her reflection in the small handheld mirror. But the face staring back at her wasn't just her own.

She spun on her heel. "Goodness, Will! You shouldn't sneak up on a body like that. You nearly scared me to death." Her hand went to cover her chest and her rapidly beating heart.

His smile was cocky and full of self-assurance, reminding her of why she'd never truly felt comfortable in his presence. "I'm sorry, Hannah Louise. You just looked so pretty standing there. I didn't want to disturb the image by speaking."

She forced a smile and held out her hand. "Still the flatterer, I see."

"I don't have to flatter when it comes to you, my dear. You're looking as lovely as ever. I've missed you." He brought her gloved hand to his lips, then squeezed it tightly.

Hannah pulled back, uncomfortable with the gesture. "Thank you." She gazed over his shoulder, looking about hopefully. "Is there a Mrs. McGrath that I should meet?"

There was a slight tightening to his lips. "No. After you, no other woman could ever measure up."

She laughed, as if to make light of the statement. "You flatter me, Will. But we both know that there was never anything between us except friendship."

"There could have been, Hannah Louise, if you hadn't lost your heart to Bodine. There still could be, if you were willing. I've never forgotten you." He stepped forward, prompting her to step back and change the subject.

"I understand that you're prosecutor for Taylor County now. Congratulations. Who would have thought all those years ago that you, Travis, and I would have ended up being attorneys?"

He stiffened. "Are you referring to my impoverished beginnings?"

She shook her head, unwilling to offend, and he relaxed. "No. Not at all. I was merely referring to the fact that we three seemed like such unlikely candidates for the law. We were more apt to get into trouble than defend against it."

"Children grow up. And so do women, I'm happy to note. And you certainly have grown up, Hannah Louise."

The lascivious way he stared at her breasts made her grossly uncomfortable. "Well, I have to be going now, Will. It was very nice seeing you again."

"Why don't you join me for dinner this evening. We can catch up on old times. Perhaps renew our acquaintance in a more mature way."

There was no mistaking his meaning, and Hannah fought the shudder running through her. It would give her nothing but pleasure to defeat this pompous jackanapes in a court of law. "I'm sorry, but I already have plans."

He bowed his head. "Some other time then. I'm sure we'll be seeing each other again. I won't let you slip away so easily this time, Hannah Louise."

Setting the ribbons back down on the counter, Hannah hurried out of the store, unmindful of the clerk who was calling after her.

Will McGrath's comments sounded more like

threats than promises, and she wanted to put distance between them. Maybe he was just bragging. Or maybe he was just happy to see an old friend. But the tingles marching down her spine had nothing to do with the joy of renewing an old acquaintance and everything to do with fear.

Chapter Four

"ARE YOU CRAZY? I WOULD NEVER AGREE TO SUCH a stupid ridiculous idea."

Travis's face reddened in anger, even his ears were turning bright red, and Hannah knew that she'd been correct in assuming that he wouldn't be pleased by her offer to act as cocounsel during Rafe's criminal trial. He'd just confirmed that belief emphatically and rudely.

Seating herself in the rickety oak chair that looked as unstable as she felt at the moment, she said in as reasonable a voice as she could muster, "Let me assure you that I am very qualified and capable of assisting you with this trial. Emmaline confided that she was a bit nervous about the difficulty of this case, and your lack of experience in criminal matters, so I decided to offer my assistance in preparing your brother's defense."

Travis's mouth fell open, then he snapped it shut. "After everything that's happened between us, you certainly do have a lot of nerve. I'll give you that." He snorted rudely. "Back in town only a few days and already stirring up trouble, huh, Hannah Louise?"

Bolting to her feet, she swallowed all the nasty invectives teetering on the edge of her tongue. "I don't know why I bothered coming here this morning, Travis. I knew that you would never agree to accept my help. Your male pride and ego will not allow it. You could never stand to compete with a woman, if memory serves." And it did, oh so painfully.

Rising to his feet, his palms braced on the desktop, he leaned toward her, blue eyes blazing. "I don't think now is the proper time to dredge up past history. We've said all we had to say on the subject of our *almost* marriage years ago, and I won't waste my time and energy on it now." Or the heartache. He thought the pain of their failed relationship had healed, but it was coming back in full force, eating away at his composure.

"Regardless of what you choose to think, I didn't come here to dwell on the past. I came to offer my assistance in the hope of saving your brother's life. I would think that you'd want to put his welfare above your own. I can be a great deal of help to you, if only you'll let me. I've tried many criminal cases, and—"

He shook his head emphatically. "I don't want or need your help. I think I've made myself clear on that point, Hannah Louise. Your bluestocking ways don't interest me."

The man was stubborn to a fault. Always had been, always would be. She had held out a tiny hope that he might have changed, mellowed over the years, but she could see now that he hadn't. He was still the same intractable, impossible, arrogant—

Sighing, she silently berated herself for thinking of past hurts. "Just because you resent me for obtaining a law degree and making something of myself, Travis, is no reason to blind yourself to the facts. You need help to win this case. And I'm the best person for the job. Don't let foolish pride stand in the way of saving your brother's life."

The truth hurt, especially coming from Hannah, but Travis wasn't about to accept it. Or her. "Perhaps your assistance would be valuable, but I think it's clear that you wouldn't be able to put aside your animosity toward me to assist with this trial. There's still too much anger and resentment between us." And how could he stand being near her day after day, remembering how she felt in his arms, how it had been between them?

Her chin came up. "Maybe on your part, Travis. But quite frankly, I don't care enough to resent you any longer. I've grown up. Maybe you should, too."

The vein in his neck started to throb. The woman had a way of exasperating him to the boiling point, making him lose whatever tenuous hold he had on his emotions. Without thinking, he grabbed hold of her, startling them both.

"If you've come here to find out if I still want you, Hannah, then here's your answer." Drawing her to his chest, he kissed her passionately. All the hurt, longing, and resentment he'd experienced in the past five years was communicated in that one kiss. But there was something else, too. Something Travis hadn't counted on. Feelings he'd thought dead and buried were still very much alive and fighting to reach the surface.

Hannah was stunned by the ferocity of the kiss, of the tumultuous way it made her feel. But not too stunned to react. She hauled her arm back and slapped him fully on the face. The sound seemed to echo off the office walls. "How dare you! I came here to offer my help, and you attack me like I'm some common trollop.

"You haven't changed one bit, Travis Bodine. You're still the same immature boy that I was once engaged to. When are you going to grow up and become a man?"

When she finally stormed out, all five feet, five inches of righteous indignation, slamming the door loudly behind her, Travis felt enormously relieved.

He didn't know what had possessed him to behave in such a fashion. He didn't know why he had kissed Hannah Louise. And he sure as hell didn't know why he had liked it so much. He never meant for any of it to happen.

Travis didn't like losing control. He took great pride in the fact that he always held on to his temper, that he rarely ever let his emotions show, even at the most difficult times.

But today had been different. Hannah had gotten to him. She'd made a shambles of his feelings, had driven him to the point of no return, had made him react in a most unconventional way.

And those powerful feelings he had experienced

served to convince him more than ever that he and Hannah Louise could never work together. They were either going to kill each other or bed each other. And he couldn't quite decide which would be worse.

Hannah Louise couldn't remember when she'd ever been so angry. Not even when Travis had broken their engagement had she felt such murderous rage. Having worked up a full head of steam by the time she arrived home, she was pacing back and forth across the carpet of the parlor, still steaming enough to blow the roof off the house.

Imagine Travis's arrogance! Imagine his audacity! She'd gone to his office to offer her assistance and support and what had been his response—he'd kissed her, that's what.

And it hadn't been a tender kiss, but one delivered in anger, one meant to punish.

Well, it hadn't punished. In fact, she'd rather enjoyed the stimulation of it. The sheer animal magnetism of being taken so forcefully. But she'd die before letting that horrible man know it.

The knock on the parlor door halted her in mid-stride. "Yes, what is it? I want to be left alone."

Maude stuck her head in, and her smile was gloating. "Can't do that, missy. There's someone to see you. And he's got humble pie smeared all over his face."

Before she could utter a word—NO! came to mind—Travis came bursting through the doorway, thanks to Maude shoving him from behind. He looked horribly embarrassed. Which could have been attributed to the fact that he'd just tripped over his own feet.

Righting himself, he cleared his throat. "Hannah Louise, I came to apologize."

She crossed her arms over her chest. "Really? And you think that's going to make everything all better? You really do need to grow up, Travis."

"Are you going to shut up long enough to allow me to apologize or not?"

Her chin came up. "Go on."

"Perhaps you're right. Maybe I do need help with this murder case. I've never tried one before."

"And?"

"And what?"

"And that's your idea of an apology? You grab me, molest me, nearly rape me, and that's it?"

He bit the inside of his cheek. "First of all, I didn't try to rape you. Trust me. You would have known the difference." Her cheeks crimsoned. "I apologize for kissing you. I shouldn't have done it. You just made me mad, and I retaliated."

"Is that how you retaliate whenever anyone makes you mad? My, my, this is going to be an interesting trial. I hope Will McGrath is ready for your kisses."

His color deepened, and he took a breath before saying, "Will McGrath and I weren't engaged to be married."

"Well, if you kiss him enough I'm sure he'll—"

"Hannah Louise! You're making it very difficult for me to say I'm sorry about what happened, and to ask you to assist me with my brother's trial." He'd thought long and hard after she'd left and realized that Rafe's life was far more important than his bruised ego. Hannah had the experience that could help him help his brother.

"Let me make certain I'm understanding you correctly: You want me to assist you with your brother's case? You want me, a mere woman, to help you with a legal matter? Is that correct?"

Figuring that he deserved her wrath, he ignored her sarcasm and nodded. "I'm willing to try and put aside our differences, if you are. My brother's life is more important to me than holding a grudge. And contrary to what you may believe, I'd like to think that I've matured in the last five years. Perhaps even learned a few things."

Her eyebrow shot up at the unexpected admission. "I'd like to think so, too. And you aren't the only one who has matured, Travis. I've grown up. A great deal. I was a mere child five years ago." They both were, apparently. Too bad neither had realized it then. Maybe things would have worked out differently.

"I'm a grown woman now," she added.

"So I've noticed." His eyes danced over every inch of her body, warming her, warning her.

"Someone else recently said the same thing to me." But then it had made her feel dirty. Funny, when Travis said it she felt good.

"Who, your father?"

"No. Papa will always think of me as his little girl.

It was McGrath. Apparently he likes the way I've grown up."

His eyes hardened. "Will always did fancy himself in love with you."

"So did you, once, Travis."

He stilled at her comment, chose not to respond, then said, "I'll expect you at my office bright and early tomorrow. Don't be late."

By the following morning everyone in Misery knew that Hannah Louise Barkley would be assisting Travis Bodine with Rafe's criminal trial.

It was the chief topic of conversation at the tonsorial parlor, saloon, and post office. There also had been a three-column article on the front page of the newspaper, along with a terse editorial devoted to women who overstepped the bounds of decency, and the unseemly behavior of some female attorneys who didn't seem to know their place in polite society.

The news had spread faster than a prairie fire burning out of control, and Travis was annoyed as hell at having to defend his decision to accept Hannah's help, especially in light of their past relationship and the town's fascination with it. And he especially didn't like having to defend Hannah Louise herself. But he had no intention of letting someone like Will McGrath have the last word in the matter.

"Well, well, Bodine. I suppose you think you're really smart for putting Hannah Louise on your defense team. I suppose you think her influential father can help get your brother off," the prosecutor had said, halting him on the street not fifteen minutes before.

A vicious sneer lit the man's features. "I hope you know that I intend to protest your unethical behavior through the court. It's highly unprofessional that Hannah would be allowed to assist you under these circumstances. Her father is the presiding judge, after all."

"I've already spoken to Judge Barkley about it, McGrath. Because he's turning over the case to another judge and won't be presiding himself, he didn't see anything wrong with Hannah lending a hand. I'll be conducting the trial myself, not Hannah Louise."

"Bet you'd like to be conducting more than the trial, hey, Travis?" McGrath's innuendo had almost earned him a bloody lip, but Travis let the remark pass.

After uttering a few more comments about conflict of interest and the like, Will had stalked off, and it wasn't difficult for Travis to figure out who'd been spreading some of the malicious comments he'd heard, like the fabrication that he and Hannah had taken up where they'd left off, or that Travis was such an inadequate, incompetent attorney that he had to rely on a woman for help.

It was this attitude, this condemnation, he had feared when Hannah had first announced her intention to practice law. A strong woman could make a man look not only incompetent but impotent. Something he'd felt his whole life while growing up under the shadows of his older brothers and strong-willed father.

The law had been his salvation, a chance to make

his mark in the world. He couldn't allow false accusations to undermine all he had worked for. All Hannah had accomplished, too.

Lies could destroy reputations and undermine confidence in a lawyer's abilities. Not that the facts had ever stopped gossip from being spread as thick as manure on pasture grass.

Hannah Louise's reputation was already being torn to shreds, and it was barely ten o'clock in the morning. At the bakery where Travis had stopped on his way to work to buy a sweet roll, he'd overheard Mrs. Fasbinder tell her friend Mrs. Willoughby that Hannah Louise was a loose woman with no moral fiber.

He'd nearly lost his temper at that and almost said something to the two gossipy old biddies. But when he overheard the Reverend Potter remark that women who rise above their station were an abomination unto the Lord, he knew that it would be better just to let the talk die down rather than add more fuel to the fire.

Stopping at the general store to purchase another pound of the candy he was so fond of, Travis did his best to ignore the curious stares and hushed whispers that greeted him. It was painfully obvious that his brother's defense had just gotten ten times more difficult, and he had no one to blame for that but himself.

"And did you hear about that hussy, Hannah Louise Barkley, who's dared to compared herself with a man and offer herself as an attorney? Well, I was shocked, I tell you."

The shorter of the two women tsked and shook her head. "It's that big-city influence. There never was a woman raised in the East who wasn't free with herself. It's simply disgraceful. Well, I—"

The woman had more to say, but Hannah Louise had chosen not to listen as she hurried past the two matrons, who obviously didn't know who she was, or didn't care, which was more likely the case. Sighing, she wondered what terrible, shameful thing she had done to be the object of such scorn and ridicule. And the topic of this morning's edition of the *Sentinel*.

Her father had nearly had an apoplectic seizure when he'd read the morning newspaper, vowing to get even with the editor, Sid Barker, if it was the last thing he did. And Maude had declared in no uncertain terms, and a few colorful epithets thrown in for good measure, that she would only use the "rotten rag" as lining for her parakeet's cage, and then only as a last resort.

Thinking of the housekeeper's vehemence made Hannah smile, though she knew that this was certainly no laughing matter. She dreaded having to face Travis this morning. His original reluctance to have her as co-counsel had been made crystal clear. Why he'd chosen to change his mind, she had no idea. But the town's narrow-minded vision of her role would only reinforce his opinion that she had no business being a lawyer. And certainly no business being Rafe's lawyer. She sighed at the impossibility of the situation and continued on, reaching the law office a few minutes later.

"Good morning," she said almost too cheerfully

upon entering. She looked about for somewhere to hang her cape amid the squalor, and finally settled for tossing it on the sofa when she couldn't find a coatrack.

His eyebrow arched. "Is it? I assume you've already read the paper?"

"Yes. And I've had my ears blistered by a couple of gossiping ladies on the street."

He seemed genuinely sorry to hear that. "Ignore them. It's a small town, and this is big news apparently."

"I'm sorry to say that this town will never change. Folks here have nothing better to do than gossip and mind other people's business."

"Misery has its flaws, like any small town. But it's also got its good side. People here care about each other, help each other out in times of trouble, unlike large cities where nobody knows your name."

She shrugged. "I like New York. Anonymity has its rewards."

"At any rate, we've got more to worry about than your reputation. Finding an impartial jury is going to be next to impossible now."

The truth of his words stung. The jury pool would be tainted by the gossip, or Will McGrath, who she suspected was behind the whole thing. But she wasn't about to turn tail and run. "I won't quit."

"Somehow I doubted you would. But this isn't going to be easy for either one of us." The rose scent of her perfume drifted over him, and he moved restlessly in his seat.

"I'm use to ridicule and scorn. I'm a woman, remember? A woman doing a 'man's' job." Hannah pushed aside a year's worth of law journals and seated herself on the cracked-leather sofa, dusting the cushions with her gloved hand. The once white glove turned a disgusting shade of gray, and she grimaced. "You don't clean much, do you?"

"Nope." He reached for a gumdrop and popped it into his mouth. "Don't have the time for it. So, if that's a requirement of your staying, you may as well leave now."

"It isn't. But I find that orderliness tends to be a help when preparing a case of this magnitude. We're going to generate lots of paperwork, and we'll need to keep good track of our notes, files, and such."

She was absolutely correct, but he had no intention of agreeing with her, finding comfort in the chaos he created for himself. "I know where everything is."

"I doubt that." Staring at the stacks of books on the floor, at the piles of papers scattered over his desk, on the carpet, and anywhere else there was an empty smidgen of space, she was clearly skeptical. "I hope your office isn't a reflection of your mind. You used to be fairly neat, as I recall."

"Things change."

Her eyebrows shot up. "Well, apparently not always for the better. I see you still haven't lost your sweet tooth." She used to buy him gumdrops by the bagful, teasing him that his teeth would surely fall out one day. But she'd been wrong. They were white, straight, and strong as ever, his smile still devastatingly handsome. Though she hadn't seen much of it lately. Which was just as well, she supposed, since it always made her weak in the knees to see that dimple of his.

"Do you intend to discuss my brother's case, or did you come here to offer cleaning critiques and advice about my eating habits?"

"Both." Unable to help herself, she began to straighten the stacks of books and journals while she talked.

"Leave those alone."

She ignored him. "I'll do whatever's necessary to assist you with your brother's defense. I wouldn't have made the offer if I didn't think I could help."

He hadn't yet had a chance to discuss this situation with Rafe, but he was sure that his brother would agree with the arrangement. After all, according to Hannah, Emmaline had doubts about his ability to defend her husband.

"I'm of the opinion that we should start by interviewing witnesses," she said, interrupting his thoughts.

Travis continued to stare out the window, noticing how much grime had accumulated on the glass this past year, and hating himself for it. It was something he wouldn't have paid any attention to before Hannah's arrival. Silently berating himself, he finally said, "I agree. We need to interrogate Judy DeBerry, the prosecution witness. I was thinking about asking Ethan to ride over to Justiceburg and do it."

Hannah's eyes widened in disbelief. "What? You've actually considered sending that tactless, overbearing brute-of-a-man to talk to a prospective witness?" She shook her head. "Are you trying to sabotage this case before it even goes to trial, counselor?"

He stiffened, and the old chair he was seated in creaked in protest. "Ethan's talked to the woman before."

"And he had no luck getting anything out of her the first time, did he?" When he admitted as much, she added, "It's extremely doubtful that he would be able to this time either. The man is like a bull charging a red cape. He has no finesse in dealing with witnesses, certainly not hostile ones."

As if conjured up by her rude comments, Ethan took that moment to enter, covered with dust and looking tired and haggard. Hannah Louise felt vastly relieved that the Ranger hadn't overheard her unflattering opinion of his disposition. She was wearing a red dress and didn't relish being charged.

Tipping his hat to Hannah Louise, Ethan marched in and perched himself on the edge of the desk. "How's things going, little brother? I've been out rounding up strays for Pa and only just got back."

"It's going. That's about all I can say. Hannah and I were just discussing the DeBerry woman. We need to interrogate her."

"If you want, I can ride over to Justiceburg and try talking to her, use stronger tactics than I did the last time." The Ranger appeared elated by the prospect.

"We don't." Hannah stepped forward, determined to set a few things straight with the lawman. "Travis and

I will handle things from here on out, Ranger Bodine. But we appreciate the offer."

Ethan's eyes widened, his lips thinning beneath his mustache. "Pardon me for asking, ma'am, but what gives you the right to come butting into things concerning my brother's case?"

"Travis has agreed to let me help him with Rafe's defense."

"The hell you say!" He jumped to his feet, glaring at Travis, willing him to deny it. "When did this happen? And who made such a stupid decision?"

Travis cleared his throat, feeling uncomfortable about his brother's rudeness toward Hannah Louise. Ethan had never made any bones about disliking Hannah and had objected strenuously to Travis's plan to wed her.

A man who always preferred the company of men, Ethan had never cared much for any woman, or been a proponent of marriage, so Travis hadn't really thought much about his animosity toward Hannah Louise. But now it was starting to rankle him, and he couldn't figure out why.

"Hannah's right, Ethan. I decided that she would be a great deal of help since she has such an extensive background in criminal law. And I'd think you'd be appreciative of the fact that she's offered to help save our brother's life."

Ethan had the grace to smile sheepishly at Hannah Louise, then moved toward the door. "Guess I'd best be getting on home. Don't want to keep my wife waiting. Willy's temper hasn't been the best of late."

"I thought Rangers were known for not retreating in the face of danger." A teasing smile curved Hannah's lips as she watched Ethan make a hasty departure.

"Like me, Ethan's learned that women, especially Bodine women, are not to be taken lightly."

"I knew there was a reason I liked those sisters-in-law of yours."

Ignoring the comment, Travis dropped back down into his swivel chair. "What are we going to do about Judy DeBerry? Guess I could go to Justiceburg and try to talk to her."

Surprised that he was actually asking her advice, Hannah felt a rush of pleasure. "I don't believe that would be wise. I think we should just wait until the trial and question the woman on the stand while she's under oath. It's obvious that she's going to be a hostile witness. I don't see the point in creating more animosity. That can only hurt us in the long run."

"There's a bartender at the bordello who Rafe claims to have spoken to. I could try talking to him."

"No doubt the bartender, who's employed by the DeBerry woman and looks to her for his livelihood, will testify to the fact that Rafe came looking for Bobby. I doubt he'll be much help."

Travis heaved a dispirited sigh. "Things don't look too promising."

Perching herself on the edge of the desk that Ethan had so recently occupied, Hannah studied his forlorn expression, and her heart went out to him. She knew it couldn't be easy for Travis having to shoulder the burden of his brother's defense. His close-knit family had always expected a lot from Travis and would be relying on him to perform miracles.

Travis had a good heart and a kind disposition, especially when it came to his family. Funny she hadn't remembered that about him.

"As I'm sure you realize, Travis, this case is not going to be an easy one to win. Which is why we need to work a few things out between us."

"Such as?"

"Such as agreeing that we should put aside our personal differences for the time being and declare a truce until this trial is over. We have enough obstacles to face without fighting each other."

He grinned, and that damn dimple appeared. "There's something to be said for fighting. The making up is always fun."

She swallowed, her gaze zeroing in on his lips. "I think it would be best to keep our relationship strictly professional. You have your own life to live, and I have mine. If we're to work together successfully to acquit your brother, then that's the way it should be. Agreed?"

She held out her hand to seal their bargain, but instead of taking it, or responding to her suggestion, he opened her palm and dropped a gumdrop into it.

Hannah stared at the candy, then at the man, and her heart quickened at the promise in his eyes. Travis had never shared his candy with her before.

Chapter Five

WITH A BRIGHT RED BANDANNA WRAPPED AROUND her head and a long apron covering most of her conservative navy blue dress, Hannah Louise didn't look much like an attorney this morning. Rather, she resembled one of the maids from the Upper East Side of Manhattan.

She'd been unable to stand the filthy room that Travis laughingly referred to as his law office and had arrived shortly after dawn in the hope of putting it to rights before he could take her to task for it.

With wire brush in hand, she scrubbed the pine-planked floor with a combination of lye soap, water, and determination, hoping to eradicate whatever vermin lived in and beneath the once attractive wood surface. She had been forced to take a knife to several deeply embedded pieces of gumdrops that had been rolled into the floor by Travis's swivel chair. A sticky, messy job, it had all but ruined her fingernails.

How anyone could pretend to enjoy working in such horrible surroundings was a mystery to her. She'd already spent the better part of two hours organizing the bookshelves and filing system. It had taken that long to sort out the important papers from the trash that had been accumulating over the years. It was a wonder the man could find a thing amid the chaos he'd created.

Hannah was still kneeling on the floor behind the desk when she heard the front door open. Peeking around the corner of the furniture, she observed two pair of serviceable black high-button shoes and felt relieved that she would be spared Travis's wrath for the time being. No doubt he'd be upset by her efforts to tidy up the place.

Whatever relief she felt was short-lived when she looked up to discover that her callers were none other than Olive Fasbinder and Margaret Willoughby. She groaned inwardly. They were the last persons in the world she wished to see, especially now when she looked like a German *haus frau*.

"Hello?" they called out.

Thinking seriously about taking refuge under Travis's desk until the two women departed, Hannah realized her actions would only be construed as childish and immature—something she'd vowed never to be again—and she decided to just make the best of it and pray that they left soon.

Pulling herself to her feet, she whipped off her kerchief, stuffing it into the pocket of her apron, and pasted on a welcoming smile she didn't feel. "Good morning, Olive . . . Margaret. I'm sorry, but if you've come to see Travis, he isn't in yet." Though their eyes widened at her disheveled appearance, to their credit they said nothing about it.

"Actually," Olive began in a high-pitched, grating voice that Hannah likened to a cat's wail, "we came to see you, Miss Barkley."

"Really? Well, here I am. But as you can see, I'm rather busy at the moment."

"This won't take long." Margaret took up where her cohort left off. "We just thought you should be made aware that Travis is already spoken for."

Hannah's eyebrows rose so high they nearly disappeared into her hairline. "Really! Well, I hadn't heard. Who is the . . ." she was tempted to say *un*lucky woman, but then thought better of it, "lucky woman?"

Olive, who'd always been highly allergic to lye soap, began to sneeze, then dabbed daintily at her nose with a lace handkerchief. "Travis hasn't actually declared himself yet, Miss Barkley," she admitted. "But Miss Willoughby and I have the greatest hope that he will confess his intention to marry one of us soon. You shouldn't think that you can come back to Misery and take up where you left off."

Olive was not an attractive woman by any stretch of the imagination. Her angular face and nonexistent chin stamped her homely. Her lack of good looks could have been overlooked if she'd possessed a pleasing personality, but unfortunately she was sadly lacking in that area, too.

Wondering if the two women were going to convert Travis to Mormonism so they could share him,

Hannah felt like laughing, but she was too annoyed to do anything but grit her teeth. "I came back to Misery to care for my father, who is ailing. I've subsequently been asked to assist with Rafe Bodine's criminal trial."

At the mention of the trial, Margaret puckered up like a tart lemon. "And that's another thing, Miss Barkley. Your unseemly unfeminine behavior is making it very difficult for Travis to hold his head high."

"Women have no place outside the home, as my mother has said to me so often," Olive piped in, looking very self-righteous in her condemnation of Hannah Louise. "You should be ashamed of yourself for daring to compete in a man's world."

Always in agreement with her lifelong friend, Margaret nodded. "You'll make Travis the laughingstock of this town if you don't desist in your actions, Miss Barkley. Men's egos are fragile, as I'm sure you know."

Hannah's smile never reached her eyes. "Why, yes I do know, Margaret Willoughby. But I didn't think you did, since you've never been married or had a serious beau." She ignored the woman's sharp intake of breath, adding, "And don't you think it's silly for both of you to keep calling me 'Miss Barkley' when we grew up together and have seen each other in our drawers?"

Red-faced, Olive fanned herself with her hand. "What a shocking thing to say, Hannah Louise Barkley! But then, you always were doing and saying things no decent woman ever would."

"And you've never gotten over the fact that Travis wanted to marry me, not you, did you, Olive? I remember when our engagement was announced, you took to your bed for two whole weeks."

"But it didn't last, did it?" Margaret reminded her with a spiteful smile, and Hannah wasn't the least bit surprised that the spinster hadn't married. Beneath Margaret's meek and mild exterior lay a nasty streak a mile wide.

"No. That's true," Hannah admitted finally. "But that's none of your or Olive's concern, and neither are my reasons for coming back to Misery or working on this murder trial. So I suggest you leave before I douse you both with that bucket of soapy water." She pointed at the metal pail, her intention quite clear.

"Well, I never—"

"And you're not likely to," Hannah told Margaret, her vow to remain mature suddenly forgotten.

The red-haired woman turned various shades of crimson and dashed from the room. Olive followed close on her heels, but not before flashing Hannah a hate-filled look that promised retribution.

When they were gone, and it was blissfully quiet once again, Hannah couldn't help the satisfied smile that now covered her face. And it wasn't just because Travis's office looked so clean and tidy, though that was certainly cause for glee, but because she had finally stood up to Olive and Margaret and told them exactly what she thought of them.

The two women had been the bane of her childhood existence, always ganging up on her, playing dirty tricks, spoiling whatever amusements she took pleasure in. Well, she wasn't going to allow them to spoil her gratification at working on this murder case.

The Bodines needed her. Travis certainly needed her help. And she needed to prove once and for all that women were far more intelligent and capable of holding their own in a male-dominated society than the people of this town were willing to allow.

There had been those who doubted her abilities when she'd first entered Hastings School of Law in San Francisco. Professors humored her questions, her classmates, mostly male, ridiculed her desire to study law in the first place, and the few colleagues who pretended to take her seriously merely did so out of pity.

Finishing fourth in her graduating class, she had won many honors, including the respect of her classmates. It felt good to be measured by her own worth and achievements, not because she was a woman, not because she was someone's wife or daughter, but because of what she had accomplished through her own hard work and determination.

Travis wasn't in the best of moods as he headed to his law office later that same morning. He'd just come from visiting Rafe, who had seemed inordinately pleased, if not downright elated, that Hannah Louise would be working on his defense case with Travis. Admittedly, his ego had taken a bit of a bruising.

Taking the stairs two at a time, he opened the door to his office only to pull up short. Thinking he must be in the wrong place, he looked up at the shingle hanging over the door that read, "Travis Bodine, Esq." He wasn't lost. But what the hell had happened to his office?

Hannah was nowhere to be found when he entered, so he assumed that she hadn't the courage to face him after doing her good deed for the day. Surveying her handiwork, he discovered that the floors had been scrubbed and waxed, the books on the shelves were lined up according to size, correspondence papers, which had previously been strewn everywhere, were stacked neatly in piles on his desk. And his law journals were now filed in alphabetical order in a wooden cabinet he had never seen before.

Everything looked extremely organized and orderly, and not the least bit like his office. If he hadn't just read the shingle outside, he would have sworn he was in the wrong place.

Hanging his jacket on a brass coatrack that had mysteriously appeared for that purpose, he shook his head, wondering again where Hannah Louise had gone. They were supposed to begin in earnest today preparing Rafe's defense, and he didn't have time to waste on womanly excuses or justifications.

Just then, the door opened and Hannah sailed in, wearing a smile as bright as a newly minted penny, and holding a wicker basket filled with something that smelled positively delicious. His heart skipped a beat at the sight of her.

"I thought since we'd be working straight through lunch today, I'd bring in some sandwiches and cookies for later."

His stomach rumbled in appreciation, but he chose to ignore the thoughtful gesture. "What have you done with my office? I can't find it."

"It does smell nice, doesn't it?" The beeswax she'd pasted on the floor and the ammonia-clean windows gave off nice fresh scents.

She looked inordinately pleased with her interference, and that did not set well with the annoyed attorney. "I think you've overstepped your bounds, Hannah Louise. This is my place of work, not yours."

"And now it's a clean place of work that we can both be proud to share. I didn't relish contracting some dread disease because you didn't have time to clean. You needn't thank me, Travis. I was happy to do it."

Plopping down in his chair to find a glass jar filled with gumdrops sitting on his desk, he bit back a rejoinder, touched by the thoughtful gesture. She'd always brought him candy in the past. "Thanks for the gumdrops," he said grudgingly.

"You're welcome. By the way, you had visitors this morning."

Knowing he'd made no appointments, Travis's forehead wrinkled in confusion. "Who was it?"

"I understand congratulations are in order." She swallowed her smile.

"For what?"

"I'm told you'll be getting married soon."

He paled considerably. "Who told you that?"

"Why, Margaret and Olive did," she replied innocently, proud that she'd managed to keep a straight face.

"They said you'd be declaring for one of them any day now." At his outraged look, she almost lost her composure. "I'm delighted for you, Travis."

"I'm not marrying anybody. And certainly not one of the spinsters."

Relief flooded through her at his words. She chided herself for caring and quickly changed the subject.

"Did you research those case histories we discussed yesterday?"

"Yes. But I'm not sure they apply to Rafe's case. Both of the defendants cited were judged not guilty by reason of insanity. I don't think that can be applied to Rafe. It's obvious his intentions, having been thought out ahead of time, were premeditated."

She hung her cape on the rack she had purloined from her father's attic, then sat in the chair in front of the desk. The sunlight glinting off her hair made it look like spun gold. Travis's fingers began to itch, and he drummed them nervously on the desktop.

"Your brother was under a great deal of duress at the time of the murder. We can stress that fact. It might be construed as temporary insanity."

Forcing his attention back to the matter at hand, he said, "I doubt Rafe will hold with us portraying him as some kind of lunatic. He's too damn proud for that."

"Pride and a hangman's noose don't make good companions. Rafe will need to agree to whatever type of defense strategy we come up with. It's his neck they're wanting to stretch. He'll have to listen to reason, no matter how farfetched or unmanly he thinks it is."

"That's easy for you to say, Hannah. You're not a man."

"I've been made painfully aware of that fact for years." She noted the slight flush to his cheeks and saw that she'd made her point. "Gender has nothing to do with this. Your brother is our client. He must trust us to make the right decisions and then abide by those decisions. It's the only way we can properly defend him."

"Yeah. But how are we going to come up with the right defense? That's easier said than done."

"True. But we've got time and a lot more research to do before we formulate any strategies. I'll get started on reviewing some previous court decisions, and perhaps you can—"

He shot her a menacing look that halted her in midsentence. "Just who's in charge of this case? And since when are you giving the orders?"

She shrugged. "I was under the impression that we were going to put our egos aside and find a solution to your brother's problem."

Her comment made him feel small and stupid. "I don't see how a man can work with all that damn sunlight pouring into the office," he said, changing the subject. "I'm about to go blind with all that clean glass we've got in here."

Rising to her feet, Hannah smiled knowingly and headed for the bookcase. "You're welcome, Travis."

The following morning when Travis arrived at his law office he found blue-gingham curtains hanging at the window and a vase of spring flowers on his desk. Two days after that a banjo clock was hanging on the rear wall, and a faded but still usable oriental carpet graced the center of the room.

His office was starting to take on the appearance and fragrance of a bordello, but he didn't make any more comments about the changes. He and Hannah were getting along quite well, and if she wanted to clutter up his office with flowers, frills, and furbelows, it was a small price to pay for the peace that presently existed between them.

Their bickering now centered solely on legal matters, not personal ones, and he found himself looking forward to their daily debates of legal points and issues. Hannah had an astute mind and a remarkable memory when it came to reeling off criminal statutes and judicial opinions. And he found her mind only slightly less appealing than the rose scent of the perfume she was fond of wearing.

It was difficult keeping his mind on legal matters when the plump curves of her breasts looked so damn tempting beneath the crisp cotton blouses she wore, or the way her hair always escaped her chignon and framed her face in charming disarray.

Travis cursed aloud, hating the fact that he was beginning to notice intimate details about Hannah, like how her nose crinkled when she concentrated on something important, or how tiny laugh lines edged the corners of her lovely eyes. Lost in disquieting thoughts, he didn't hear the door open.

"What's wrong, little brother? Your face is practically hanging down to your boots. Is your new partner proving to be a pain in your backside?" Ethan sauntered into the room and ground to a halt, his eyes widening at the changes before him. "Jesus! What the hell happened to your office? And where in hell did you get those flowers?" The yellow prickly pear flowers on Travis's desk bore a striking resemblance to Hannah Louise— lovely to look at, but hurtful to the touch—and Ethan wondered if his brother had noticed the resemblance. Probably not. He had the distinct feeling that his little brother was becoming enamored of the female attorney. Again.

Not in the mood for lengthy explanations, Travis replied, "I've been redecorating. What's on your mind?"

"Apparently not the same thing that's on yours, little brother. You and the lady lawyer ain't picking up where you left off, are you?" Ethan frowned deeply at the prospect.

"That's none of your business. But since you asked, the answer is no. We're working together, that's all." He couldn't even classify his association with Hannah as friendship. But some of his hostility had melted under her soft smiles. Smiles, he realized, he'd missed.

"No need to get as prickly as that cactus flower. I just don't want you getting hurt again."

Travis's brow arched in disbelief. "Like you're one to talk? After your previous experience I wouldn't have thought you'd have jumped so quickly into marriage with Willy."

"That's different. Willy's different."

Travis had found over the years that arguing with his older brother was a futile experience. Ethan liked being right about everything, and he very rarely relinquished the last word in an argument. "You've no cause to worry at any rate, Ethan. I hear it's all over town that I'm going to marry one of the spinsters."

The Ranger's mouth fell open, then he burst out laughing. "Is that what they're telling everyone?" he asked when he finally regained his composure. "Jesus!"

"That's what they told Hannah Louise."

Ethan's eyes twinkled mischievously, and he rubbed his chin as if contemplating the matter. "Well now, little brother, you're not getting any younger. Maybe you should think about settling down with one of the spinsters. They sure as heck are stuck on you. And if you hitch up with Margaret, you might end up with a dozen or so little woodpeckers running about the house. That would surely make Pa happy."

Not in the mood for more of his brother's teasing remarks, Travis seated himself behind the desk. "Was there something else you wanted? I don't have time to sit here and listen to you bellow like some goddamn hyena. I've got work to do."

Swallowing his laughter, Ethan said, "Lavinia's birthday is next Saturday, and Pa is fixing to give her a party. She wants you to come and bring Hannah Louise with you. She said to tell you that she won't take no for an answer."

"I can't speak for Hannah Louise, but tell Lavinia that I'll be there."

"I'll be sure to tell her to invite Olive and Margaret, so you'll have plenty of ladies at your beck and call."

The legal tome hit the door just as Ethan slammed it shut behind him, missing the Ranger by a mere fraction of an inch.

A few moments later, Hannah stepped through the doorway, nearly tripping over the law book lying on the floor. She bent to pick it up, a puzzled look on her face. "What's your brother laughing so hard about, Travis? I can't recall ever seeing Ethan with a grin on his face, let alone hearing him laugh." The Ranger was actually quite handsome when he smiled. But that still didn't mean she liked him.

Travis didn't bother to hide his disgust. "Nothing worth talking about." He noted the large package under her arm. "What's that?"

Moving forward, she placed it on the desk in front of him. "It's a typewriting machine." She removed the cloth cover as if she were unveiling a prized piece of art to display a black metal object. When he made no comment, but only stared at her strangely, Hannah went on to explain, "It's a machine for writing in characters. The keys strike the inked ribbon, then—"

"I know what a typewriter is, Hannah. I went to college, remember? I'm just wondering what you're doing with one. And why you've brought it here to my office."

"I bought it in New York, and I intend to use it to prepare the paperwork for the trial."

He shook his head. "That's a ridiculous idea. We don't need any of your highfalutin machines to—"

"Don't be such a pigheaded fool, Travis Bodine," she said, her eyes flashing fire. "Your male ego is showing again, and it's not a pretty sight."

Her remark made a direct hit, especially after his conversation with Rafe, and he swallowed his retort, striking a key on the machine instead. "Nothing happened. It must be broken."

She shook her head. "I don't have any paper rolled into it. It needs paper before it can print."

Feeling only slightly dumber than an ox, Travis shrugged. "I knew that. I was just fooling around."

"Don't be touching it, if you don't know how to use it. This typewriting machine was frightfully expensive, and I doubt there's anyone in town who's capable of fixing it if you should break it."

Perhaps he should ask her to sit on his lap and show him how to use it. Intriguing as that thought was, he said instead, "Are you ready to get down to work? It's nearly lunchtime, and we haven't gotten anything accomplished today."

"I've done some work at home, so you needn't worry that I'm not pulling my weight. But I'm afraid that we're going to have to postpone our discussion until after lunch."

"Well if you're that hungry, I guess we could go down to Bennett's Café and grab a bite to eat."

"Thank you. But I already have a luncheon engagement with Will McGrath."

"Will McGrath!" The spark of jealousy Travis felt took him totally by surprise. Not so, his anger. "Why are you having lunch with McGrath? He's trying to hang my brother, for chrissake!"

"That's exactly why, Travis. I thought it would be wise to see what McGrath has up his sleeve. When I received his note this morning, asking me to lunch to discuss Rafe's case, I thought it odd that he would want to meet with me and not you. But then, remembering that you two never got along all that well—"

"And that Will always had a crush on you," he interjected.

"His request didn't seem quite so unusual," she continued, as if he hadn't spoken. "It's only lunch. I won't be gone long. And when I return we can go over everything." She didn't mention that the thought of lunching alone with McGrath had made her extremely nervous in light of their previous encounter. But if she was going to help Rafe, she would have to ferret out information in any way possible, even if that included cozying up to McGrath.

"Just don't be giving away any of our secrets to that slimy snake."

Annoyed that he thought so little of her abilities and common sense, Hannah retorted, "Why, Travis, I wasn't aware that you and I had any secrets."

Heat climbed his neck. "I meant about Rafe's case."

"I'll be sure to be extremely circumspect in my dealings with McGrath. You needn't worry."

"See that you are." And this time he wasn't talking about the trial.

Chapter Six

WILL MCGRATH WAS WAITING AT A TABLE BY THE window, drumming his fingers impatiently on the red-and-white checkered tablecloth, when Hannah Louise entered Bennett's Café a short time later. Glancing at the regulator clock on the wall, Hannah noted that despite her usual punctuality she was fifteen minutes late for their appointment.

Stopping at the post office on her way to lunch, she had sent a letter to her mother informing Fiona of her appointment as Travis's cocounsel. Considering Hannah's past history with Travis, her mother would be surprised and not at all pleased that her daughter would remain in Misery for an undetermined length of time.

Because of the trial, and the continued puzzling circumstance of the judge's poor health, Hannah doubted that she would return to New York by summer as she had originally promised her mother. Her father's health had taken a turn for the worse. He seemed listless most of the time, constantly complaining of one ailment or another. And though Doc Leahy had assured her only yesterday that most of the judge's afflictions were in his head and not his heart, Hannah worried nevertheless.

She also felt a large measure of guilt, wondering if his latest relapse was caused by her excessive absences due to the upcoming trial. She'd come back to Misery to take care of him and instead had shirked that responsibility to pursue another. And though her father insisted that she remain on the case, she just wasn't sure she was doing the right thing.

"There you are, Hannah Louise. I was beginning to think you had stood me up." The copper-haired prosecutor smiled, revealing a wide gap between his two front teeth, then rose to his feet as she approached the table.

Smiling apologetically, she slid into the seat across from him. "I'm sorry to be so late, William, but I stopped to post a letter, and Myra Semple kept me talking about one thing or another. That woman does love to gossip."

"Nor surprising, since there's no shortage of it in town these days."

Waiting for him to make some snide remark about her and Travis working together, she relaxed when he said, "How's your father? I hear the judge hasn't been feeling well of late." Not that he cared. Will had always despised Thaddeus Barkley. In fact, if the old bastard died tomorrow, he would dance on his grave. Barkley had never liked him, had even gone so far as to accuse him of some underhanded tactics during a murder trial a few years back. But he'd never been able to prove his suspicions that a witness had been bribed, and the judge had been unable to carry out his threat of having him disbarred.

Hannah forced a smile, wishing she liked Will better. She had never warmed up to him in all the years she had known him. Maybe it was because he'd always been so outwardly jealous of the Bodine brothers and had never bothered to hide his dislike. Will had often vocalized that the Bodines were an uncouth bunch of braggarts who hid behind the law to further their own ambitions, which sounded more like Will than any of the Bodines, in Hannah's opinion. Or maybe it was because she had always seen through his fawning, insincere ways. The man was a master at manipulation.

"My father's doing as well as can be expected for a man his age," she finally replied. "Thank you for asking."

"I'm glad you consented to see me today, Hannah Louise. There's something I've been wanting to talk to you—"

"If it's about Rafe Bodine's case, then I'm afraid—"

He held up his hand. "Not directly. Though I did want to tell you how surprised I am that you'll be assisting Travis with the case. Lord knows he needs the help. Quite frankly, I think he's out of his element. But I never thought he'd allow such a thing.

"And there's also a conflict of interest problem because of your father's position as presiding judge. You should know that I intend to file a complaint with the court as soon as the new judge arrives."

"You must do whatever you feel is necessary, Will. But I can assure you that if my father found no conflict of interest, the new judge won't either. Papa is a stickler for doing things by the book. He knows the law like the back of his hand.

"And Travis is quite a competent attorney, as I'm sure you'll find out, if you haven't already." She knew Travis had defeated Will in court on several occasions. That the prosecutor still smarted over that fact was evident by the high color staining his cheekbones.

"Your reputation is already tarnished, Hannah Louise. Are you sure you want to damage it further? You know what small towns are like. People talk."

Gossip and innuendo had been hounding her since her arrival back in Misery. Unkind comments always found their way to the intended victim—she'd already experienced that firsthand—as did well-meaning advice. It was another of the many things Hannah disliked about small-town living.

But there were a few things she enjoyed—the smell of chicken frying, for one, which seemed to be a small-town specialty. No one in New York City could have fried up a decent chicken if their life depended on it.

Her stomach grumbled loudly at the tantalizing aroma surrounding her, but if Will heard, he gave no clue. He was obviously more in tune with his own thoughts than her hunger pains. "Are you trying to scare me off this case, Will, or are you threatening me?"

"You wound me, Hannah Louise. I've always respected your abilities. If we had been engaged to marry, I would have been man enough to accept your desire to practice law."

Hannah held the menu up in front of her face, so Will wouldn't notice the disgust registered there. The self-serving prosecutor was good at attacking others when they weren't around to defend themselves.

"How's the fried chicken today?" she asked. "I've always been partial to it."

Reaching across the table, he grabbed the edge of her menu and lowered it to the table, an intent look on his face. Hannah felt like bashing the damn thing over his head.

"We can order in a minute. First, there's something important I'd like to discuss with you."

"So you said. Go on."

"I'd like you to reconsider your decision to act as cocounsel on the defense team. I won't petition the court if you do.

"This is an open-and-shut case. We've got an eyewitness who'll testify that Rafe shot Bobby Slaughter in cold blood, the accused has a reputation for violence, and there's not a jury in this land who'll vote to acquit. You're backing a loser, Hannah Louise."

Though she did her best to keep her face perfectly impassive, Hannah Louise was boiling like a geyser ready to erupt. "Let me get this straight—you want me to just walk away from Rafe Bodine's defense team and leave Travis at your mercy?"

He reached for her hand, but she pulled back just in the nick of time to avoid contact. "It's no secret that I've always harbored a deep affection for you, Hannah Louise. How would it look if we were to renew our acquaintance and you continued to work for your ex-fiancé?"

"I'm afraid that your suggestions are out of the question, William. Not only would it be unethical for me to abandon Travis and his brother at this point, I'm not interested in pursuing a personal relationship with anyone in this town, including you. My life's in New York. I intend to go back there when the trial is over." His angry expression indicated that she had offended him, but she just didn't care.

What kind of a man would ask her, or any attorney, for that matter, to abandon a client, to enter into a personal alliance during a murder trial?

Perhaps one who was afraid he would lose. She filed the intriguing thought away for future reference.

"Thank you for lunch, William, but I'm afraid that I've lost my appetite. And I must get back to work." She had no intention of listening to any more of his ridiculous suggestions. Ignoring the fact that his mouth was hanging open wide enough to catch flies, she bade him farewell.

Will watched Hannah walk away and his mind was made up. The woman couldn't be used as an ally. No doubt she was still in love with Bodine and having an affair right under everyone's nose. The possibility infuriated him.

Olive and Margaret would no doubt be interested in his suspicions. They would be very effective in spreading the gossip before the jury was selected. And his friend, Sid Barker, the editor of the newspaper, would love to speculate in print about the legalities of Judge Barkley's daughter working for the defense. And if all else failed, there was still the matter of Roy Lee Slaughter, a man who had a very big ax to grind against the Bodine family.

"That weasly, no good bastard! I should have expected something like this from McGrath. But I didn't think even he would stoop so low as to try to intimidate my cocounsel to resign."

Hannah had anticipated that Travis would be mildly upset at the news, but she hadn't expected this full-fledged fury that had erupted upon his learning of Will's suggestion. She hadn't mentioned the prosecutor's other, more personal, proposition. Now, observing Travis's anger, she was glad.

"For someone who didn't want me as cocounsel, Travis, your reaction to Will's offer is somewhat surprising, if you don't mind me saying so. Careful, or I might think you actually need me."

Travis's shirt collar suddenly felt two sizes too small for his neck. He swallowed with some difficulty before answering. "I was wrong, okay? From what I've seen, you're a very competent attorney."

"But I'm still a woman? And you're still not one hundred percent comfortable working with me?"

She knew him too well for Travis to deny it. "I'm trying to overcome my pride and prejudice in the matter of women in the workplace."

If only you'd made that concession five years before. The startling thought flashing through Hannah's mind was quickly squelched.

"Well, I guess that's something then, isn't it?" She went on to say, "I never seriously entertained any of McGrath's suggestions. Though I admit that some small part of me was happy to see him humble himself by asking. It only proves that he's less than confident about winning this case."

Leaning back in his chair, Travis steepled his fingers before his face, contemplating her deduction. "Not necessarily. Will has always disliked me. I suspect he hated the fact that my brothers and I were close and that he was an only child. At any rate, his suggestion that you quit—not to take anything away from you, mind you," he added quickly, "could very well have been made just to spite me. He's not above that sort of childish behavior."

"Well, whatever the reason, it just makes me want to defeat him that much more. And if we're to do so, we'd better get to work."

Time seemed to fly by as they worked out their strategies, studied relevant case law, and took copious notes, which Hannah would transcribe later on her typewriter. The sun had long since disappeared into the horizon, and the kerosene lamps burned brightly against the encroaching darkness.

When Hannah finally pulled her nose out of *Blackstone's Commentaries*, it was to find that Travis had fallen asleep at his desk, his head buried in his arms.

The sight tugged at her heart. Travis had been working very diligently of late to make himself proficient with the difficult criminal statutes and case law he needed to master before the trial. She admired both his determination and unwavering dedication to his brother.

She also couldn't help but admire how tanned and muscular he'd become compared to five years before, and she credited his new house construction with the change. No doubt he'd been working long hours out in the sun, doing all sorts of physical labor that resulted in those impressive biceps.

The lamplight played over his dark hair, and she could distinctly remember how it felt to run her fingers through the soft strands. His hair was unusually silky for a man, and always much too long, as it was now, brushing the collar of his shirt.

The rich timbre of his voice still had the power to send tingles down her spine. And on those rare occasions when he smiled, she found herself staring at the dimples in his cheeks, at the soft contours of his lips . . .

She shook her head. Remembering would likely get her in trouble, Hannah reminded herself as she crossed the room and cleared her throat loudly.

Travis awoke with a start. He'd been having the most wonderful dream about Hannah Louise, about making love to her in a field of wildflowers. No wonder he was sweating so profusely and that his groin actually ached. "Sorry. I must have dozed off."

"You've been working hard. There's no need to apologize. This trial is likely to take its toll on both of us before we're through."

He nodded, then stretched like a sinewy jungle cat, watching as she crossed to the coatrack to fetch her wrap. "There's something I need to ask you before you leave."

She tied the dark blue woolen cape around her neck and sighed. "Something about the case? I'm tired. Can it wait until morning?" Her brain felt like mush, and she could barely keep her eyes open. As worn-out as she felt, she might have to borrow some of her father's Peruvian Syrup elixir, touted to increase the iron and vitalizing agents in one's blood.

Pushing back his chair, Travis stood. "I'll walk you home. It's late. You shouldn't be out on the street by yourself."

The protective offer made her laugh. Misery was hardly the crime-infested city of the West, certainly not as bad as New York. "I walk home by myself every evening, Travis. And I doubt that I'll be accosted, except perhaps by Olive or Margaret, who feel I've trespassed on their territory, namely, you."

He looked chagrined. "I'm sorry you've had to put up with them."

"It's no matter," she said with a shrug. "They don't really bother me anymore. Not like they did when we were kids."

Chuckling, Travis moved to the door and opened it, waiting for her to precede him out. "You mean like the time when they tackled you to the ground, and Olive sat on your back while Margaret forced you to eat poison oak?" Ethan had done the very same thing to Rafe once, he recalled.

"You wouldn't think it so funny if you'd been the one with the rash inside your mouth. I couldn't eat for over a week. I remember my mother marching over to Olive's and Margaret's houses and giving the Fasbinders and the Willoughbys a blistering setdown." Fiona could always be counted on to speak her mind. That was one of her mother's most endearing, and most exasperating, qualities.

The days had turned warmer, but the nights were still brisk, and Hannah wrapped her cape more securely about her to ward off the chill. Stars twinkled like brilliant diamonds against the black canvas sky, and the moon shone half-full like a crescent.

"What was it you wished to ask me?" She remembered another time, another place, another question. Travis had been nervous, tongue-tied, and distracted, as he was now. It was the night he had proposed marriage. She sighed. *Oh, Travis, what happened to us?*

Strolling alongside Hannah brought back memories, feelings of happier times they'd shared, and Travis fought against them. What was in the past, was in the past, he told himself. But he wondered if that were really true. Lately, he'd been questioning his wisdom about breaking their engagement, wondering if he'd made a mistake. There was still something between him and Hannah, feelings, unfinished business. But love? That was the one thing he wasn't sure about.

"My stepmother's birthday is tomorrow, and Pa is holding a party for her out at the ranch. She wants you to come."

Hannah chewed her lower lip, indecision furrowing her brow. "I don't know. Papa isn't feeling well, and I don't think I should leave him. Besides, how would I get there?"

"I can drive you out in the buggy, and Mrs. Fogarty will remain to take good care of the judge."

What he said was true, but still she hesitated. Hannah liked Lavinia a great deal, but being alone with Travis was just asking for trouble. She still hadn't gotten that impetuous kiss out of her mind, and she'd been wondering what it would be like to kiss him again. "I'm not sure if it's such a good idea."

"Lavinia will be very disappointed if you don't come. It's her birthday, after all."

Reaching the Barkley home, they halted. Light shone from within, indicating to Hannah that Maude had waited up, had dinner warming on the stove, and would no doubt be looking out the window at any moment. Circumspection was not one of the housekeeper's traits.

"I'd hate to disappoint Lavinia. She's always been so nice to me," Hannah said, not realizing she'd spoken her thoughts aloud.

"Then you'll come?"

Though she'd probably regret it later, she nodded. "What time can I expect you?"

"How does six sound? That'll give me time to clean up after working on the house all day."

"And you'll actually be on time?" Her smile teased. "As I recall, you have a penchant for lateness."

"In case you haven't noticed, I've changed."

"We'll see," was all she said.

Hannah entered to find Maude standing in the front hallway, guarding the door like a sentinel. Maude had obviously been watching from the window and appeared ready to do battle if the granite set of her chin was any indication. There'd be no escaping the nosy housekeeper's probing questions this night.

"Well, young missy. What have you to say for yourself?"

Feigning innocence, Hannah purposely side-stepped the question. "I'm just famished. Has Papa already eaten?"

"And why shouldn't he?" She took Hannah's cape, hanging it on the coatrack. "It's hours past dinner, and you're late getting home again. And don't think I didn't see you outside chatting with the Bodine boy."

"In case you haven't heard, Travis and I are working on a criminal case together. It's often going to be necessary to work late, as I did tonight, and conversation cannot be avoided."

"*Hmph!* You two looked too cozy by half," she said.

Hannah sighed, trailing the older woman into the kitchen. The distinctive smell of onions rose up to greet her. As tired as she was, she wasn't in the mood for one of Maude's lectures, especially one that centered on her relationship with Travis—a relationship she had yet to figure out.

"What's for dinner? I'm starved."

The housekeeper practically shoved Hannah into one of the kitchen chairs then proceeded to fill a splatterware bowl with a generous portion of beef stew. "I've made one of your favorites, Hannah Louise."

Stew was one of the few things Maude made passably well. Of course, it didn't take much culinary expertise to toss some meat and vegetables into a pot and cook them. The housekeeper had once tried adding dumplings to the mixture with disastrous results. They had cooked up as hard as one of Abner Doubleday's baseballs, and the judge claimed he could have broken every single one of the windows in the house with them.

"How's Papa been feeling today?" Hannah asked, hoping to change the subject. The judge's health was one of Maude's favorite topics and a sure way to distract her.

The woman tsked and shook her head. "The poor man's in a bad way, I tell you. He hardly ate a thing at lunch, and he stayed in his room most of the day. And when he hears that you've taken up with that Bodine boy again . . . Well, it's likely to put him into a permanent decline."

Hannah swallowed her smile and her stew before

saying, "I haven't taken up with Travis, though I am planning to attend his stepmother's birthday party with him tomorrow evening. He offered to drive me, since Papa isn't feeling well and won't be able to attend."

Maude's deep frown creased her forehead in two as she seated herself at the table. Since Fiona's departure there was little formality in the household, and the housekeeper often took her meals with Hannah Louise. "I can't help thinking that this new association you've got with Travis is going to come to no good, just like the last one did, Hannah Louise. Have you forgotten how heartsick you were when he broke your engagement? How you cried your eyes out until they was all red and puffy and you resembled one of them frogs out in Cooper's Pond?"

Reaching out, Hannah patted the woman's hand. "I haven't forgotten any of that, Maude, so you needn't worry that anything will come of our working together. We're just business associates. I've got more experience in criminal law than Travis. He needs my help to win this case." *So why then am I eager to see him every morning and so loath to leave him every night?*

The older woman didn't look at all convinced. "*Hmph!* So you say. But things have a way of happening before you know it. Take the judge, for example. He was lucky your ma left when she did and decided never to come back. It spared him the hurt a reunion with her might have caused."

"Perhaps a reunion would have gotten them back together," Hannah pointed out.

Maude looked horrified by the possibility. "The only thing worse than you getting back together with the Bodine boy is the judge getting back together with Mrs. High-and-Mighty Barkley."

To say that Fiona and Maude hadn't gotten along well would have been a gross understatement. Both women were stubborn and strong-willed, and they liked doing things their own way. Hannah suspected that her father was at the center of the discord, but no one had ever admitted as much. Not Maude, and certainly not her mother.

"You'll not have to worry about either one of us, Maude. Especially not Papa. Hell would freeze over before Mama stepped foot in this town again. If she told me once, she told me a hundred times, 'Hannah Louise, I am through with Texas for good.' " Hannah flailed her arms dramatically, mimicking her mother, and Maude smiled. " 'I would rather burn in hell than set eyes on that man I call husband. Thaddeus Barkley will rue the day he chose the law over me.' "

"Did she ever say what that meant? 'Cause both were pretty closemouthed about what caused their breakup to begin with."

"No. Though I asked innumerable times, Mama refused to discuss it, saying it wasn't worth her time."

"Well, I ain't gonna beat a dead horse, Hannah Louise, but I truly hope you're going to let your head and not your heart rule you this time. I don't want to see you hurt again, baby. I don't think I could stand it."

"I'm five years older and a great deal wiser,

Maude, so you needn't worry. I can take care of myself."

Maude looked clearly skeptical. Hannah Louise felt just plain scared, despite her words to the contrary.

Chapter Seven

"PRETTY. PRETTY."

Hannah gazed down to discover a small child tugging determinedly on the hem of her skirt. Big brown eyes with an achingly sweet smile looked up at her, and Hannah found herself enraptured by the sight of Emmaline's youngest adopted daughter, Theodora, or Pansy, as she was called.

"Hello, sweetheart." She held out her arms and was surprised when the child came readily to her. Hoisting Pansy in the air, she hugged her to her breast. "You're a precious bundle, aren't you?" Every maternal instinct she possessed came rushing to the forefront. She could tell herself and everyone else that she didn't desire or need marriage and family, but she'd be lying. And it was times like these that those lies were most evident.

"Pretty," Pansy said again, patting Hannah's hair and the glittering tortoiseshell comb resting there. The comb had been a gift from Travis on the occasion of Hannah's eighteenth birthday. The comb, and the kiss that had accompanied it, would always remain a treasured remembrance. "I'd let you play with it, sweetheart, but my hair'll fall down if I do and then I'll look just dreadful."

Pansy's attention shifted suddenly, and she pointed at Travis, who was making his way over toward them, holding two glasses of wine punch. "Papa!" the child squealed excitedly, and Hannah felt tears well in her eyes. Travis bore a striking resemblance to Rafe, and the small child was obviously confused.

"That's your Uncle Travis," she explained. Her heart fluttered strangely, and she took a deep breath to calm herself, wondering if he would always have the power to affect her that way.

"I see you've got your hands full," Travis said, staring at the drinks he held, then at Hannah, an odd expression on his face as he observed her with his niece. "I'll hold on to yours for a bit," he offered.

"Papa!" Pansy flailed her arms wide at Travis, who looked exceedingly uncomfortable at the child's mistake.

"I think she's got me confused with Rafe."

"You and your brother do look a lot alike. And I'm sure this sweet baby misses her papa a great deal. Do you want to hold her? I can take the punch glasses if you like."

Travis had an affinity for dogs and babies, though he was out of his element with the latter. "I guess," he said with a great deal of uncertainty before they exchanged burdens.

Setting the drinks down on a nearby table, Hannah watched as Travis hugged Pansy to his chest and nuzzled her soft cheek affectionately. She sighed deeply, thinking what a wonderful father he would make. *Would have made*, she amended, a queer ache replacing the flutter in her chest. Before she could dwell on the disturbing thought, Emmaline approached, looking very distraught.

"There you are, Pansy." Exasperation and relief filled her voice at the sight of her daughter. "I wondered where she had toddled off to." She shook her head. "If I turn my back for even one minute, this child disappears into thin air." Her pronouncement made Pansy giggle, then shout, "Mama! Mama!" at the top of her lungs, as she clapped her tiny hands excitedly.

A loving look infused Emma's face—a look that said all was forgiven. "I hope Pansy hasn't been too much of a nuisance."

"Not at all," Hannah reassured her. "I think she's perfectly precious. And she smells wonderful."

"Rafe calls her his little flowerpot. But there have been times when—Well, let's just say that she hasn't always been fragrant."

Travis wrinkled his nose in disgust, then a horrified look crossed his face. "I think this is one of those times." He held the child out to her mother.

"Timing is everything with children," Emma advised, smiling ruefully. "You'll find that out when you have some of your own."

Hannah's face heated. Travis shifted his feet nervously, feeling very uncomfortable at where the discussion was headed, and was relieved when Emma departed to take Pansy upstairs

He changed the subject. "You look very pretty tonight, Hannah. I can't remember if I told you so or not." The pink-and-white-striped gown she wore reminded him of a tasty confection—taffy or sugar-spun cotton candy. His eyes drifted down to the eyelet lace scooped neckline and the expanse of flesh there. He'd always had a fondness for sweets, and Hannah Louise looked mighty tasty. He shifted again, this time for entirely different reasons.

Hannah was pleased by the compliment and smiled widely. "As a matter of fact you did. But it's something no woman ever tires of hearing."

The fiddler began a toe-tapping rendition of "Buffalo Gals," and Travis cleared his throat, knowing how much Hannah loved to dance. And how much he loved dancing with her. "Would you care to take a turn around the floor? It's a shame to waste all this good music."

Spying Olive and Margaret coming toward them, Hannah groaned inwardly. She had no intention of ruining her evening by engaging the two spinsters in conversation. Travis's timing couldn't have been more perfect.

Despite her earlier reservations, she decided that dancing with Travis was an awfully appealing prospect. And if she were entirely truthful with herself, the idea of being held in his arms, however briefly, was not something she wanted to pass up. "I'd love to. It's been ages since I've danced."

Five years to be exact. Hannah hadn't had a serious beau since moving to New York and rarely dated, much to her mother's displeasure. Fiona was always trying to match her up with one fellow or another, but Hannah had gotten adept at dodging her mother's human male bullets.

"I'm surprised. You always loved dancing."

"Things change," she replied, her voice soft and filled with something akin to regret, and she was eager to change the subject.

Across the room, Hannah spied Lavinia chatting with her daughter-in-law, Willy. "Your stepmother looks positively radiant tonight, Travis." And it wasn't just the lovely peach-and-green calico dress she wore either, Hannah decided, though Lavinia certainly looked stunning in it. An inner glow radiated from the older woman that Hannah couldn't quite put her finger on.

"Lavinia's goodness shines from within. She's a wonderful woman. My father is a very lucky man. Whether or not he realizes that is another matter." He watched Ben sidle up next to his wife, and the look he wore was far from festive. Travis decided that he'd much rather concentrate on the lovely woman he held in his arms rather than his father's nasty disposition, which, after all, was nothing new.

"I hope you're not still planning to do what you threatened, Vin," Ben Bodine said. "I wasn't joking last night when I said that I wouldn't approve."

Hurt crossed the older woman's face, and her chin jutted out mutinously. "This is my party, and I will decide when to make the announcement. And that will be shortly, Ben, so I hope you act your age and be polite."

"Look who's talking about acting their age," he said, and Lavinia's cheeks flushed hot. Watching him walk away, she fought against the hot rush of tears threatening to spill. Never in a million years would she have thought Ben would object to having another child. But when she had told him last night that she was pregnant, he'd been anything but overjoyed.

"I can't believe such a thing, Vin." He stared at her accusingly over the special celebratory dinner she had prepared. The beef had been cooked rare, the potatoes slathered in butter, just the way he liked them, but his expression registered indigestion just the same.

"I'm too damn old to be having another child. Can't you see that? And I don't feel right about it. Not with my son in jail and facing murder charges."

"But you've known for years that I wanted a child, Ben. Why can't you be happy about it? It's a child conceived by the love we share for each other." And she did love him, with all her heart and soul. Despite the fact he was irascible and hardheaded, she found him to be also good-hearted and generous. And his faults only endeared him to her that much more. Perfection was dull; Ben was anything but.

"I've got three sons. I don't need another child. *We* don't need a child at our age. For chrissake, Vin! I'll be the laughingstock of the entire town for having another kid at my age."

At that, she threw down her napkin, jumped to her feet, and shouted, "Well I've got no sons, no daughters, and I will have this child, with or without your approval. And there's not a damn thing you can do about it, Benjamin Bodine, except be happy."

She fled the room then, and it wasn't until morning that they had discussed the situation again. Though Ben had seemed somewhat contrite about his earlier behavior, he hadn't changed his negative attitude about the baby: He didn't want it.

Lavinia wondered if he ever would.

"Your stepmother looks madder than a wet hen," Willy told Travis after the song ended and he and Hannah had quit the dance floor. "And that's pretty darn mad where I come from."

"I believe Willy's right." Hannah watched the older woman storm across the room at a hurried pace. She was heading in their direction, but not looking directly at them. "I wonder what's wrong."

"Guess we'll find out soon enough," he replied. "She's heading straight for the bandstand."

Frowning, Ethan shook his head. "Don't know why everyone's so surprised. It's her birthday. Pa probably said something rude to her about her age. You know how ornery he can be."

Patting her husband's cheek affectionately, Willy's

smile bordered on mischievous. "I believe he's the one whom you take after, Ethan dear."

Ethan had been on the blunt end of his father's anger many times. The two men mixed together like oil and water, never agreeing on much of anything, and he resented, even jokingly, being compared to him. "I'm nothing like the old man. I'd shoot myself if I thought I was."

Hannah's eyes widened at the vehement remark, and Travis thought she was probably glad she hadn't entered into his strange, combative family after all.

Staring out from the bandstand that Ben had hastily erected, Lavinia gestured for everyone to quiet down, then took a deep breath. She purposely avoided looking at her husband, who she knew would be furious, but she could feel his blue eyes shooting into her like bullets just the same. Be that as it might, nothing was going to spoil this moment that she had waited too many years for, she decided.

The room finally quieted. "I'd like to thank everyone for coming tonight to share in my birthday celebration. You've made it a very special occasion for me. Most of all, I'd like to thank my husband for making all of the arrangements." Lavinia saw their neighbor, Rafe's former father-in-law Will Masters, slap Ben on the back good-naturedly, heard him say, "Good going, Ben. You finally did something right," and she almost winced.

Ben's face took on the hue of long red underwear, and color filled Lavinia's cheeks as well. "Actually, Ben has done a lot more right than just arrange for this wonderful party," she started to explain, hoping to interject a note of levity into the moment.

"Lavinia!"

There was no mistaking the warning note in her husband's voice. Swallowing with some difficulty, she chose to ignore it. "I have a very happy announcement to make."

Travis and Ethan exchanged confused glances.

"What's going on, do you think?" Ethan asked.

"*Sssh!*" Travis said. "Lavinia's about to talk."

"I'm happy to announce that Ben and I are going to have a baby."

At that moment, the room grew so deathly quiet you could have heard a pin drop. The crowd stared at each other in surprise and confusion, then someone, a woman in the back of the room, began clapping and shouting, "Three cheers for Lavinia."

Soon the room was in total chaos as the Bodines' friends and neighbors rushed forward to congratulate the new mother-to-be.

Ben beat a hasty retreat.

Ethan and Travis stood stock-still with their mouths hanging open.

"Well, I never thought I'd live to see the day that those two had nothing to say." Emmaline came forward to stand beside the two couples.

Ethan ignored her amused grin. "Aren't they a bit old for that sort of thing?" he whispered, and Wilhemina burst out laughing.

"There's not an age moratorium on having sex or babies."

His wife's remark made his cheeks fill with color. "What the hell's a moratorium?" he asked, flashing Willy an annoyed look. "And why aren't we giving the expectant mother a kiss?"

With apologies to Hannah, Travis rushed forward to do just that. "Congratulations, Lavinia! I'm very happy for you and Pa. Where is he?" He looked about the crowded room, but saw no sign of him. "I wanted to shake his hand, offer my congratulations."

Her happiness faded a bit; her eyes filled with uncertainty. "I'm . . . I'm not sure, Travis. You go find him though and give him a hug. I think he needs one. The news about the baby was a bit of a shock to him."

"There's nothing wrong, is there?"

She kissed her stepson's cheek. Of the three boys, Travis had always been the sensitive one. "We'll talk later. Go find your father now. Do it for me, okay?"

Travis did as she asked, locating Ben a few minutes later standing outside on the front porch. Even in darkness, he could see that his father was troubled. The way Ben rubbed the back of his neck was a sure sign something was agitating the heck out of him. Travis pretended not to notice. "I understand congratulations are in order, Pa. I'd like to be the first to shake your hand."

"Damn woman! Doesn't she know that I'm too damn old to be saddled with another young'n? I finally get a bunch of grandkids I can dote on, and now I'm going to have me another kid of my own." He cursed aloud. "I'm sorry to say, but I ain't happy about it, boy."

Before he could respond the front door banged shut and Ethan approached, grinning like the cat who had just eaten the canary. Travis gritted his teeth. His brother was not known for his tact or subtlety.

"Why you sly old dog. Why didn't you tell us you and Lavinia were fixin' to have a baby? And here I was thinking you were too old for that sort of thing." He slapped his father on the back, clearly amused by the old man's annoyed reaction.

"I can run circles around you on my worst day, Ethan, so don't be giving me any of that old-age crap, you hear?"

Grinning despite the insult, Ethan replied, "Sounds like you're not real thrilled about the prospect of having another kid, Pa. Could it be you're worried about not getting one as handsome or smart as the first three?"

"Jesus, Ethan! Shut up!" Travis warned. "Can't you see Pa's upset about Lavinia's announcement?"

"But why? I'm happy as hell about Willy having a baby. I'd think at Pa's age he'd be tickled pink. It's a sure sign of his potency. And at his age, that ain't nothing to shake a stick at. No pun intended."

Ben lunged for Ethan, but Travis stepped between them just in time to avoid possible bloodshed. Ethan made a hasty retreat back into the house, grumbling the whole time about the ungratefulness of some men.

"Don't mind Ethan, Pa. He's just getting back at you for all the times you teased him. And you were awfully hard on him when you first heard the news about Willy being pregnant," he reminded his father, who sighed in response. When it came to temperament, Ethan and Ben were like two peas in a pod. Travis couldn't figure out why neither one of them could see it.

"Care to take a walk? I don't relish talking to anyone else right now. I'm too upset."

Travis followed Ben off the porch and into the yard. Cottonwood leaves snapped loudly in the soft breeze, and the music emanating from the house almost drowned out the chirping crickets and hooting owl.

"How have you left things with Lavinia?" Travis asked. His father could be hard, and his stepmother needed all of their support right now. Forty-seven wasn't ancient, but Lavinia's age was bound to make her pregnancy more difficult than most. "She's going to need you, Pa."

"Don't you think I know that, boy? But I can't help the way I feel. Did you see the shocked looks on my neighbors' faces? I feel like some old reprobate who got caught with his pants down at the local whorehouse."

Travis swallowed his smile. His father's reaction was just the opposite of what he'd expected. Ben's ego had never been what one could call small. In fact, he bragged louder and more often than most. His mother used to say it was part of Ben's charm, and one of the reasons she'd decided to marry him. Patsy Bodine had always enjoyed a challenge.

"Ethan's right, you know. This is going to make you somewhat of a big shot around here. Not many men

your age have children. You should be proud, not embarrassed."

"Sixty-two ain't that old, boy. And I'm in good
health. It's just aggravating that everyone knows my
personal business. That they know me and Vin—Well,
you know." His cheeks filled with color, and Travis
couldn't remember a time when he'd seen his father
blush like a schoolboy.

"I'd think you'd have more cause to complain if
you weren't able to—You know. Many older men can't
cut it between the sheets. You ought to be proud you can
still do the deed and do it right, Pa. I'd be, if I was your
age."

"You can't do the deed right at the age you're at
now, boy," Ben tossed back. "And why are you sashay-
ing about with that Barkley woman? I thought you and
her were quits. Now I see you cozying up to her again.
Why don't you make up your mind about what you
want?"

His father had very effectively turned the tables on
him, and there wasn't a whole hell of a lot Travis could
do about it, unless he wanted to get into an argument,
which he didn't. Arguing with Pa was a lot like sparring
with Ethan—an exercise in frustration.

"Hannah's been helping me with Rafe's case. You
know that. We're just business associates, that's all."

The old man harrumphed, clearly not convinced.
"Don't look that way from where I'm standing. You
ain't getting any younger, boy. Instead of mooning after
some woman you tossed away, why don't you find a

nice woman and settle down? Mrs. Fasbinder tells me that Olive is sweet on you."

Travis almost choked on the suggestion. He gazed at his father in disbelief. "Olive Fasbinder is sweet on anyone who's wearing pants. And in case it's escaped your notice, Pa, she's not exactly my type."

"Well who the hell is? You thought Hannah Louise was at one time, then changed your mind. Now you're keeping company with her again." Ben shook his head. "My boys are all fools." With one last contemptuous look, he stalked away, leaving Travis alone in the moonlight.

While Travis pondered his foolishness in consoling his father, Hannah joined Emmaline and Wilhemina in offering her heartfelt congratulations to Lavinia, who was now seated on the leather sofa beside her two daughters-in-law.

Hannah was nearly as excited as the two Bodine women about the prospect of their mother-in-law's baby. Lavinia had confided in the past about her desire to have a child, so Hannah was thrilled to hear that she was finally getting her wish.

"Ben must be so excited, Lavinia," she said, and Wilhemina and Emmaline exchanged worried glances, making the young woman think that she'd said something wrong. "I'm sorry. Did I—"

Clasping Hannah's hand, Lavinia shook her head. "It's quite all right, dear. Ben is a little upset about the baby, that's all. I was just telling Willy and Emma about his reaction to the news that I was pregnant."

"Well I think it's just so exciting." Emmaline patted her own swollen stomach. "Now all the Bodine women can be fat and sassy, and no one can say a word about it."

Willy laughed. "If I get much fatter, I'm not going to be able to see my feet." She thrust the swollen appendages out in front of her and made a face. "Sometimes I wonder if there's more than one child stuck inside me."

"Do you really think so, Willy?" Hannah's eyes glowed with childish excitement. "Having twins would be such a thrill."

The horticulturist smiled. "I suppose Ethan would think he was the cock of the walk if that happened. Not that he doesn't already."

"Have you given any thought to children, Hannah dear?" Lavinia patted the space next to her, and Emmaline scooted over to make room on the sofa for her. "With your law career going so well, I guess you don't have time for a family right now. But I'm sure someday you'll meet the right man and want to settle down."

Hannah thought about Lavinia's words the entire way home. She hadn't given children a great deal of thought up until now. She had always thought she and Travis, had they married, would have eventually had a child. But it had never been a priority, not like obtaining her law degree.

And she still had niggling doubts about the entire institution of marriage. Her parents' union had failed after many years of bliss, and there were no guarantees that her own wouldn't end up the same way. That possibility had haunted her even before her breakup with Travis.

She had wondered on occasion, when her mind had wandered back to those blissful days with Travis, what it would have been like to have married him and had his baby. To produce an exact replica of the man she loved. To suckle a wee babe at her breast and watch her husband's face fill with awe at the miracle they'd created from their love. Hannah sighed wistfully at the notion.

"You're awfully quiet," Travis commented, very aware of the soft body pressed up against him. The smell of rosewater filled his nostrils, and heat emanated from where their bodies touched.

The horse plodded along at a slow pace, which was just fine with the young lawyer. He wasn't in any hurry to have the pleasant evening come to an end. Even his father's surly ways couldn't dispel his joy at being with Hannah.

Hannah was grateful for the darkness that hid her heated cheeks. She had no business dwelling on the past. But as many times as she'd told herself that the past just kept creeping back, like a stubborn ivy vine that refused to die. "I was just thinking about how happy Lavinia is to be pregnant. I'm very pleased for her."

"Do you miss not having a child?"

She swallowed the lump in her throat. "Yes. Sometimes I think about what I've missed. But I have my career now, and I'm content as I am." It was a partial truth, but she couldn't admit to more right then.

And what would I say? That maybe I'd made a mistake?

No. She would never admit that. She hadn't made a mistake. She was sure of it.

Travis cast a sidelong glance at Hannah, at the perfect profile, the pert nose, the creamy skin, and he wondered what their child would have looked like. Who it would have resembled. He'd always envisioned a boy with dark hair and light eyes. The girl would have looked like Hannah. He would have insisted on that.

"I understand your father wasn't too pleased to discover he is going to be a father again?"

"He wasn't. But he'll come around. Pa's just got a quick temper and speaks before he thinks. As soon as he gets used to the idea of the baby, he'll accept it. He loves Lavinia too much not to."

"They seem very happy together."

"They are. She was the best thing that could have happened to him after Ma died. She made him human again. He was a bear to live with before that."

"With Ethan and Rafe gone so much of the time, you're the one who took the brunt of his anger and frustration." She remembered quite distinctly some of the cruel barbs Travis's father had flung at him and wondered at his capacity for forgiveness. It was one of the things she had always admired about him.

He shrugged his shoulders. "Pa was devastated by

the loss of my mother. And he never understood my wanting to leave the ranch and pursue a law career. At first, he had pinned all of his hopes for the ranch on Ethan, but my brother found ranching too sedate for his tastes and Rangering more to his liking. Rafe would have stayed on and helped, but Ethan convinced him to join the Rangers. That left me. And when I decided to pursue a law career, Pa felt betrayed that none of his sons wanted to follow in his footsteps.

"And even though he's proud of the man I've become, I still think he believes that one day I'll come to my senses, move back to the ranch, and take up raising cattle and pigs."

"You as a rancher?" Her brows lifted, and she giggled. "I can hardly believe that, any more than I can believe you're building a house. You never used to be all that skilled with your hands."

"That's not what you used to say, Hannah Louise." The suggestive tone, his measured look, made her face turn bright red. She stammered over her next words, even as her heart thudded loudly in her chest, remembering.

"How . . . how is the new house coming along? I haven't seen it yet."

"Slower than a three-legged turtle. But I'm building it pretty much by myself with occasional help from Ethan when he's not chasing after that new wife of his. It'll be a while yet before it's done. Why don't you come by sometime, and I'll show you around?"

"I'd like that," she said.

He pulled the buggy to a halt and turned to face her. "And do you think you'd also like it if I kissed you? I want to. I've been thinking about little else for weeks, Hannah."

She saw the passion in his eyes, and her throat went dry. She could say no. Put an end to things right now. But she didn't want to. And so instead she said, "I'd like that."

He pulled her into his arms and covered her mouth with his. The kiss was very different from the first one he'd given her. From any he'd given her before. It was masterful, emotional, passionate, and very tender. And as his tongue sought entry into her mouth, and she admitted him past five years of barriers that she had erected, Hannah's toes curled heavenward, and her heart opened up once more.

Chapter Eight

"So Pa and Lavinia are fixin' to have a baby?"
Rafe grinned, pacing back and forth across the narrow
confines of his cell. Walking and doing exercises—the
same exercises he'd chided Emmaline about when
they'd first met—were the only things that kept his muscles limber, the only thing keeping him sane.

Travis nodded. "Yep. And Pa's none too pleased
about it, I can tell you that." He went on to explain their
father's feelings on impending fatherhood.

Rafe scratched his head in bewilderment. "You'd
think the old man would be strutting about like a pea-
cock instead of growling like a bear. I sure as hell
would. Having a baby is got to be about the greatest
thing in the world. Next to having sex, that is." The grin
he flashed melted quickly into a frown. "Not that I've
had any lately."

"We're doing everything we can, Rafe. Hang in
there. The new judge should be here soon, then we can

get this trial started and get you freed, so you can go home to your wife and kids."

Freedom. Would that ever happen? Rafe was delighted that he was to have a new stepbrother or -sister, and absolutely ecstatic about becoming a father on his own. But in both instances he wondered if he'd live long enough to see the children born. The notion that he might not haunted his every waking moment.

It wasn't that he was afraid to die. He'd faced death more than once during his career as a Texas Ranger. But the thought of never seeing Emma again, or holding her in his arms, making love to her, of kissing Pansy's soft cheek, listening to David and Daniel argue, hear Miriam and Miranda sing one of their childish songs . . . He couldn't bear that. And he couldn't bear thinking that a child of his would grow up never knowing his father. Never knowing how much Rafe loved and wanted him.

He pushed the troubling thoughts aside. "Has Hannah Louise been any help to you? She seems to have a lot of experience in these matters."

"Hannah's very astute when it comes to legal strategies and such. She's been a great deal of help." In fact, he didn't know what he would do without her. And he wasn't just talking about the case. She'd become a fever in his blood. He wanted to do more than kiss her. He wanted to make love to her. Make her his own. Which was why he hadn't kissed her again. He wasn't sure he could control himself the next time. And there was still the trial to consider. Guilt gnawed at him for thinking about Hannah at such a time.

The clouds of uncertainty in Rafe's eyes brightened a bit, and Travis dragged his attention back to the matter at hand. "Then you think we've got a fighting chance, even with the DeBerry woman's testimony?"

"Yes." Travis hesitated, unwilling to offer false hope. "But we haven't had any luck in finding witnesses who can corroborate your version of what happened. It's probably going to boil down to her word against yours.

"There's also the additional killings of Hank and Luther Slaughter to contend with. McGrath is sure to bring that up, though I'll do my best to keep it out. I won't kid you, Rafe. This is going to be an uphill battle all the way."

"But Hank and Luther were going to kill me and Emma. I acted in self-defense."

"And those facts will be testified to when, and if, the time comes. But bear in mind that McGrath is going to portray you as a cold-blooded killer. He's going to say that you stalked the Slaughters to their lair and killed them, just like you killed Bobby. He's going to paint an ugly picture of a vengeful man who took the law into his own hands—a man who acted as judge, jury, and executioner."

Rafe dropped dejectedly to his bunk and clenched the sides of his head. "What's the good news?"

"I'm afraid there isn't any at the moment, big brother. Though we're doing our best to dig up some. I can't tell you how many cases we've researched, how many notes we've taken." He wouldn't bother to mention how many hours Hannah'd spent transcribing all of the notes on her typewriter. Admittedly, they were a lot easier to read that way.

The typewriter was another thing he'd been wrong about. One of many, he feared.

"What you're telling me, Travis, is that I'm screwed—finished—going to hang."

Sitting down next to his brother on the narrow bunk, Travis placed a comforting hand on his shoulders. A rat scurried across the floor, and he felt a mixture of anger and pity at what Rafe had to endure.

From what Ethan had related, the Slaughters were murdering scum. They'd been in and out of trouble and prison most of their miserable lives. In Travis's opinion, Rafe should have been given a medal for killing the bastards, not condemned for it. But that was his brotherly side speaking, not the voice of legal reason.

He sighed deeply. "You're not giving me much credit, Rafe. How can you think that I'd let you hang? That's not going to happen."

"I've never been much of a praying man, little brother, but I'm going to start praying you're right."

"Look on the bright side," Travis said, hoping to cheer him up. "Ethan says if you're convicted, he's going to bust you outta here. With such brotherly devotion, how can you be so down in the mouth?"

The former Texas Ranger's face whitened. "You can't allow that to happen, Travis. I want you to promise me you won't. I'm not going to allow any of my family, Ethan included, to suffer the consequences of my actions. It would kill Ethan to go against the Ranger code."

Ethan might be a hardheaded, hard-assed Ranger, but he was a principled man. And for him to go against everything he believed in would tear him up inside, destroy him. Rafe knew that, just as surely as he knew his eldest brother would do everything in his power to see that Rafe didn't hang. They'd been as close as any two brothers could be their whole lives. It was what Rafe would do if the circumstances were reversed.

"Promise me you'll reason with him, if the time comes."

Travis wanted to laugh. Reason with Ethan? Ha! He'd sooner reason with a mule. Come to think of it— it was about the same thing. "I'll do my best, Rafe. But keep in mind that Ethan is not a reasonable man and will most likely do whatever he damn well pleases, regardless of what I say."

Rafe nodded at the truth of his words. Ethan marched to his own drummer, that was for damn certain. "The way to get to Ethan is through his wife. Willy will set him straight. And he's gonna have a new baby to think about soon."

"So will you. So get out of this maudlin state you're in and start helping me find a way to get you out of this place."

Rafe studied the conviction, the raw determination, on his younger brother's face, and it filled him with pride at the man Travis had become. The boy had lived his whole life in his and Ethan's shadow. But he was standing tall now, and casting a mighty big shadow of his own.

"Good thing you decided to become a lawyer and not a doctor, little brother. You've got a hell of a bedside manner."

Rising to his feet, Travis flashed his brother a cocky grin. "That's what all the women tell me."

Rafe leaned back against the wall, crossing his arms over his chest, the temptation to tease too strong to resist. "Even Olive and Margaret?"

His cheeks flaming, Travis cursed aloud and grabbed hold of the metal bars. "Damn Ethan's big mouth!" Casting Rafe a disgusted look over his shoulder, he yelled, "Deputy Barnes, get me the hell outta here!"

Rafe threw back his head and roared.

While Travis visited his brother at the jail, Hannah took the opportunity to spend time with her father. They hadn't seen each other in days, and she felt guilty about it. She knew he enjoyed her company, perked up whenever she was around, and she felt the need to see for herself that he was all right and not at death's door as Maude claimed.

The irregular hours she'd been forced to keep had her arriving home late most evenings, and the judge was usually retired. In the mornings before she left for work, he was sequestered in his office. And if there was one thing Hannah'd learned as a child, it was that when her father's study door was closed he did not want to be disturbed for any reason, other than a dire emergency. And sometimes not even then.

As a child, it had been horribly frustrating not to have him at her beck and call. As an adult, she understood well the burdens the law placed upon his shoulders. And even though he was retired now, he kept abreast of the latest court rulings through his journals—usually disagreeing with them—still offered opinions to his colleagues through regular correspondence, and took an inordinate amount of interest in everything going on around him. All of which she credited with keeping his mind sharp as a tack.

The judge's door stood open. Hannah entered to find him seated behind his desk, a shawl draped over his shoulders, his nose buried in the thick tome spread out before him. He looked somewhat pale, but not as ill as Maude would have had her believe.

Placing the tray of ham sandwiches and milk on the corner of the desk, she waited for him to acknowledge her presence. Another lesson she'd learned was that it wasn't wise to disturb the judge when he was absorbed in his work. That could result in a serious tongue-lashing, and Thaddeus Barkley's tongue could be razor sharp and bitterly acerbic when the situation warranted. In court they had referred to him as Justice 'Grizzly Bear' Barkley because his words were so biting they could tear a man in two.

Finally, he looked up, mock annoyance registered on his face. "You may as well sit down, Hannah Louise. You've already broken my concentration."

She slid into the chair across from him. "You can't be as sick as Maude claims, if you've still got that nasty temper of yours, Papa."

"*Hmph!* Other than being poisoned by Mrs. Fogarty's meals on a regular basis, I'm feeling all right I guess. I have my good days and my bad ones." Today was one of the good ones. Hannah Louise had taken the time to visit, and that pleased him.

"I made the sandwiches, so they're safe to eat." She smiled at his relieved expression.

Grabbing one, he bit into it and made a noise of appreciation. "Don't know why the old bat can't cook. Should have fired her years ago." He shook his head. "It's a wonder we all haven't died from starvation. She thinks I don't eat because I'm sick. I don't have the heart to tell her it's because her meals make me gag."

Hannah grinned, knowing her father's bark was usually much worse than his bite. As much as he grumbled and groused about Maude's cooking, Hannah knew he was fond of the woman and respected her for speaking her mind when the occasion called for it. Respect wasn't something Thaddeus Barkley gave easily.

"Mama's a good cook. I like to think I take after her."

His dark eyes softened momentarily. "Yes. Yes, she was. There's no one on the face of this earth who can make an apple pie as good as Fiona's. My mouth waters just thinking about it." He licked his lips. "The crust was flaky as I recall. The apples had just the right amount of cinnamon and sugar. Not too tart, not too sweet."

"She still bakes them. I had one before I left to come here. I think Mama wanted to let me know what I'd be missing."

He heaved a sigh. "Damn good pies."

"I can bake one, if you like."

His eyes brightened momentarily, then his lips pinched into a frown, and he shook his head. "I don't want any reminders of your mother." Grabbing another sandwich, he swallowed half of his milk before saying, "I've missed you, Hannah Louise. You and the boy have been working long hours this past week."

It was obvious that the judge didn't want to discuss her mother any further, so Hannah dropped the subject. Though she wondered why, after all these years, the mere mention of Fiona Barkley still had the power to hurt him. Love was like that, she thought, shifting uncomfortably in her seat.

"Travis and I have been doing mostly research. We haven't really spoken to any witnesses yet." And they hadn't kissed again, which she found very disappointing and worrisome. What if Travis had decided that renewing their relationship wasn't a good idea, especially now that she'd decided it was?

The judge straightened at that. "And why the hell not? I'd think that would be the first thing you'd want to do."

She sighed. "Travis was going to send Ethan to depose the DeBerry woman. Can you imagine? It would have been a total disaster. She won't talk to anyone except McGrath. And I decided that most of the other witnesses would likely be hostile, since they work for Madam DeBerry, so I think it's best we wait until the trial."

"Your reasoning is sound. But don't forget about character witnesses. I'm sure you'll have no trouble finding those who'll speak on Rafe's behalf. I'll testify myself, if need be. Of course, that'll have to wait until the new judge takes over. Wouldn't want it said that I was taking sides."

His lip curled in distaste. "I never could stomach McGrath. The man's a weasel." And corrupt. He'd wager a great deal of money on that.

Hannah related her conversation with McGrath and his suggestion that she quit the trial. After which, the judge threw back his head and laughed. "Sounds like the little bastard is running scared."

"I hope so. We're going to need a miracle to pull off an acquittal in this case."

"The law is full of miracles, child. You're living proof of that. You almost died of scarlet fever when you were a baby, but you survived to become a respected member of the bar. A woman lawyer in this day and age is nothing short of a goddamn miracle, and I'm proud as hell of you, Hannah Louise."

Tears clogged her throat. She circled the desk to seat herself upon her father's lap, throwing her arms about his neck. "Thank you, Papa. You don't know what your words mean to me. I was never sure you approved of what I'd done."

His voice sounded strangely affected as he said, "A

man can be proud without being all gushy about it, daughter. But I just wanted you to know how I felt before I died."

Patting his grizzled cheek, she rose to her feet. "You're not going to die, Papa. I won't allow it. Now drink the rest of your milk and finish your lunch."

He harrumphed loudly. "You're beginning to sound like Mrs. Fogarty."

"And what's wrong with that? The girl could do a lot worse, Judge." Maude Fogarty barreled into the room like a lead bull in a stampede, pulling up short at the sight of the sandwiches. "I come to tell you lunch was ready." She cast both parties an accusing look. "But I see now that you've already eaten."

Hannah and her father shared a conspiratorial smile, then the judge said, "What the hell did you make, Mrs. Fogarty? Not more of that watered-down soup that tastes like donkey piss I hope."

The housekeeper ignored the insult. "I made some of my famous chili, Judge. Hot and spicy, just the way you like it." Maude beamed from ear to ear.

Judge Barkley clutched his stomach and turned an alarming shade of green.

Hannah Louise tiptoed quietly out of the room, hoping her father's emesis basin wasn't too far out of reach.

Travis looked up when Hannah entered the office. She looked happier than he'd seen her in days, but he couldn't bring himself to share in that happiness. He was far too worried about Rafe. "You're looking awfully cheery this afternoon," he said, frowning deeply. "It's nice to know one of us has something to be happy about."

Hannah's smile melted quicker than ice on a hot skillet. How could she tell Travis, someone whose father always withheld praise and offered little in the way of encouragement or emotional support, that her father was proud of her? That knowing he was proud made a gloomy day brighter and a difficult situation more palatable to deal with? She couldn't. There was no way she would ever be that cruel. So she said, "I just had a nice chat with my father. He seems better today."

Driving rain pelted the glass like hailstones. The howling wind banged the wooden shutters loudly against the building. But the menacing look Travis wore made the inclement weather seem tame by comparison. "That's nice. Did he offer any suggestions on how we're going to win this damn case?" Since he'd returned to the office, he couldn't get Rafe's despondent mood out of his mind. His brother had tried to be brave, even cracking an occasional joke, but Travis knew how much he hurt inside. And that bothered him even more.

"Whatever's the matter? Is something wrong with Rafe?"

Slapping the flat of his hand against the desktop, he said, "I can't stand seeing him so upset and not being able to do anything about it."

"You are doing something. You're helping to find a way to get him out of jail."

"Am I?" He sneered. "We've been researching cases for days and nights on end, and I don't think we've gotten any closer to finding a suitable defense for my brother. For chrissake, Hannah! He killed three men. They're going to hang him for it."

Crossing to the desk, her eyes blazing blue fire, she impaled him with a censorious look. "Hush up, Travis Bodine! I won't stand for that kind of defeatist talk. If you give up on Rafe, what chance does he have? I don't intend to allow your brother to hang. We're going to find a way out of this mess. And I think that instead of feeling sorry for yourself and for Rafe, you should get back to work and find a strategy we can use."

The veracity of her words stung. He bolted to his feet, his face only inches from her. "You've got no call to talk to me like that, Hannah Louise. I've got every right in the world to be worried. It's my brother they're fixing to hang, not yours."

She heard the worry in his voice, glimpsed the utter despair on his face, and she suddenly felt sorry that she'd spoken to him so harshly. He bore the weight of the world on his shoulders, and it was driving him into the ground. She wished she could carry some of the burden, but she knew it was his alone to bear.

"I'm sorry, Travis. I shouldn't have spoken so bluntly. I'm afraid living in the East has worn off many of my polite Southern ways."

He ran agitated fingers through his hair and heaved a sigh. "No. You're right. Whining and feeling sorry for oneself never did accomplish much. There's got to be something, someone we've overlooked."

Hannah pondered his statement, then suddenly her eyes lit with excitement. "There is. I don't know why I didn't think of it before."

"What? Who?"

"Roy Lee Slaughter. He's in the Wyoming Territorial Prison. I'm going up there to talk to him."

Travis's eyes widened at the absurdity of the idea. "Like hell you are! That's out of the question."

"Don't you see, Travis? The man might be willing to corroborate Rafe's story. He was there. He survived. Rafe could have killed him, but he didn't. Maybe, just maybe, there's enough humanity in Roy Lee Slaughter for him to tell the truth about what happened."

Fear clutched his heart at the very idea. "No!" He shook his head emphatically. "There's no way in hell that I'd allow you to travel to Wyoming to talk to that ruthless murderer. He's no better than the rest of them. You heard what they did to Ellie Bodine? Cut her up like a piece of meat, until she was practically unrecognizable. Those bastards raped her, murdered her unborn child—" Horror crossed her face as he recounted the details. "No! We'll find another way. I won't have that murdering bastard within a thousand miles of you. And that's final."

"You? You won't have? May I remind you, Travis Bodine, that I am a free and capable woman, an attorney, and I must do what I deem best for my client? I won't be ordered about like some lackey. Like some *wife*."

He rocked back on his heels as if slapped. "Goddamn it, Hannah Louise! You haven't changed a bit. Still trying to call all the shots, no matter who you hurt. Even if it's yourself."

"And you're still trying to control my life, even though you're no longer a part of it."

He blanched at that. "Do you really think I would countenance such a plan, knowing what I know about the Slaughters? Well I won't. And if you persist in defying me, I'll have you thrown off this case so fast your head'll spin."

"Well, you've been looking for an excuse all along, haven't you, counselor?"

"Don't be ridiculous. I hate it when women let emotion rule their head instead of logic." He rose to his feet, clutching her arms, hoping he could talk sense into her. If anything ever happened to Hannah like what happened to Rafe's first wife, he wouldn't be able to live with himself.

"Hannah, be reasonable. Can't you see the danger involved in what you're wanting to do? I'd never risk your life. Not even to save my brother's."

She swallowed the lump in her throat, not daring to delve too deeply into the meaning of his words. But she clutched them to her heart just the same. "This might be our only chance, Travis. You said yourself that our case was thin at best. We need something strong to present to the jury. Roy Lee Slaughter's testimony could be the critical piece of evidence—"

"I said no." He dropped into the chair behind his desk, the matter settled in his opinion.

But it wasn't in Hannah's. "You are the most rigid, the most pigheaded man on the face of the earth." She crossed her arms over her chest, impaling him with a look that would have withered lesser men.

"And you are the most stubborn woman on the face of this earth!" he shouted loud enough to be heard by the patrons of the barbershop downstairs.

Suddenly the door opened, and a gust of wind ruffled the papers on Travis's desk. Hannah's sharp intake of breath had him following her gaze to find a woman standing there. She was garbed in a dark cloak, soaking wet from the rain.

"And here I thought I was the most stubborn woman on the face of this earth," Fiona Barkley stated.

"Mama!" Hannah rushed forward, wrapping her arms about the sodden woman. "What on earth are you doing here?"

"I didn't see any lights on over at the house, and I was afraid I'd disturb your father if I knocked, so I came here instead."

Hannah shook her head. "I mean—what are you doing in Misery? Why are you here?"

Patting her daughter's cheek, she looked over Hannah's shoulder at the man seated behind the desk. "Hello, Travis. It's been awhile. You're looking good, I must say."

He rose to his feet. "As are you, Mrs. Barkley. Nice to see you again."

"My daughter wrote that she's working on your brother's case with you," she said, removing her gloves. "I can only assume that you two must be getting along. Or is that commotion I overheard a few minutes ago consistent with your professional relationship?"

Hannah's cheeks pinkened. "Travis and I were just having a little difference of opinion, Mama. We're getting along quite well. Aren't we, Travis?"

"You should have spanked Hannah more when she was little, Mrs. Barkley. She's a handful now."

Hannah shot him a baleful look. "Travis Bodine! What an awful thing to say."

He exchanged a smile with Hannah's mother. "Awful but true, nonetheless."

"And is my daughter every bit as good a lawyer as I think she is?"

"Better. Hannah's one of the brightest attorneys I've ever met." Hannah's smile was so brilliant that it nearly took Travis's breath away.

Noting the interaction between the two, Fiona smiled knowingly. It was obvious as the lovesick smile on her daughter's face and the smitten one on Travis's that the two young people were still very much in love and just didn't realize it yet.

Fiona concluded that she had arrived at a very propitious time.

Chapter Nine

FIONA STARED AT THE THICK LAYER OF DUST COVERING the master bedroom's walnut dresser and sniffed disdainfully. "I can see Maude Fogarty's housekeeping skills are still as poor as ever. It's a wonder your father keeps her on. The woman is useless, in my opinion. Always has been, always will be."

Still bewildered by her mother's unexpected arrival, but unwilling to countenance an attack on Maude's housekeeping abilities, whether or not it was justified, Hannah voiced her disapproval. "You should have sent word that you were coming, Mama. I would have seen to it that your room was prepared properly. I don't think it's fair to blame Maude, or anyone else for that matter, because your room wasn't ready. If we had known—"

Fiona turned from the mirror, which she had just wiped with her gloved hand and was now showing to Hannah with obvious distaste. "And give your father an excuse to refuse me admittance? I think not, Hannah dear." Her chin tilted skyward, a determined glint shining in her eyes. "Thaddeus will have no choice but to accept that I've come home for a while."

Her father's acceptance of the matter was still very much in question. He had taken to his bedroom and had not been heard from since Fiona had stepped foot into the house thirty minutes before. Hannah glanced at the ormolu clock on the mantel and sighed. *Thirty-five* minutes before. It seemed an eternity already, for she knew the problems her mother's visit was likely to cause. *Had* caused already.

Maude had nearly fainted at the sight of her employer's estranged wife and had refused to speak to Fiona directly, banging pots and pans loudly as she made a great pretense of cooking dinner. Hannah had been forced to act as go-between, and she wasn't looking forward to refereeing further the ongoing animosity between the two strong-willed women.

Easing herself onto the white-crocheted bed covering slightly yellowed by time, Hannah leaned back on her palms. "I don't understand any of this, Mama. Why have you come back? You told me in New York that you would never again set foot in Misery. And then you pop up quite unexpectedly."

The blond woman shrugged. "Your letter intrigued me."

"My letter?" Hannah's brow wrinkled as she tried to recall just what she had written. It must have been very compelling to have lured her mother back to a home she'd never made any bones about hating.

"You said you were assisting Travis with his brother's murder trial—"

Hannah's eyes suddenly brimmed with awareness. "And that Papa was not doing well," she finished.

Fiona began to unpack her clothing and hang it in the closet. The verbena-scented garments emitted a familiar fragrance. "I admit that I was concerned about your father's health. It's not like Thaddeus to languish and allow others to wait on him."

"May I remind you, Mama, that it's been ten years since you've seen the man? For all you know he could have become quite dotty and dependent on others by now."

Fiona's laughter filled the room. "Thaddeus dotty? That's rich. Exasperating. Mean-tempered. Rude beyond reasonable. But dotty?" She shook her head. "I think not. The man is too intelligent by half, and too proud to be cosseted like a child. Something's wrong with him, and I'll find out soon enough what it is."

Good heavens! Her mother's extended stay was likely to have all sorts of ramifications. The least of which was Maude's reaction when she heard the news. Hannah didn't want to contemplate what her father would say. Nothing civilized, she was certain. "How long are you planning to stay in Misery, Mama?"

"I'm not sure, dear. I met Carlton . . . Judge Hix in New York. He was there visiting his sister. And when he told me that he'd be the presiding judge in the Bodine case. Well—My plan to come was a bit impulsive I admit. I haven't given much thought to the future. I guess I'll just have to wait and see what unfolds."

Unravels would be a better word, Hannah thought. The whole fabric of the family was likely to come apart at the seams again, as it had ten years before. She remembered quite vividly the tears, the heartache, the mournful months that had passed for her father. And she didn't want a repeat of that. It would be too painful for all of them. And it just might send her ailing father over the edge.

"Would it do any good to pull the bell pull and ring for tea?" Fiona stared at the frayed rope and felt a twinge of regret that her once lovely room and furnishings had been so terribly neglected. She could clearly remember the day she and Thaddeus had stood on the platform of the train station eagerly awaiting the arrival of the bedroom furniture they'd ordered from an East Coast manufacturer.

The furniture, and their ability to pay for it, had been a symbol that Thaddeus's law career had taken off, that after many years of hard work and self-sacrifice Mr. and Mrs. Thaddeus James Barkley had finally arrived.

"It doesn't work anymore, Mama. And it's doubtful Maude would come willingly anyway." Hannah doubted she could drag the housekeeper upstairs with a rope. "I can fetch you some if you like."

Fiona tugged her thoughts back to the present. "Would you, dear? I'd be ever so grateful. And it'll give me time to look in on your father."

At the door, Hannah's eyes widened, and she spun

on her heel. "Mama, you cannot just go waltzing into Papa's room unannounced. You'll give him a heart attack. He's sick enough as it is."

Fiona stiffened, and her blue eyes, so much like Hannah's own, darkened to midnight. "Are you implying that I'm trying to kill my husband?"

"Not intentionally. But the shock of seeing you again might be too much for him."

"Balderdash! The man's had over forty-five minutes or longer—if Maude still peers out the window at people, and I'm sure she does—to grow used to the idea that I'm home. I promise I'll not do or say anything to upset him. I'm just going to go into his room and see how he's feeling. Have a little chat. We're long overdue, don't you think?"

Hannah rolled her eyes heavenward. "Perhaps I should just go ahead and tell him—"

"Run along and fetch the tea, Hannah Louise," her mother ordered in that inflexible tone Hannah recognized all too well and had learned over the years not to oppose, if she wanted to preserve her sanity. "I can handle Thaddeus by myself. After all, I did it rather successfully for years without any help from you."

With an audible sigh, Hannah departed, and Fiona smoothed down the folds of her gown. She'd given some thought to changing—the black foulard silk was horribly wrinkled from the train trip and the rainstorm—but decided that she wouldn't give Thaddeus the pleasure of thinking that she cared enough about him to alter her appearance.

At fifty years of age a woman had a right to ignore what others thought. Unfortunately, Fiona was not that kind of woman. She very much wanted to look her best, and not her age, which was why she was relieved that her hair showed not the slightest bit of gray, that her complexion remained smooth and unwrinkled. Hannah's skin was much like Fiona's, and her daughter would be grateful for that fact in another twenty-five years.

Growing old was no fun at all. And growing old alone was even less appealing.

She moved down the hall, noting that the walls still displayed the same red-flocked wallpaper she'd installed over fifteen years ago, though it was torn and faded now. Pausing before the last door on her left—the guest room—she made a mental note of the intriguing fact that Thaddeus had abandoned the bedroom suite they'd shared for so many years.

Breathing deeply to quiet the churning in her stomach, she knocked softly and entered, not waiting for the invitation she knew would not be forthcoming.

Thaddeus sat in a wing chair by the fireplace, looking much older than his sixty-one years, much older than she had remembered. His hair was snowy white, his hands aged with brown liver spots. His shoulders, though still broad, were stooped, as if he bore the weight of the world upon them. But despite all that he still looked wonderful to her. And as handsome as the day she'd married him over thirty years ago.

"Hello, Grizzly," she said, using the nickname

most people dared not call him and stepping farther into the room until she stood directly in front of him.

Thaddeus looked up, and ten years of longing swamped over him like a tidal wave. He drank in the sight of Fiona greedily, like an alcoholic forced from the bottle. She was still a strikingly beautiful woman. Perhaps a few pounds heavier. But then, weren't they all?

His eyes registering pleasure before he shuttered out his feelings, Thaddeus replied with as much disinterest as he could muster. "Fiona." She moved forward and took a seat opposite him in the matching wing chair, and he did his best to ignore the enticing fragrance of her cologne. It was difficult.

"Hannah wrote that you weren't feeling well."

He shrugged. "How can that possibly matter to you? I've been ill many times these last ten years." It was a lie, but he could see he'd made his point. Her face blanched.

"I wasn't aware of that."

"How could you be, living in New York? What happens here is of little concern to you."

"Still bitter after all these years, Thaddeus?"

"I've learned to accept what cannot be changed."

"You could have come after me, begged me to come back. Written me a letter. But you did none of those things. Your pride would not allow it."

And what of my foolish pride? she thought.

"Would it have done any good? Would you have come back, Fiona?"

She shrugged. "I honestly don't know. Maybe. No.

I don't know. It was such a long time ago." Another lifetime. She recalled what had sent her away—one of Thaddeus's harsh case rulings—though it didn't seem nearly so important now.

A young prostitute had killed a man who she claimed had brutalized her savagely. There had been evidence to prove her assertion, and Fiona had taken her side, championed her cause, arguing to her husband that the woman's action had been self-defense.

Because of her less than sterling profession, the prostitute had opted to forgo a jury trial and had thrown herself on the mercy of the court. But Thaddeus had shown no mercy. He had found her guilty of murder and had sentenced her to hang.

On the day of her execution, Fiona had packed her bags and left Misery and her husband, vowing never to return.

But she had returned. And now she had to question why.

"Is Miss High-and-Mighty planning to grace us with her presence at dinner this evening?" Maude asked Hannah with a sneer.

"Why, yes I am," Fiona answered as she stepped through the swinging door and into the kitchen. "And you don't need to be so formal, Mrs. Fogarty. Just plain old Fiona will do. Or Mrs. Barkley, if you prefer. Perhaps the latter would be best, so it will serve as a reminder that I am still mistress of this house, and you're still the housekeeper, no matter how much we may wish otherwise."

Pecking away at the keys of her typewriter, Hannah thought back to the previous night's ugly scene and heaved a sigh of pure frustration. Because of it, and because she didn't feel like taking sides between two women she loved, she had purposely avoided going home, staying at work later than necessary. Travis had gone to his boardinghouse to eat dinner, but she had remained at the office, using the excuse of transcribing her notes.

It was cowardly, she knew. But if she was to preserve her sanity and remain focused on the upcoming trial, it was something she had to do.

Now that Judge Carlton Hix had arrived the trial would begin soon. The distinguished man had a reputation for fairness, so Hannah thought they were fortunate to have him presiding. A jury would then be selected and seated, the preliminary motions made, and the prosecution would begin to present their case.

She had spent the better part of the afternoon compiling a list of possible witnesses the defense team could call. Rafe's family would be included, as would Ethan, who would be able to testify to the circumstances surrounding Hank Slaughter's initial arrest and conviction for bank robbery five years before. Hannah felt it was imperative that Rafe and Emma take the stand. Their testimony would be the most compelling of all, since they had experienced the cruelty of the Slaughters firsthand. And Emma's being a woman was sure to gain sympathy from some of the male jurors.

The door opened. Hannah looked up, surprised to find Travis entering. "What are you doing back here? I thought you went home to eat."

The basket he held emitted a tantalizing aroma, and he placed it on the desk. "I had Mrs. Langley put together some dinner for you. I figured you'd still be here banging away on that infernal machine. And I guessed you might be hungry. Am I right?"

His thoughtfulness poured over her like warm syrup. It was a very sweet thing to do. "It smells delicious. What's in it?"

"Just some fried chicken, biscuits—"

She lunged for the basket before he could finish, and he laughed. "I thought that might appeal to you."

"Thank you! I'm starved." She began gnawing on a leg.

"Why didn't you go home for dinner?" Hannah was seated behind his desk, so Travis took the chair in front of it. "Is Maude making something particularly disgusting this evening?"

"No more than usual." She went on to explain about the turmoil her mother's presence had created. "My mother and Maude fight like cats and dogs when I'm around."

"From what you've just told me, they may end up killing each other if you're not there."

She sighed, knowing he was probably right, but not caring at the moment. "I've got to focus my energy on this trial, not on their petty squabbles. They're both grown women who should know better. If push comes to shove, I'll be making up that sofa and sleeping here."

Travis's heartbeat quickened at the enticing possibility. Bedding Hannah had been uppermost on his mind lately. He'd been doing a lot of fantasizing about kissing her again, caressing her, slipping into her warmth and making her his own. He felt himself harden and realized that he needed to do more than just think about it. He needed to act.

This overwhelming urge to make love with Hannah surprised him in light of everything that had happened between them. He was usually a very cautious man, weighing everything out, considering all the possibilities and ramifications. But where Hannah was concerned caution was not on his mind.

"To complicate matters, my father has taken it in his head that my mother is having an affair with Judge Hix." Hannah could have been knocked over with a feather when she'd had that little tidbit dropped on her like a ton of cement the previous evening. Her father had called her to his room to reveal his suspicion, insisting that it was true. Though she had told him repeatedly that the notion was absurd, he could, and would, not be convinced.

"Should my father choose to vocalize that belief to the judge," Hannah continued, "we may have some serious problems facing us."

"What?" His ardor deflating quickly, Travis immediately refocused his attention on what Hannah was telling him. "What did you say? Your father thinks what?"

"That my mother and Carlton Hix are lovers. She denies it, of course. Says they're only friends and have been for years. Apparently there was some kind of competition between my father and Judge Hix over my mother some years back. Because my mother chose to travel here escorted by the judge, Papa has decided to think the worst."

Travis's frustration began to mount, and he let loose a string of curses. "This is just great! What else can go wrong?" The job of defending Rafe was becoming nearly impossible.

"We need to concentrate on what can go right," she reminded him. "I've put together a list of possible witnesses. I believe your brother should be one of the first to testify."

He looked at her as if she'd just grown two heads. "That's preposterous! McGrath would have a field day with Rafe if we did that." He jumped to his feet, and she came around the desk to face him. It was always easier to convince a man to your way of thinking if you were staring him in the eye, her father had taught her.

"I disagree totally, Travis."

"I'm in charge, and I say Rafe doesn't testify. My brother's hatred of the Slaughters will become all too apparent to the jury. He'll be damned by his own words. What kind of stupid strategy is that for you to come up with? I thought you were a brilliant lawyer."

The remark was anything but a compliment, and

her spine stiffened ramrod straight. Biting the inside of her cheek, she tried to restrain her temper, which was hanging by a thread. Travis was obviously distraught and taking out his frustration on her. "You're not thinking clearly about this. Rafe's emotional reaction to his first wife's death is just what the jury needs to see and hear. And yes, I do have a lot of experience in these matters. Experience you should take advantage of."

It wasn't Hannah's experience that Travis wanted to take advantage of, but Hannah herself. He listened to the passion in her voice, saw the glittering determination in her eyes, the way her breast rose and fell in indignation, and he wanted her more in that moment than he'd ever wanted anyone. And by God he was going to have her.

Grasping her hand, he pulled her to him. Hannah's mouth fell open in surprise . . . and invitation. "I know I'll probably regret this, Hannah Louise, but I've just got to kiss you."

When his lips touched hers, all thoughts of protest melted, and she lost herself in the wonder of his kiss. His mouth covered hers hungrily, his tongue tracing the soft contours of her lips, creating a need within that surprised her. Her lips parted on a sigh, and she allowed his tongue to enter and duel hungrily with her own.

Passion flared brightly between them—hot, fast, and all-consuming. Thoughts were centered only on the moment and each other—on the hands that caressed, the bodies that craved for more, the lips that melded two hearts together.

Five years of pent-up emotion came gushing forth like a geyser ready to explode. Hannah and Travis were lost to everything else but each other and the need they shared.

"Well, well. Isn't this an interesting picture?"

At the sound of a man's sinister laughter, they broke apart quickly—guiltily—and turned to find Will McGrath standing in the open doorway. Neither had heard him enter.

Hannah's stomach dropped to her feet, and she felt suddenly ill. The look of triumph on Will's face spelled nothing but trouble.

"Looks like you found a use for Hannah's talent after all, huh, Travis?" There was no mistaking his meaning. "If I'd have waited a few more minutes I bet I would have seen a lot more than—"

Travis didn't wait for the second insult and slammed his fist into McGrath's mouth. "Shut your trap, you bastard, or I'll shut it for you." He hit him again, punching him hard in the stomach. McGrath grunted, falling backward.

Hannah screamed, grabbing Travis's arm. "Travis, stop! It's what he wants. Don't you see? He wants you to lose control."

Travis grabbed the prosecutor by the scruff of the neck. "Get the hell out of here, McGrath. I don't want to see your ugly face until the trial begins, or I may be tempted to wipe the floor with it."

The man blotted his bloodied lip on the sleeve of his coat, and his eyes glowed maniacally. "You'll be sorry, Bodine. I'm going to take great pleasure in seeing your brother hang."

"Please leave, Will. I think you've caused enough trouble for one evening," Hannah pleaded, leery of the killing rage reflected in the depths of Travis's eyes.

"I'll go. But know this, Hannah Louise, you're going back to New York in disgrace, and not just because you're going to lose this case."

Travis started after him again, but McGrath beat a hasty retreat out the door, running down the steps as if the devil were on his heels.

"That bastard!" Travis dropped into the chair and blew on his bruised knuckles. "Wish I'd knocked his teeth down his throat."

"This is all my fault." Hannah's eyes brimmed with unshed tears. "I should never have allowed myself—" She bit her lip.

"Hannah." Travis heard the anguish and self-recrimination in her voice and rose to comfort her.

She shook her head. "No. Don't touch me, Travis. What happened between us must never happen again. I must go. I'll see you in the morning."

The door slammed shut. Travis dropped back down into his chair, heaving a deep sigh as he ran agitated fingers through his hair. Then he winced in pain, his swollen knuckles a painful reminder that everything that had transpired tonight had been his fault, not Hannah's.

If he hadn't lost control, pushed himself on her . . . But dammit! He wanted her. Needed her. Loved her?

No! He shook his head. He couldn't be in love with her. He wouldn't make that mistake again. It was lust, pure and simple. He was a man. Hannah was all woman. There'd always been an attraction between them. What had happened was a natural hazard of their working together. It was what he had feared from the outset.

Being with Hannah again, kissing her, wanting her, made him forget what was truly important: saving Rafe's life. He didn't have the time or the emotion to spare on renewing a relationship. And he felt guilty as hell for what he'd done.

He didn't want Hannah Louise Barkley back in his life.

But he sure as hell wanted her in his bed.

Hannah banged her hairbrush down on the dresser, angry at herself, McGrath, and most especially at Travis for making her want him so.

The professional reputation she had worked so hard to establish and maintain had now been compromised. Will McGrath would see to it that everyone in Misery, prospective jurors included, would know of her shameful behavior with Travis, her colleague and partner. Her former fiancé. The man who rejected her, didn't view her as an equal.

And the man she still loved.

"Damn, damn, damn!" she cursed, punctuating each "damn" with the bang of her brush and wishing it was Travis's head. If he'd just kept his distance, stayed away, then maybe she could have ignored all those tingly feelings that formed in the pit of her stomach whenever she was near him, the spicy scent of his cologne when they had their heads bent close in concentration on a legal matter. Maybe she wouldn't have remembered all the wonderful, endearing things about him that had drawn her to him in the first place those many years ago—the crookedness of his smile, those damn gumdrops he loved to chew.

When his lips touched hers tonight, she knew she was doomed. All those old feelings, the pent-up emotions, came rushing back to turn her insides to mush, her feet to puddles of quicksand.

She pressed her hands to her chest, trying to soothe the ache centered there. Her heart ached. Her body yearned. But her mind knew that for now there wasn't a thing she could do about it.

Rafe Bodine was on trial for his life. She had vowed to defend him to the best of her ability. She would let nothing stand in the way of performing her duties as an attorney.

She would do everything in her power to get Rafe Bodine acquitted of murder. Then she would get out of Misery, regain her sanity, and get on with her life.

Chapter Ten

"YOU'VE BEEN IN A FOUL TEMPER FOR DAYS, HAN-nah Louise. Do you want to tell me what's wrong? Or should I guess that it has something to do with Travis?"

Hannah pushed her oatmeal aside and heaved a sigh. Her mother had always been too perceptive for her own good. "I'm troubled by a great many things, Mama. Not just Travis. Though he's certainly part of it."

"Feelings take time to sort out, dear. Don't rush it. If things are meant to be between you and Travis, you'll know it in your heart.

"Now tell me what else is wrong. Maybe I can help."

"Only if you know a way to get Rafe Bodine acquitted of murder."

Worry lines creased Fiona's brow. "I take it that things are not going well with the case?"

"I've just about exhausted all the possible defense strategies, save for one. And Travis is dead set against my going to see Roy Lee Slaughter, one of the outlaws who killed Ellie Bodine."

Fiona took the seat next to her daughter and filled a cup with coffee. "Since when did you start listening to Travis? If you'd listened to him five years ago, you wouldn't be an attorney now."

Hannah pondered her mother's words, then she reached out to clasp Fiona's hand and squeezed it tightly. "You know something, Mama? You're absolutely right. Just because Travis doesn't want me to talk to Slaughter doesn't mean that I shouldn't, can't. He could be the whole key to Rafe's defense."

"Where is this Mr. Slaughter, dear? Would you have to travel far to see him?"

"He's in the Wyoming Territorial Prison, Mama, serving a life sentence for the killing of Ellie Bodine."

Fiona gasped, her face paling considerably. "Well no wonder Travis doesn't want you to go. It sounds terribly dangerous, dear."

Hannah shook her head. "Mama, you're beginning to sound like Travis. Roy Lee Slaughter is in prison, for heaven's sake. What could happen there? There would be plenty of guards around to see to my protection."

Fiona thought a moment, then said, "Maybe it wouldn't be so worrisome if you had an escort, Hannah Louise."

Hannah's brow wrinkled in confusion. "An escort? I told you—Travis doesn't want me to go. I can't ask him to—"

"I wasn't thinking about Travis, dear. I was thinking about myself."

"You, Mama!" Hannah's cup clattered noisily to the table. "Don't be ridiculous. You're much too—" She was going to say "old," but she knew her mother was growing increasingly sensitive about her age. "—too important to Papa's health," she amended. "He needs you here to take care of him."

"Thaddeus has been doing fine without me for ten years, so if I'm gone a few weeks to see to the safety of my only daughter, I doubt he'll mind." The thought of a real adventure had Fiona's eyes wild with anticipation. "When do you intend to go?"

"I haven't planned that far ahead, Mama. I've only just this moment decided to do it. It's going to take some time to make the arrangements. The warden will have to be contacted. And there's no guarantee that Roy Lee will consent to talk to me. I am Rafe's attorney, after all, and Rafe did kill Slaughter's brother and other members of his family."

"Well, once you've got it all worked out, let me know. In the meantime, I think we should pay a visit to the milliner's and do some shopping. We'll want to look our best for the trip."

Unable to believe what she was hearing, Hannah rolled her eyes heavenward, wishing she'd just kept her big mouth shut.

Staring at the attractive house under construction, at the man pounding the nails with great resolve, Fiona wondered why the Barkley women were doomed to love difficult, exasperating men.

By Hannah Louise's decidedly foul mood, it was plain to Fiona that her foolish daughter had once again fallen under young Bodine's spell. History, it seemed, was destined to repeat itself. But she was determined to see a much happier ending this time.

"Well, Travis, I see you've become a carpenter, in addition to all your other skills."

Standing on the ladder attempting to affix a piece of decorative molding over the doorframe, Travis started at the woman's remark and would have fallen had he not grabbed on to the doorframe. His heart pounding loud in his ears, he looked down to find Hannah's mother standing below. The hostile look she wore made him suspect that she'd heard about what had transpired between him and Hannah the other night. It was all he could do not to groan.

The weekend had spared both him and Hannah from having to face the passionate kiss they'd shared, and their reactions to it. Unfortunately, it didn't look like he'd be spared Fiona Barkley's wrath.

Mrs. Barkley was a forthright woman, who would no doubt take him to task over what had happened. He'd always liked her directness, but not when it was aimed at him, as it appeared to be now. "Nice to see you again, Mrs. Barkley." Climbing down off the ladder, he faced her with an uncertain smile, wiping his sweaty forehead and face with a blue bandanna, then stuffing it into the back pocket of his denims.

Scrutinizing him from top to bottom, Fiona decided that the skinny man her daughter had once been engaged to had filled out rather nicely. Quite nicely, in fact, judging by the width of his shoulders that even an older woman like her couldn't fail to appreciate. She might be aging fast, but she wasn't dead yet. "You're a good-looking man, Travis Bodine. It's no wonder you've got the ability to break women's hearts."

The left-handed compliment took him by surprise. "Ma'am, about what happened—"

Her brow shot up. "I wasn't aware that anything had happened, young man. But if you'd care to enlighten me, I'd be most appreciative. My daughter has not been in good spirits of late. I suspect it has something to do with you. Am I correct in this assumption?"

He swallowed with some difficulty. How did one confess to stealing a kiss? To having impure thoughts? One didn't, if one wanted to keep his head from being bashed in by an irate mother. "Uh . . . Perhaps I spoke out of turn. Nothing really happened."

"Well, if that's the case then why are you blushing so hard? Your cheeks are positively glowing. And why is my daughter so upset and distracted? It was bad enough having to console her five years ago when you broke off your engagement. I don't mind telling you Hannah Louise was devastated. And I don't relish having to go through that again." Before he could spit out the apology teetering on the edge of his tongue, she added, "I'd like to know what your intentions are concerning my daughter, Mr. Bodine?" She folded her arms across her chest. "And I'm not inclined to leave until you tell me."

"My intentions?" He swallowed again. "I . . . I'm not sure what you mean, Mrs. Barkley. Hannah and I are cocounsels on my brother's murder case. I'd like to think we're friends. If she's led you to believe something else—"

"My daughter is too proud to ever admit to anything. I find that you young people are unbearably polite and civilized when it comes to matters of the heart. Are you trying to stand there and tell me that you don't have feelings for my daughter? That she means nothing to you?"

The sun beating down on Travis's neck had little to do with the heated flush covering his face. "Of course I have feelings for Hannah." What those feelings were still remained a mystery. But they were far from the anger and resentment he had felt when she first arrived.

Fiona stared into the blue brilliance of the young lawyer's eyes and saw the same misery and uncertainty that she'd recognized in her own daughter. It was obvious Travis was telling the truth. He had feelings for Hannah Louise, but he just didn't know the depth of them yet. She suspected he still loved Hannah, she was positive Hannah still loved him. But love hadn't been enough the last time the two headstrong people were together. Perhaps they had matured. She hoped so for both their sakes.

"Hannah Louise tells me that your stepmother Lavinia is expecting a child. Please give her my heart-

felt congratulations." She'd known the woman for
years. Lavinia had been Misery's schoolteacher when
Fiona had resided there previously.

"I can't tell you how happy I was to learn of her
marriage to your father after dear Patsy's death. Lavinia
and your mother were such good friends that it seemed
only natural that she would be there to console Ben."

Travis's mouth curved into a smile. "Lavinia's
been good for Pa. And she's quite beside herself at the
prospect of becoming a mother."

"And your father? How does he feel about it?"

"Old and embarrassed," Travis admitted, seeing no
point in lying to her. The Barkleys and Bodines went
way back, and she'd no doubt discover the truth anyway.

"I may just have to pay him a visit, straighten the
old fool out. He doesn't know just how lucky he is, how
lucky they both are." Ben Bodine was the only man she
knew who could make Thaddeus appear reasonable by
comparison.

"Yes, ma'am. I'm sure they'd love to see you."
And his father could do with a little outside pressure.
Lord knows everyone in the family had talked to the
stubborn man until they were blue in the face. Not that
it had done any good. Ben remained fast in his foolish
resentment of Lavinia's pregnancy.

She nodded absently, tapping her chin as she
spoke. "Yes. That's just what I'll do. Well, I must be
going. I'm to meet Hannah at the milliner's at eleven. If
I'm late, she's likely to turn tail and run home. She isn't

as fond of shopping as I am." She shook her head, as if the notion was totally absurd.

"Nice seeing you again, Mrs. Barkley," Travis remarked to the departing woman, breathing a sigh of relief that he'd come out of their encounter relatively unscathed.

She paused at the end of the walkway and looked back. "Oh, we'll see each other again, young man. I'm quite sure of that." She disappeared down the street, leaving Travis to ponder her words and wonder just what she knew that he didn't.

Hannah Louise's heart wasn't into shopping, and she wished for the hundredth time that she hadn't agreed to meet her mother at the milliner's. But Fiona was insistent that they both needed new hats for their "upcoming trip," and it had been easier to agree than to argue.

It didn't appear from the selection before her that Mrs. Hobbs' millinery creations were going to compete with anything she'd previously purchased on New York's Fifth Avenue. But she was certain that her mother, who loved to shop, would find something to buy.

The bell over the door tinkled loudly. Turning, Hannah expected to find her mother. What she found instead was trouble. Olive and Margaret had entered, and the malicious looks they wore could only spell harassment with a capital H. She gritted her teeth and steeled herself for the inevitable.

With an airy wave at Mrs. Hobbs, both women

marched straight toward Hannah, not bothering to peruse any of the finery displayed in the glass cases or hanging on the racks.

"Have you no shame whatsoever, Hannah Louise Barkley?" Olive pointed an accusing finger at Hannah Louise. "It's all over town about what you and Travis were doing at his office the other night. It's shocking. Simply shocking."

Margaret's lips thinned. "My mother always warned that you were fast and loose. I guess she knew what she was talking about. A decent woman doesn't carry on in the middle of the night unchaperoned, involving herself in all sorts of . . . indecencies." Her lips puckered on the last word, as if she had a difficult time forcing it out of her mouth.

Hannah took a deep breath, trying to quell her anger and conceal her embarrassment. "Not that it's any of your business, but it wasn't the middle of the night. Travis and I shared an innocent kiss—a kiss between good friends. That's all."

Olive's smirk screwed up her face in a most unattractive manner, like a rabid dog in the throes of extreme agony. "That's not what Mr. McGrath says, and I'm more inclined to believe him than you.

"I knew you'd go to any lengths to lure Travis back to the altar. I just never imagined you would go so far as to take him to your bed."

Her face whitening, Hannah rocked back on her heels as if slapped, balling her hands into fists of anger. *How dare these jealous harpies sit in judgment of me?*

Accuse me falsely without hearing my side of the story?
Not that they'd believe the truth anyway.

At that moment, Fiona stepped from behind a rack
of dresses. She had entered the store on the heels of
Olive and Margaret but had gone unnoticed during their
offensive attack on her daughter. The look she directed
at the spinsters was anything but polite.

"Well, well, if it isn't the two troublemakers. I
swear, but nothing much ever changes in this town."
She turned her attention to her daughter's stricken face.
"Hannah dear, you really should mind the company you
keep. You know how some small-minded people will
talk, and Miss Fasbinder and Miss Willoughby don't
have such sterling reputations. I really wouldn't want
you to besmirch yours by associating with them."

Olive's gasp was audible; Margaret stiffened in
outrage, then said, "Really, Mrs. Barkley! You are
hardly in a position to speak. A married woman arriving
in town in the company of a single man. What are decent folks to think?"

"That's right," Olive tossed out. "Like mother like
daughter, I always say."

"What a nice compliment. Thank you so much."
Hannah's forced smile never reached her eyes. "I'm always proud to be compared to my lovely mother."

"Why, thank you, dear." Fiona preened for everyone's benefit.

"*Hmph!*" Olive crossed her arms over a nonexistent bosom. "You have misconstrued my words entirely,
Hannah Louise."

Fiona's voice filled with mock indignation. "What? You don't think I'm lovely? Well, what a rude young woman you are." She shook her head. "I must have a talk with your mother, Olive. Yours too, Margaret. If I remember the last time we spoke—"

Paling considerably, Margaret gasped, clasping her cohort's hand tightly, as if it would give her strength to fight such a formidable foe. Her mother still hadn't recovered from the tongue-lashing she took from Mrs. Barkley those many years ago over the poison oak incident, and continued to harangue Margaret over it whenever she was displeased about something. Which was often. "Mama's not well. I don't think you should call on her, Mrs. Barkley."

"Come, Margaret," Olive insisted, dragging her unresisting and thoroughly relieved friend toward the door. "We'll be late for our luncheon appointment with Mr. McGrath. He wants us to help him with some important matters."

Matters like spreading gossip, Hannah thought. And no one was better suited to the task than the two spinsters. McGrath was clever. And he was doing just as he'd promised—ruining her reputation.

"Yes, do run along, girls, before I am sorely tempted to tell your parents what a horrible job they did in raising you."

Their horrified looks were enough to make Hannah smile, and when the door slammed shut behind them so hard the tiny brass bell fell to the floor with a clunk, she threw back her head and laughed, then her mother joined in. Soon the two women were laughing uproariously and hugging each other, while Mrs. Hobbs stared strangely at them and departed for the back room, shaking her head at the oddness of some Eastern folk.

"Oh, Mama, you are absolutely priceless." Hannah wiped tears from her face with the sleeve of her shirtwaist. "If only I could expel such brilliance in court." She kissed Fiona on the cheek. "Thank you for such a wonderful defense."

"And here I always thought you considered me an interfering woman bent on destruction."

"Well, there is that, too."

Patting her daughter's cheek affectionately, Fiona said, "You mustn't let the Olive Fasbinders and Margaret Willoughbys of the world bother you, my dear. They are spiteful, small-minded women who are envious of your beauty and your brains. And of your blossoming relationship with Travis.

"Speaking of which, I'd like to hear more about this kiss you mentioned. Travis never said a thing about it when I stopped by to see him this morning. Guess he was just too—"

"Mama!" Hannah's eyes widened in alarm. "You went to visit Travis? I hope you didn't say anything horrible to him. You know how you are."

"Brilliant?" Fiona offered, smiling inwardly at her daughter's reaction. "You needn't look so terrified, Hannah Louise. I merely went there to find out what his intentions are toward you."

"You didn't ask him that? Oh, Mama! I am so mortified. How can I ever face him again?"

"*Tsk, tsk,* dear. You are blowing our innocent chat entirely out of proportion. I merely mentioned that you had been in quite a foul mood these last few days—"

"You didn't?" She palmed her burning cheeks. "I can never face him again. I'm going to resign from the case."

"You needn't be so dramatic, dear. Travis said you were friends. He admitted having feelings for you, but didn't elaborate on what those feelings were."

Hannah looked up, slightly mollified. "He said that?"

"Well of course, my dear. I never lie. Well hardly ever. Unless it's absolutely necessary. And even then I give it a lot of thought before I do."

"Mama, that is absolute nonsense and you know it. You've been lying these past ten years, telling yourself and everyone else that you don't love Papa when you know you do. When are you going to face the fact that you two belong back together?"

It was Fiona's turn to blush. "Your father and I are miles apart from a reconciliation. Not nearly as close as you and Travis seem to be. Why, we haven't even shared so much as a chaste peck on the cheek, while you have shared—"

"I think we should go home and discuss this, Mama," Hannah interrupted, pointing to the rear wall and lowering her voice to a whisper. "Mrs. Hobbs prob-

ably has her ear glued to the wall at this very moment."
The milliner was a notorious gossip.

"Yes. I believe you're right on all counts, my dear.
Good-bye, Mrs. Hobbs," Fiona called out as they made
to depart. The next sound they heard was the crash of a
shelf and a woman's loud shriek as several bolts of fabric hit the milliner squarely on the head.

"Shouldn't we go back to make sure Mrs. Hobbs is
all right, Mama?" Hannah asked when they'd reached
the sidewalk, ignoring the whistles and catcalls coming
from the two cowboys riding hurriedly out of town. Dirt
tossed in their wake, and she stepped back to avoid
being hit by a flying clod.

"No, dear. The busybody needed to have some
sense knocked into her anyway. And I abhor people who
listen at peepholes."

Hannah asked skeptically, "But wasn't that what
you were doing when Olive and Margaret were taking
me to task?"

Fiona smiled, threading her arm through Hannah's
as they strolled farther down the street. "That's entirely
different, Hannah Louise."

"How so?"

"I was preparing your defense and needed to hear
incriminating testimony that would bolster my case."

The young woman couldn't contain her laughter. "I
think you may have missed your calling, Mama. The
way you twist facts and perform legal maneuvers, not to
mention interrogate former fiancés, I think you should
have been an attorney."

"Actually, Hannah Louise, I was thinking more along the lines of a judgeship."

"Everyone in town's talking about you and Hannah Louise, little brother. About what happened the other night. Should have locked the door if you was fixin' to ravish the woman." Ethan grinned, scooping up another bite of mashed potatoes. "Didn't I teach you right?"

All eyes at the table turned on Travis, who ignored his brother's teasing remarks and continued eating. It was customary for the Bodines to gather on Saturday evening to have dinner together. It was a time to catch up on weekly events, share accomplishments, and exchange the juiciest bits of town gossip.

"These pork chops are mighty good, Lavinia," Travis said. "Thanks for having me to supper."

"You know you don't need an invitation, dear. You're welcome here anytime." Pain clouded his stepmother's eyes, and Travis feared that she and his father'd had another go-around about the baby. The man needed to be taken out to the woodshed and thrashed, just like he'd taken them out there as kids when they'd been stupid and stubborn about things.

"How are you feeling?" he asked. "Willy tells me you've been overdoing. I hope that's not the case."

"It is," Wilhemina interjected before her mother-in-law could respond. "She's always trying to spare me and Emma chores and taking on more than she should. It's one of the reasons we decided to send the children to bed early this evening. Lavinia's doing way too much." She gazed accusingly at her father-in-law. "I'd think her husband would have cautioned her against it."

Sopping up the thick milk gravy with a biscuit, Ben paused, returning Willy's stare without flinching an eye. If he possessed any guilt over his callous treatment of his wife, it didn't show. "That's what happens when older women take it in their heads to get themselves with child."

Lavinia stiffened. Willy drew a sharp breath. Travis rolled his eyes heavenward.

"I doubt Lavinia did it all by herself, Pa," Ethan remarked, noting his wife's agitation, and wondering if the old man possessed even one ounce of tact. He sincerely doubted it.

"Have you been to see Doc Leahy yet, Lavinia?" Emma asked. "I have an appointment next week. You should come with me. Let the doctor take a look at you to make sure everything is all right with the baby."

The older woman hesitated. "I don't know—"

Willy nodded. "I think you should. We'll all go and see what Doc has to say about when these babies might be due. I'm getting awfully tired of hauling this belly around."

"But it's such a pretty belly, darlin'." Ethan leaned over to kiss his wife's cheek. "It's a good idea, Lavinia," he told his stepmother. "I'd be happy to drive you to town. Just let me know when."

Ignoring her husband's fierce frown, Lavinia smiled gratefully at her brood. They had rallied around her from the moment they'd learned of her pregnancy. For that she would always be grateful.

Ben, on the other hand, continued to be his usual obstinate self. She'd become so annoyed with him of late, she had taken to sleeping in Travis's old room, which she later intended to turn into a nursery, providing she ever decided to return to her husband's bed.

The thought depressed her, so she changed the subject. "I hope Hannah Louise is bearing up well under all the gossip, Travis. It's a lot more difficult for a woman to face scorn and ridicule than a man. Folks tend to forgive men just about anything . . . but not everything."

Her husband shifted uneasily in his chair but didn't comment.

"It's all McGrath's fault," Travis stated. "I just kissed Hannah, for heaven's sake. I don't know why everyone is making such a big deal out of it."

Ben leveled a castigating look at his son. "I doubt you're doing your brother's case any good by carrying on with your law partner. I thought you had more sense than that, boy."

"It was only a damn kiss!" he insisted.

"In my day a man didn't kiss a woman until he was fixin' to marry her."

Ethan and Willy exchanged amused looks.

Travis pushed back his chair, his appetite suddenly gone. "I'm not fixing to marry anyone, and I'd appreciate it if you would all mind your own business about what Hannah and I do."

"Can't do that, boy," Ben said. "What you do affects others, like your brother."

"Ben," Emma said softly, "I'm sure Travis is aware that his actions are scrutinized closely by everyone. I doubt he needs to be reminded of his responsibilities as a lawyer. And if he chooses to court Hannah Louise, then I think he should be allowed to do so without interference from any of us. I, for one, am in favor of it."

"So am I." Willy turned to look at Lavinia, who she hoped would lend support.

"I . . . I think Travis should follow his heart and do what he thinks best," the older woman finally said, unwilling to be drawn into any matchmaking efforts. She'd learned her lesson about interfering the day of the barbecue.

"*Hmph!* What a lot of nonsense. Hearts and flowers. And babies. That's all you women know about. It's enough to make a grown man sick."

"Well, if you were a grown man, Benjamin Bodine, I might be worried about that," Lavinia lashed out. "But from where I sit all I can see is a petulant child who didn't get his own way and has decided to make everyone else suffer for it."

Willy and Emma gasped at Lavinia's unexpected outburst. Then silence filled the room except for the repetitive tick, tick, tick of the clock on the sideboard.

A red-faced Ben pushed back his chair and stood, throwing down his napkin. "I've had my fill of dinner conversation. I'm going for a walk. Care to come, Ethan?"

The Ranger looked somewhat startled by the invitation and turned to look at his wife, who smiled her encouragement. Looking like a calf about to be taken to slaughter, he nodded. "Yeah. Sure. I'll come. I could do with a bit of fresh air."

Travis placed a comforting hand on his distraught stepmother's shoulder. "Don't pay attention to Pa, Lavinia. He's just got to work out all of this baby stuff on his own. He'll come around. You'll see."

"Quite frankly, I don't care at this point if he does or not." Looking weary and heartsick, she pushed herself to her feet. "I'm going upstairs to *my* room—your old room, Travis. It's where I sleep now. It might only be temporary or it could be a permanent arrangement. That'll be up to your father."

Travis watched his stepmother walk out, then shook his head in disgust at the old man's stubbornness. "I just love these weekend dinners at home, don't you?" he said to no one in particular.

"Have a piece of pie, Travis. You look like you could use one." Willy cut a large wedge of pecan pie and put it on a china plate, then handed it to him. "If I could bake pies as good as Lavinia's, I'd open a bakery."

"I've discovered that a great deal of problems can be solved by eating pie and other assorted confections," Emma stated, patting her growing mound. "I'll be as fat as a cow soon, if I don't stop gorging myself like I've been doing lately."

"Guess you'll just have to do more calisthenics then," Willy said, turning from her sister-in-law to

Travis. "Did you know Emma exercises regularly? She does these crazy scissorslike dances every morning with the kids. I just love watching them bounce up and down."

Remembering someone else who was fond of the activity, Travis smiled. "Rafe's been doing them over at the jailhouse. Says he learned them from Emma."

The young woman looked up at that. "Really? And he used to tease me about them." She sighed, a faraway look lighting her eyes.

"Have you seen Hannah since all the gossip started?" Willy bit into her pie, savoring the sticky sweetness. "I hope she's doing okay."

He shook his head. "No. But her mother came by the house this morning to ask me about my intentions."

Emma raised a brow at that.

"As a professional woman, I can understand why Hannah would be upset to have her reputation tarnished," Willy said. "It's much harder for a woman to establish a good reputation in the workplace and to be taken seriously. She's probably devastated over what happened because of that."

"I should never have kissed her. I just couldn't help myself."

"Love's like that," Emma said, almost absently.

"Love? Who said anything about love?" Travis's face turned three shades of crimson before he pushed back his chair and stood. "I'm going outside to join the men."

Willy smiled knowingly. "There's safety in numbers, huh, Travis?"

Emma grinned. "Never took you for a coward."

"I can't believe my brothers married such opinionated, loose-tongued women."

"The Bodine men need women with spirit. That's what Ethan says," Willy told him.

"Rafe, too. He said he'd be bored to tears if I was the shy, retiring type."

With a resigned expression, Travis replied, "I suspect my brothers never knew what hit 'em." Then he quickly quit the room.

Chapter Eleven

As clerk of the court Malcomb Beezley announced the beginning of Rafe Bodine's murder trial and introduced the esteemed presiding Judge Carlton Hix, who'd arrived forty-five minutes late and had just taken his seat behind the bench, the butterflies in Hannah Louise's stomach multiplied with disgusting rapidity.

She was always nervous the first day of a new trial. But today she had even more reason to be discomforted, agitated, and annoyed. Travis's furtive, guilt-ridden looks had filled her with unease but fortunately, she had come straight to the courthouse this Monday morning and hadn't yet confronted him. Everyone in town was talking about what had supposedly happened between them. Her mother had stuck her nose into something she had absolutely no business interfering with. And poor Rafe Bodine had paled two shades whiter than freshly laundered sheets since entering the courtroom.

And if all that wasn't bad enough, Judge Hix had

decided to make examples of the defense counsel by reminding everyone in the courtroom just why they were all here to begin with.

"We have come here today to determine if Rafferty Bodine, the defendant who stands accused of the murder of one Robert Slaughter, commonly known as Bobby Slaughter, has broken the law. If Mr. McGrath, who represents the state of Texas in his capacity as prosecuting attorney, can prove his case against Mr. Bodine beyond a reasonable doubt, then the jury—that's you," he said pointing to the twelve solemn men seated in the jury box—"will be required to bring forth a unanimous guilty verdict, whereby the court will prescribe a penalty for his illegal behavior. On the other hand, if the state fails to prove Mr. Bodine's guilt, then the jury will have no recourse but to acquit.

"Let me remind you and everyone else in this courtroom that Mr. Bodine is considered innocent in the eyes of the law and must be proven guilty. That burden of proof rests with the prosecution. And it is my job as overseer of these proceedings to see to it that he receives a fair and impartial hearing."

"Bodine's guilty. Lynch the bastard!" someone in the back of the room shouted. A chorus of angry voices soon erupted, turning the room into chaos.

"Order! Order in the court!" Judge Hix banged his gavel furiously, his face reddening in anger, and the courtroom quieted once again. "Bailiff, throw that man out of my courtroom. And if anyone dares make a similar outburst they'll be thrown out as well. I will not tolerate that kind of uncivilized behavior. Do I make myself clear?"

Travis turned to see Flint Black being forcibly ejected from the room by Deputy Barnes. Black, he recalled, had been arrested by Rafe some time back for horse stealing and had served two years in the state penitentiary for his crime. The cattle rustler and horse thief was lucky he hadn't been hanged, which was the usual penalty for horse thieves in Texas.

"You'll find that I run a tight ship. I won't permit any snide innuendoes," the judge added, staring directly at McGrath, making the prosecutor squirm nervously in his seat. "Nor will I allow any emotional outbursts or personal relationships to interfere with the accused receiving a fair trial."

Hannah and Travis stared straight ahead, not daring to look at each other, though they were mindful of the curious stares of others upon them. Hannah's face flushed hot, while Travis rubbed his throat in an unconscious gesture.

"We are here to conduct some very serious business. A man's life is at stake. And though this may be a backwater town by some people's standards, far removed from the bright lights of the big city, let me assure you that this trial will be conducted with the same decorum and adherence to the law as if we were seated in downtown Manhattan. That's in New York City," he told the jurors, who nodded gravely when he asked if he'd made himself clear, and offered to repeat himself if he hadn't.

Just then, the clerk of the court whispered something in the judge's ear that made Carlton Hix frown deeply. After a brief discussion, he addressed the court. "As much as it pains me to delay the start of this trial, something important has come up that I need to attend to right away. Court will adjourn until after lunch. At such time, we will begin hearing the opening arguments of the prosecution and defense, which will hopefully be of short duration.

"Pontificating is a sin. Be mindful of that when you come back here this afternoon," he instructed both parties. Banging his gavel to punctuate the warning, he rose and quit the room, his black-satin robe billowing out like ominous thunderclouds behind him, a portent of things to come.

"I'll tell you what's a sin," Travis said to Hannah fifteen minutes later, loosening his tie as he seated himself behind the desk. "Having that old reprobate on the bench. I sure do wish Judge Barkley was presiding over my brother's case. I'd feel a whole lot better about things if he were."

So would Hannah, but she was too professional to admit such a thing. At any rate, her father would have had to excuse himself if she'd been part of the proceedings. "Judge Hix is tough but fair. I've never tried a case before him, but my mother believes Rafe will get an impartial hearing, and that the judge will hold tight rein on McGrath's attempts to grandstand."

Her voice was velvet-edged but strong, husky, and

sensual, sending ripples of awareness through him. Travis was grateful that Hannah was seated across the room on the sofa, for despite what he was about to say, he didn't believe one word of it. "I'm sorry about what happened the other night, Hannah. I won't let it happen again."

Her cheeks blossomed pink. "We were just caught up by the emotional stress of the trial. As long as we maintain a proper distance I don't anticipate any further problems." *Liar!* she told herself. All she could think about was being wrapped in Travis's arms once again.

"Your mother came by to visit me at the new house the other day. She was worried about you."

"Mama tends to overreact. You know how older people are? And she isn't happy unless she's interfering in my business."

"Well in that case, how about having dinner with me tonight? McGrath is going to call the DeBerry woman tomorrow to testify, and I'd like to go over my questioning of her with you. I thought maybe we could eat here to avoid any further public scrutiny."

A lump formed in her throat, and she had difficulty swallowing around it. "Dinner? Here?" That sounded like one big problem to her. It was a perfectly reasonable request; one that she wouldn't normally consider denying. But things had changed. The kiss they'd shared changed everything. She had changed. Her feelings, her needs . . . But yet, she couldn't bring herself to refuse. "I suppose it would be smarter to stay in. We can lock the door, shut the curtains. Just to make sure there's no repeat of the other night."

Her suggestions were sensible, so why then was his heart beating fast, his palms sweating in anticipation of being alone with her? "I'll bring some food from the boardinghouse."

"And I'll bring a few things from home as well. Mama promised to make two apple pies today. We can make it a potluck of sorts."

"I love juicy, ripe . . ." He stared at her lips, then her breasts, and his manhood hardened. "Apples."

Tingles marched up her spine like determined soldiers on their way to battle. She leaned back against the sofa to squash them. "Me too," she said, sounding very much like a croaking bullfrog. "Shall we practice the opening statement again? I wouldn't want you to get tongue-tied." Her gaze drifted to his mouth, and she remembered distinctly where that tongue had recently been. Her nipples hardened. She crossed her arms over her chest, hoping he hadn't noticed.

"Shall I come sit next to you on the sofa?"

"No!" she blurted, a little too vehemently. "I mean—why don't you stand like you would do in court? I can critique you more effectively that way."

But when he stood, his crotch was at her eye level and there was no mistaking the bulge that projected his desire for her quite clearly. "It's awfully warm in here, isn't it?" she asked, blotting her damp forehead with the back of her hand. "Do you think we should open the window?"

He rushed to do it, grateful for the diversion, hoping his swollen member would subside by the time he returned. Gulping in great amounts of fresh air, he waited in vain.

"Shall we begin?"

Yeah, he replied silently. *Why don't you lie down on that sofa, take off your dress, pull off your drawers, and I'll—* He swallowed, biting the inside of his cheek, horrified that he'd lost control. "I'm just going to run downstairs for a minute. There's something I've got to do." He prayed that Enos's water barrel was still full. He intended to submerge himself in it.

Think about the trial, he told himself. *Think about the trial.*

Hannah's smile was pure innocence. "I'll wait right here until you get back."

With a groan, Travis quit the room, slamming the door behind him. Hannah heard him cursing all the way down the stairs.

Fiona and Thaddeus gazed at each other across the large expanse of dining-room table. Bright sunlight filtered through the lace curtains hanging at the double hung windows, landing softly on Fiona's animated face while a soft breeze ruffled the bouquet of bluebonnets, pink morning glories, and yellow prickly pear flower gracing the center of the mahogany table.

Though it seemed strange to be sharing a mea again with his wife after so many years, it also seeme very right to Thaddeus, who had missed Fiona, bu would rather have had his tongue pulled out than admit it. When she had insisted that he come down from his room to have lunch with her so she could fill him in on the morning's court proceedings, he hadn't the will or the inclination to refuse her request.

"I wish you could have been there, Thaddeus. You would have been so proud to see Hannah Louise seated at the defense table with Travis. Oh, they do make such a handsome couple." Her eyes sparkling brightly, she slathered butter on her biscuit, then made a face when she bit into the dry roll. "It was a shame court had to recess when things were just getting started."

"Why did Hix halt the proceedings?" He could barely say the man's name without choking. Carlton Hix had been Fiona's friend since childhood. Thaddeus had never liked the man, especially when he'd discovered that Hix had designs upon his wife.

She shrugged. "I suppose Carlton—Judge Hix—had a good reason. He's quite a fair man. And very mindful of his duty."

"*Hmph!* You've always been taken with the man. Must be all that white hair of his. Personally I think it makes him look as old as Methuselah."

"You know perfectly well that Carlton's been prematurely gray since the age of twenty. And I think his hair makes him look distinguished, not old. But that doesn't mean that I harbor any romantic feelings for him. If you think that, Thaddeus, then you are very much mistaken."

He sipped slowly at his split pea soup, saying without glancing up, "A married woman should be more circumspect about how she travels, and with whom."

"Carlton and I have been friends since grade school. There's nothing wrong with traveling with an old friend. Would you have preferred that I traveled here alone and unescorted?" When he didn't answer, she added, "Really, Thaddeus, if I didn't know better, I'd say you were jealous of Carlton Hix."

He snorted, hoping the flush rising to his cheeks would be credited to the hot soup. "What nonsense. A man my age doesn't get jealous." Even if Hix was rich as Croesus, had a mansion in Dallas, and had the stature of a man thirty years his junior.

Before Thaddeus could make himself any more ill with his reflections, Maude entered the room. "Will you be wanting anything else, Judge?" The housekeeper purposely avoided looking at Fiona.

"I made two apple pies this morning, Thaddeus," Fiona said. "Hannah mentioned that you might like to have some."

"I had me a piece of it, Judge. It was pretty good, considering an Easterner made it."

"Why thank you, Mrs. Fogarty. Your effusive praise overwhelms me." Fiona's sarcasm was unmistakable, and Maude's eyes narrowed.

"Don't you two start caterwauling again. I ain't well enough to be putting up with your petty squabbles." Fiona looked suitably chastised and leaned back in her seat. Maude merely glared defiantly. "Please bring two pieces of pie, Mrs. Fogarty. I'm sure my wife would like to have one."

Without a word the housekeeper spun on her heel and stormed back into the kitchen. Fiona released the deep sigh she'd been holding. "That woman despises me."

With a look that could have passed for regret, Thaddeus nodded. "Maude fancies herself mistress of this house. You've been gone a long time, Fiona, and she's had free rein here. I guess she resents having to share what she considers hers."

What Maude Fogarty resented sharing was Thaddeus. The woman was half in love with him, though Fiona doubted her husband knew it. Men were often oblivious to things like that. But Fiona had seen the affection in Maude's eyes whenever she glanced at the judge. And she could well understand the attraction. Thaddeus James Barkley was a hard man to resist. Even after all these years, after all they'd been through, he still had the power to make Fiona's heart flutter like a schoolgirl's.

"I'm home now, and I think it only proper that Mrs. Fogarty treat me with some respect. Even if she's merely pretending," she said finally.

"I'll speak to her."

"Thank you. But do be careful in what you say. I don't want to hurt her feelings. Even though she appears tough as nails, I think she's fragile beneath all that bluster and posturing."

"You've always been a soft touch, Fiona."

"Too soft, too stubborn, too stupid. But I've grown up. I know that sounds strange, considering I'm fifty years old, but it's taken me longer than most."

"We've all made mistakes, had regrets."

She heaved a sigh. "I know I've had my share."

An awkward silence ensued. Outside a redbreasted robin trilled happily while a cowboy yelled raucous, disparaging comments about his companion's ancestors.

Finally, Thaddeus cleared his throat. "I'm glad you've come home, Fiona."

She smiled softly, reaching out to touch his hand . . . and his heart. "So am I, Thaddeus. So am I."

Will McGrath had been speaking before the jury for over one hour and thirty-five minutes. The men in the jury box looked dazed, the spectators comatose, and it was all Hannah could do to keep her eyes propped open. She'd never heard such a boring, pompous opening statement in all her years as an attorney. The man's monotone voice had a lulling, anesthetizing effect, and she could tell that he was making a horrible impression on the jurors. One man was cleaning his fingernails with a penknife, another in the back row had dozed off a time or two.

"Be more animated when it's your turn," she wrote on her pad, shoving it at Travis, who nodded and rolled his eyes heavenward, as if asking the Almighty for a respite from the verbosity.

"Rafe Bodine is a murderer, gentleman of the jury, and I intend to prove that fact. I will prove through eyewitness testimony that he stalked Bobby Slaughter and shot him down in cold blood, and then proceeded to hunt down the rest of the Slaughter family and kill them one by one, without any thought to human life.

"Rafe Bodine took the law into his own hands. The same law he was sworn to uphold as a Texas Ranger . . ."

Travis wondered if the man was ever going to shut up. He'd said the same thing over and over again in at least fifteen different ways, calling Rafe a murderer, killer, butcher, assassin, slayer of innocents. McGrath was a walking thesaurus when it came to redundancy.

Judge Hix was also growing impatient with the diatribe. Travis had seen him looking at his gold pocket watch several times, then glare at the prosecutor, before clearing his throat and shaking his head in disgust. Unfortunately, McGrath was so caught up in the theatrics of what he was doing that he hadn't paid the judge the slightest bit of attention.

"And so gentlemen of the jury, do not forget that a cold-blooded killer sits before you—"

"Mr. McGrath," the judge interrupted, crooking his forefinger at him. "Would you please approach the bench?"

A perplexed look on his face, the prosecutor apologized to the jurors, then strode forward. Travis took the opportunity to speak to his brother, who looked spent by the proceedings.

"How are you holding up, big brother? You should

feel slightly better after listening to McGrath run on at the mouth."

"The jurors seem to be paying attention to what he's saying," Rafe said, not the least bit mollified.

"Not really," Hannah remarked, noting his nervousness and unable to fault him for it. Had she been in a similar circumstance, she would have felt just as uncertain and scared. "The man in the back row has nodded off several times. That can't be good for McGrath."

"I hope you're right."

She smiled, hoping to reassure him. "I've heard your brother's opening statement. I know it's good. And the jury is bound to be very impressed."

Pride mixed with fear as Travis listened to Hannah's praise, heard his brother's sigh of relief, and wondered if he'd be able to live up to everyone's expectations. The entire Bodine family was present in the courtroom. Hannah's mother, too.

Olive and Margaret were seated two rows back behind Rafe, doing their best to appear supportive. Not that he found any comfort in their presence. Quite the contrary, in fact. They'd both been instrumental in fostering McGrath's vicious lies about him and Hannah.

Ethan had been so incensed about what he'd heard at the livery the other day that he'd threatened Wally Cooper with a severe beating if he ever muttered another disparaging word about Hannah or Travis or their "wildly wanton" relationship. Wally had been conspicuously absent from the proceedings.

Sweat dripped down his neck as McGrath finally

brought his opening statement to a swift end. When the judge asked if Travis was ready to proceed, he hesitated momentarily, then replied, "Yes, Your Honor. The defense is ready to begin."

If there was one thing Hannah had stressed, it was to make eye contact with the jurors. Travis was doing that now as he led the twelve men through the horror of Ellie Bodine's murder. Eloquently and graphically, he painted word pictures of a woman's mutilated body, remnants of an unborn child lying on the floor of the barn, an anguished husband and expectant father who arrived home to find his life had just been turned upside down, his guts and heart ripped from his body. His soul tortured.

The room was hushed, the jurors hanging on to his every word. Gasps of outrage, punctuated by soft weeping, could be heard from the spectators. Hannah felt inordinately pleased that Travis was doing such a fine job of getting their points across. He had heeded her advice well. His natural flair for courtroom presentation was quite evident.

It took a lot of hard work and dedication to master the intricacies and flamboyance necessary for a successful criminal defense attorney, and Travis had done his homework well. He was as polished and proficient in front of the jury as any defense attorney she'd witnessed, and Hannah was justifiably proud of his accomplishment.

Chancing a peek at McGrath, who looked discomforted by the brilliance of Travis's oratory, she smiled inwardly. Their opponent couldn't be feeling too confident at the moment. On the other hand, Rafe seemed a bit more at ease and astonished by his brother's performance. Even Judge Hix, whose stoic countenance didn't reveal much beyond boredom, seemed enthralled by the horrific details of the case and impressed by the young lawyer's relating of them.

The student had surpassed the teacher, Hannah thought happily, a lump forming in her throat. And she'd be the first one to tell him as soon as the court session ended.

"You were absolutely brilliant! I'm so proud, so very proud of you." Hannah threw her arms about Travis's neck as soon as they entered the office and gave him an effusive hug, her smile wide, her face glowing with pride and happiness.

He set down his briefcase, a hint of color touching his cheeks. Coming from such a hard taskmaster as Hannah Louise, this was high praise indeed. And most welcome. He'd been nervous as a high-strung rooster in a henhouse during the proceedings. "Thanks. So you really think I did okay?"

"Quit fishing for compliments, Travis Bodine. You did more than okay. You were fantastic. I had no idea you would be so effective with your presentation."

He smiled gratefully, wishing he could kiss her to show his gratitude. "I have you to thank, Hannah. It was you who told me what to say and how to say it."

She brushed off his compliment with a wave of her

hand but was secretly pleased by it. "We can bask in our glory today, but tomorrow's going to be a whole lot more difficult when Madam DeBerry takes the stand. She's not going to be an easy nut to crack."

"Which is why I asked you to have dinner with me tonight, so we could go over everything," he reminded her.

She tapped her chin thoughtfully. "We'll need to explore all the possibilities."

He'd like to explore every inch of Hannah Louise, starting with her soft breasts and pert nipples, then work his way down to her—

"Travis, are you listening to me? I said I'm going to run home and get the pie. You do the same. We can meet back here in say thirty minutes and get started."

His face flushed, his tongue tied up in knots, he swallowed and blinked several times, surprised to find the object of his thoughts fully clothed and heading out the door. "Jesus, Bodine!" he said with a disgusted shake of his head.

His hunger for Hannah Louise had grown to gargantuan proportions. He wanted her badly. Needed to make love to her. And couldn't think about much else.

Five years before they had kissed and fondled as young lovers, brought themselves to the brink of madness, but never consummated their need for each other, preferring to wait until their wedding night to experience the joy of their union. But the promised wedding night had never happened—at least not for him—and he didn't know if Hannah Louise had given what rightfully should have been his to someone else, another lover . . . another man.

The idea filled him with fury. He couldn't stand to think of another man bedding Hannah Louise, touching her, kissing her. But the possibility was all too real. She was twenty-eight years old. Most women her age were married with children, had experienced life, lovemaking, or lovers.

Well, he hadn't had his wedding night. She had robbed him of that many years ago. But there was no time like the present to make up for lost time.

Hannah had become a distraction, a fever in his blood, and he couldn't concentrate on anything but her.

Tonight he intended to make Hannah Louise his, once and for all. Tomorrow, when his mind was cleared of his need for her, his thoughts would return solely to the trial.

Chapter Twelve

"YOU LOOK AS TASTY AS YOUR MOTHER'S APPLE PIE, Hannah Louise." Travis eyed her appreciatively, making her cheeks blush bright pink. "You'd best be careful, or I'm apt to take a bite out of you."

"I'd probably bite back," she retorted, hoping to disguise the mounting apprehension she felt. Seated on the rug in front of the sofa sharing their indoor picnic, Travis's close proximity was making her nervous, exceedingly warm, and very aware that they were alone with the door locked tight and the window shades drawn. There was something different in his attitude tonight. The smoldering looks he cast her way over dinner had almost succeeded in robbing her of her appetite.

She swallowed the lump that suddenly formed in her throat. "Since I'm going to assume that you've just given me a compliment, I thank you." And it warmed her heart to hear it. She had changed into a pretty lavender shirtwaist and blue-serge skirt before coming back to the office, taking extra pains with her appearance in the hope that Travis would notice. Judging by the longing she saw reflected in the depths of his eyes—longing that mirrored her own—he had.

"I love apple pie, don't you? No one makes better pie than my mama," she said, rambling on, suddenly frightened by her feelings.

"*Hmmmm.*" Travis ran his finger up her arm, down her side, then took the china dish from her hand. "But there are some things I like a whole lot better."

"I . . . I wasn't done with that yet."

Her cheeks flushed hot, and he grinned, pulling her into his chest and kissing her, making all thoughts of apple pies and mamas fly right out of her mind. The kiss was slow, thoughtful, his tongue tracing the soft fullness of her lower lip before seeking entry into her mouth, which she gave willingly.

He cupped her breasts through the thin cloth of her blouse, caressing and arousing her nipples into two stiff peaks.

She moaned. "Travis . . ." His name was a whisper, a sigh, a reflection of the deep yearning in her soul.

"I've dreamed of this for five long years, Hannah Louise. I've missed holding you, kissing you."

"I've missed you, too," she confessed and didn't protest when he moved to unbutton the pearl buttons of her shirtwaist and push it off her shoulders.

Her skin looked like peaches and cream, and he knew it would taste just as good as it looked. He kissed the soft skin at the nape of her neck, the small mole just below her left ear, and gooseflesh erupted everywhere.

His lips trailed down her chest, and he savored the soft swell of breast rising above her chemise. "You taste much better than your mama's apple pie, sweet Hannah," he said, pulling the yellow ribbons of her undergarment with his teeth and freeing her breasts to his mouth.

Shocked by his boldness, and consumed by a need she had no idea she possessed, Hannah offered no resistance. Her head lolled back, and she gave in to the sweet torture of his lovemaking.

Travis lapped at her nipples, first one, then the other, then drew them into his mouth, suckling, swirling his tongue around her nipples, making her cry out.

"Stop! Please stop!"

Pushing her back gently on the rug, he covered her body with his own. "You don't really want me to stop, do you, Hannah? Don't you want to know what we missed five years ago? What it could have been like between us?" His hand moved along her leg to push up her skirt, and he caressed the soft flesh of her calf, her inner thigh, until he reached the juncture of her womanhood. He palmed her, moving over her in slow, circular motions, applying just the right amount of sweet, torturous pressure.

"Dear God in heaven!"

"You're ready for me, Hannah. You want me as much as I want you. Let me take you, make you mine."

Desire pounded through her veins, heating her blood to a fevered pitch. She was tempted to say yes, to throw all caution to the wind and let him have his way. She loved him, wanted to be with him. But not like this. Not just for one night, for one fleeting moment of passion. She wanted forever. And she would have that or nothing.

She pushed hard against his chest, shaking her head, trying to restore her equilibrium and common sense. "I can't. I'm not willing to settle for a night of passion and nothing else."

He looked stricken by her refusal and shook his head, as if he hadn't quite heard her correctly. "You want me, Hannah. You know you do."

"I won't deny that," she said, drawing the edges of her shirtwaist together and sitting up. "But I want more than—"

"You've always wanted more, Hannah Louise." His voice was harsh with unfulfilled desire as he pulled away and took deep breaths to bring himself under control. "You wanted more five years ago, remember? Wanted everything your own way, with no thought to my needs or desires. You're doing the same thing now."

Pain replaced passion. "That's not true, Travis, and you know it. You're the one who broke our engagement, who pushed me away. And you know nothing of what I want. But that's not what's important right now."

He snorted contemptuously. "What is? Do you have another list of demands before you allow me to make love to you?"

"Actually, I do." His brow shot up at that. "But I'm not inclined to share them with you at this moment, because I doubt you'd want to comply." She wanted marriage. Nothing less would do.

"And you're forgetting something very important, Travis. Your brother's depending on us to defend him and save his life. We can't put our personal feelings before our obligation to Rafe. That wouldn't be fair to him."

She was right, of course, and Travis knew it. But he was running on pure emotion and frustration and wouldn't give an inch. "Since when do you know what's fair, Hannah Louise?"

"Trust me, I do. Now, if you're through arguing, we need to get to work. We have a hard day ahead of us."

He had something equally hard to deal with just then, though he wouldn't tell her that. He wouldn't give her the satisfaction of knowing how her rejection had hurt him, both physically and emotionally.

Maybe she was trying to get back at him for what had happened five years ago, or maybe she'd developed a sadistic streak over the years. Whatever the case, he was determined that this time around things were going to end up a whole lot differently between him and Hannah Louise.

He'd given up much too easily before. He intended to stay the course this time, see it through, and make his own happy ending. He'd already proven today how persuasive he could be in a court of law. He'd merely apply those same tactics to wooing Hannah Louise to his bed. Or die trying.

The madam of Justiceburg's most profitable bordello sat stiff-backed in the witness chair, looking as nervous as a virgin her first time out. The reddish brown henna dye she usually wore had faded, revealing the woman's natural hair to be the color of mud. Her yellow-satin dress, gaudy by anyone's standards, painted her complexion sallow, despite her rouged cheeks. Her full-figured bosom was no doubt her greatest asset, and she bore the massive mounds like badges of honor upon her chest.

McGrath stood in front of the witness box, hands clenched behind his back as he strode to and fro, caught up in his own self-importance. Hannah thought he looked like a strutting cock who was scratching hard to make his mark.

"Please tell the court, Miss DeBerry, what your relationship was to the deceased Bobby Slaughter."

Dabbing her eyes with a frilly lace handkerchief, as if the ordeal she was going through was just too much to bear, the woman sniffed several times for effect before answering. "We were affianced, me and Bobby were. And planned to be married just as soon as he could find himself a regular job."

Ethan snorted loudly from behind where the defense team was seated. "His thievin' was pretty regular, if you ask me," he whispered before his wife could shush him. Travis shot him a cautionary look.

"Please tell us to the best of your recollection, Miss DeBerry, what happened the day Bobby was shot down in cold blood."

"Objection, Your Honor. Speculation. Leading the witness."

"Objection sustained. Please, Mr. McGrath," Judge

Hix demanded, "keep your rhetoric to the actual facts. The court is not interested in hearing your opinions or embellishments."

"Me and Bobby was making love," the whore stated to the accompaniment of shocked gasps and whistles. Several of the women in the audience fanned themselves in outrage, even as their husbands leaned forward to make sure they didn't miss a word of the juicy narrative.

"All of a sudden Rafe Bodine burst into the room, gun drawn," she continued, "accusing Bobby of killing his wife and child. Though Bobby denied it, Ranger Bodine shot him dead, without so much as a by-your-leave."

"That's not how it happened," Rafe whispered through clenched teeth, and Hannah covered his hand with her own. She heard Emma whimper softly behind her, and her heart felt leaden at the pain they were going through. "You'll have your chance to explain," she told him. "For now we must be patient." Appeased for the time being, he sat back in his chair, but the look he shot the DeBerry woman could have planted her six feet under, right alongside her lover.

"Was Mr. Bodine wearing a Ranger's badge?" the prosecutor questioned. "Or was there any indication that he was there for strictly legal purposes in his capacity as a lawman?"

The witness shook her head. "No, sir. But I recognized him just the same. Rafe and his brother, Ethan, had been through Justiceburg before on the trail of desperadoes. They made quite an impression on the women in my employ."

Loud snickers filled the room, and the judge banged his gavel down hard. "Quiet! Or I shall be forced to clear this courtroom. Continue, Miss De-Berry," he instructed the witness, unable to keep his gaze off the woman's handsome figure.

She smiled knowingly and continued. "Yes, Judge. What I was going to say was that those two men could pack a powerful lot of loving into their—"

"That's just fine, Miss DeBerry," McGrath inter-rupted, mopping his red, perspiring face with a handker-chief, then pouring a glass of water from a pitcher he kept on his desk and swallowing it down in one big gulp.

"Is it your testimony then, ma'am, that Rafe Bod-ine shot Bobby Slaughter without provocation and with-out allowing him to defend himself?"

When the whore nodded, stating an emphatic "Yes!" McGrath indicated he was through with the witness, and the Judge turned over the questioning to the defense.

Travis approached, looking far more poised than he felt. "Mr. McGrath keeps referring to you as Miss De-Berry. But isn't it true that you're usually addressed as *Madam* DeBerry?"

She opened her mouth to speak, but the prosecutor jumped to his feet. "Objection, Your Honor! Irrelevant. Miss DeBerry's title has nothing to do with this case."

"I disagree, Your Honor. Her profession as owner and madam of Madam DeBerry's Pleasure Palace has a great deal to do with this case."

"I'll allow you to proceed, Mr. Bodine. But do so with caution."

"Isn't it true, madam, that Bobby Slaughter was in actuality one of your clients at the bordello, and not your fiancé? And isn't it also true that you charged him the same two-dollar rate as you would charge any other paying customer?"

She blotted her upper lip nervously. "Well, yes, but—"

"I'd think, Madam DeBerry, that if you and Bobby were really affianced you wouldn't have charged him one red cent to bed you, let alone two dollars. After all, you stated that he didn't have a regular job."

"A woman's got to make a living," she said, and the courtroom erupted once again. The gavel came down, and the judge issued another stern warning.

"Isn't it true, madam, that Rafe Bodine did not draw his gun until Bobby Slaughter pulled his weapon out from beneath his pillow and fired at him? That Rafe Bodine shot Bobby Slaughter in self-defense?"

She shook her head. "No, sir! That's not what happened. He killed Bobby. Shot him in cold blood. I seen it with my own eyes." She pointed at Rafe, her red-lacquered nail stabbing the air with accusation. "He may be your brother, but I ain't going to lie to spare him."

Hannah tapped her pencil nervously against the notepad and hoped that Travis would conclude his cross-examination of the witness quickly. This line of questioning was only succeeding in making the witness more hostile. And though Hannah was positive that the woman was lying through her teeth, it was doubtful Travis would be able to shake her testimony.

Rising to her feet, Hannah addressed the court. "Your Honor, may I have a word with cocounsel?"

The judge nodded, and Travis leaned over the defense table to hear what Hannah had to say, looking none too pleased that she'd seen fit to interrupt a cross-examination he thought was going passably well.

"You must cease this line of questioning at once, Travis," she warned. "It's doing more harm than good. Trust me. I know what I'm talking about. You'll not change that woman's mind on the stand."

Travis knew he had waded into murky waters and sensed that Madam DeBerry was going to fight him every inch of the way. McGrath had prepared her well. But having to admit that Hannah was right galled him, especially after yesterday.

After a few moments of soul searching, he turned back to the bench. "I'm done with Madam DeBerry for the time being, Your Honor. She may step down. But we reserve the right to recall her at a later time."

"Very well." The judge excused the witness, then pulled his pocket watch out of his robe. "Owing to the lateness of the hour, this court stands in recess until tomorrow afternoon. Be prompt, be brief. And for heaven's sake, let's try to interject some decorum and decency into these proceedings."

Will McGrath studied the telegram from his contact at the Wyoming Territorial Prison and smiled ferally. Hannah Louise had written to the warden asking for permission to interview Roy Lee Slaughter. She was one smart bitch, he'd give her that.

Her strategies thus far had been sound. The defense was putting up a valiant effort to acquit Bodine, but in the end it wouldn't work. Nothing they could do or say would make one bit of difference. Bodine was going to die. He intended to see to it personally. And Travis and Hannah might end up the same way, if they weren't careful.

Pulling out a sheet of paper from his desk drawer, he dipped the end of the pen in the dark ink and wrote the words that would put his plan into action.

In front of the courthouse, Travis paused to speak briefly to Ethan, with whom he had a bone to pick.

"You're not doing Rafe any good, Ethan, by sitting in the courtroom and making snide remarks. How will it look to the jury if the judge decides to toss you out, as he did Black? I'm counting on you to testify in Rafe's behalf."

Ethan had the grace to look chagrined. "I didn't mean to mess things up for you, little brother. I was just making a joke. And it angers me that that whore was trying to make Rafe out to be a villain and her fiancé some friggin' hero out of a dime novel."

It upset Travis, too, but he didn't have the luxury of admitting that to anyone, except Hannah Louise. And she'd already left to go home with her mother. "Just be more circumspect in your behavior. You and Rafe rode together for years. He'll be judged by your actions and words. Keep that in mind next time you're tempted to speak out."

"Speaking of circumspect. Did you see the way the judge was ogling that whore? The old bastard was looking at her tits like he hadn't seen any before."

Travis frowned. "I saw. And the jurors weren't immune to Miss DeBerry's charms either. Which just proves my point that we're in for a hell of a rough time. Even though Hix is a judge, and those jurors have a job to do, they're all still just men."

"I can't believe that anyone would take a whore's word over a Texas Ranger's. That don't seem right somehow."

"Not everyone is fond of lawmen, and the whore's assets are larger than most."

"Shit! I'll say. A man could get plumb tuckered out climbing those peaks of pleasure."

"Good thing your wife's not around to hear you say that, big brother," Travis said, noting Ethan's grin. "I'd venture a guess that she'd break both your legs, and certain *other* appendages, so you wouldn't be doing any climbing, poking, or prodding, for a very long time."

Ethan looked slightly discomforted by the prospect. "Just 'cause I'm married don't mean I'm dead. I can still look, even if I can't touch."

Smiling as he watched his brother walk away, Travis felt slightly envious that Ethan was so happily married and expecting a child. It was likely he and Hannah would have had a couple of kids by now if they had married.

He didn't have time to dwell on that appealing thought because Olive and Margaret were making their way toward him. The determined looks they wore were frightening.

"Ladies," he said as he tipped his white-felt Stetson.

"You were just wonderful in court today, Travis," Margaret said. "I don't think Miss Barkley had any business interrupting you when you were trying to make such valid points."

"I'm afraid it wouldn't be proper of me to discuss the case with you, but thanks for your input." He effectively cut off any further insults likely to be directed at Hannah. The two women had already done quite enough damage, in his opinion.

"We really wanted to discuss something else entirely, something different than the court case, Travis." Olive clasped his right arm while Margaret latched on to the left. "Why don't we walk toward your office while we talk? It's such a lovely day. And I'd welcome a breath of fresh air. The courtroom was so stuffy."

Feeling like a lamb being led to slaughter, Travis swallowed, wondering what the two spinsters had cooked up this time. "What's on your mind? I'm afraid I don't have much free time these days, even for church service."

Margaret giggled. Olive shook her head, saying, "You silly man. It isn't church we wish to talk about, but something far more exciting. As you probably know, the annual Founder's Day Celebration is coming up next Saturday. I have been appointed by the Ladies' Auxiliary as coordinator for this year's event."

He'd completely forgotten about it. As kids, he and his brothers used to enjoy the Founder's Day Celebration. It was a day of pie eating, sack races, and freedom from the watchful eyes of their parents, ranking second only in excitement and amusement to the town's Fourth of July observance. But over the years the celebration had grown staid, he'd grown older, and the prospect of attending had become more a chore than anything else.

"I don't usually attend," he finally admitted.

"Not many of the eligible men and ladies do anymore," Olive pointed out. "Which is why I've decided to do something very exciting, scandalous even, this year to help improve the turnout." His brow shot up, and she continued. "The town is trying to raise money for a park and a bandstand, which, I'm sure you'll agree, is a very worthwhile effort."

"I agree, it would be nice to have a real park with flowers, trees, and the like." Though he wondered who they would get to play in the bandstand. Murph Rogers and his banjo was about the only form of entertainment in town. Unless you counted the Spondella sisters, former circus performers, who were given to belting out Italian opera arias at the drop of a hat. Though the overweight twins could hardly be called entertaining.

"I just knew you'd agree to help us out with the Bachelor's Auction, Travis."

"Whoa!" Eyes wide, he skidded to a halt, making both women collapse into him. "I haven't agreed to any such thing. And what exactly is a Bachelor's Auction, if I may be so bold to ask?" The moment he did, he wished he hadn't.

"The eligible men in town are being put up for auction to the highest bidder. The purchaser is entitled to spend the entire day with the man of her choice, eat lunch . . . and," she blushed, "and whatever else may take their fancy."

Travis's face whitened as visions of spooning with Olive Fasbinder or Margaret Willoughby came into focus. "What? You're planning to sell men like slaves on an auction block? That's not only illegal, it's . . . it's . . ." *Enough to make a grown man puke.*

"It's wonderful, wholesome fun." Margaret cast adoring eyes at him, pressing her bosom into his arm, and Travis had the sudden urge to run screaming down the middle of Main Street. "And it's for such a worthwhile cause," she added.

"When we told Will McGrath about it he jumped at the chance to participate."

Travis jerked his head to stare at Olive. "McGrath is going to participate?" The wily bastard. If Travis refused to do the same, he'd be thought of as a mutineer while McGrath would be viewed by members of the jury as the savior of the town. It could sway their vote. And Travis knew that two of the jurors, Harv Preston and Clifford Otis, were on the Misery Park and Bandstand Committee.

"Do say you'll come and help us out. There are so many women who I know would just love to bid on you come Saturday." Margaret's longing was written as plain as chalk on a blackboard and was as grating as fingernails raking down the center of it.

"You know you can count on Margaret and me to bid on you, if that's what you're worried about, Travis." Olive patted his arm reassuringly and made goo-goo eyes at him.

The sight of Enos's barbershop filled Travis with relief. Escape was close at hand. But not, unfortunately, from the Founder's Day Celebration. "Count me in," he said, the words coming out as if they were plucked from the very depths of his soul. "I'd . . . I'd love to participate." He almost gagged at the bald-faced lie.

"You won't be sorry," Olive and Margaret said in unison, giggling as they made their good-byes and strolled off down the street in a flurry of linen and lace.

But Travis, who watched them go with a sinking feeling in the pit of his stomach, already was.

Chapter Thirteen

Hannah studied the ecru lace canopy over her walnut tester bed and counted the holes in it. It was something she had done quite often as a child to keep herself occupied when she couldn't sleep. Sometimes she counted the fruit in the Aubusson carpet, but she much preferred the canopy holes and was now using the process to ease her troubled mind.

Restless and unable to sleep, she had just reached number 201 in her efforts. She tried to tell herself that her agitation was caused by the anxiety of the trial and tomorrow's start of the defense case.

The prosecution had rested. Will had concluded with the testimony of Madam DeBerry's bartender, who had acknowledged serving Rafe Bodine a drink and confirmed that the former Ranger had made inquiries as to the whereabouts of Bobby Slaughter. He also put the sheriff of Justiceburg, Elmo Scruggs, on the stand, who had issued the Wanted Poster of Rafe based on DeBerry's eyewitness testimony, then finished up with several other witnesses who attested to Bodine's hasty departure the night of the murder.

The damaging testimony elicited today against Rafe was enough to give an anxious defense attorney sleepless nights, but Hannah knew that her unease had little to do with the trial and more to do with her recent amorous encounter with Travis.

Tick, tock, tick, tock. The ormolu clock on the mantel kept steady pace with the beating of her heart as she replayed over in her mind every passionate moment she had shared with Travis—the way his hands felt on her breasts, the way his tongue teased and tormented, creating a throbbing in her belly and lower that would not go away, despite cold baths and Dr. Wistar's Balsam of Wild Cherry Elixir.

Swish, swish, swish. The breeze blowing through the curtains did little to cool her heated flesh. Cold baths, medical potions, and chill winds hadn't been enough to quench her yearning.

There was only one cure for what ailed her, and Travis had it. She knew he'd be only too willing to play doctor and administer to her. He certainly had the means for it. Remembering how hard and long his maleness felt pressed against her abdomen, Hannah palmed her burning cheeks and took a ragged breath.

Unfortunately she needed more than a quick fix. She needed a lifetime of loving, and she wasn't certain he'd be willing to offer her that.

Though she knew Travis cared for her, had admitted as much to her mother, desired her friendship, she wasn't sure he still loved her. The resentment he bore for what had happened between them five years before was still evident, though he did his best to hide it.

Like her, he'd been wounded to the core, far more brutally than she'd realized.

Like her, he had placed the blame for their broken engagement squarely on his partner's shoulders.

Like her, he'd been a victim of young, idealistic love, insecurity, and selfishness.

But unlike her, he was willing to settle for an appeasement of carnal lust, one night of glorious passion.

Marriage didn't seem to be a part of Travis Bodine's vocabulary any longer.

Hannah resumed counting holes, beginning with the one now etched in her heart.

Travis wasn't counting holes. He was staring at the water-stained paper on the walls of his rented room, trying to figure out how his life had become so muddled and what he intended to do about it.

His dismal accommodations made him eager to finish his house and set up a proper home, though he knew that to have a proper home one had to have a proper wife. Hadn't Olive Fasbinder said something similar to him once? He grimaced, knowing the spinster wasn't someone he had in mind for that role.

In fact, he hadn't quite convinced himself that marriage was in his future. There was only one woman he'd even consider making his wife, and he doubted that

Hannah Louise would want to marry him, considering their past and the mess he'd made of things.

Hannah claimed she wanted more. He concluded that to mean that she wouldn't be content without pursuing her career. That she wouldn't be happy sharing his life, having his children, and living a small-town kind of life.

She'd made no bones about disliking Misery. She much preferred the fast pace of the big city, the convenience, culture, and entertainment. He didn't think the Spondella twins would measure up to a Broadway musicale.

People changed in five years. He liked to think that he'd matured, grown less rigid in his thinking, appreciated a woman's mind more than he used to. Hannah had grown even more independent. She was a career woman who knew her own mind.

She was still unmarried at twenty-eight. That meant she either hadn't met any eligible men, which seemed highly unlikely considering her beauty and intelligence, or she had no place in her life for a partner, other than in a law firm. That scenario seemed the more likely of the two.

Hannah had matured in many ways. Her mind, certainly. She was quick-witted, astute, and possessed a vocabulary that would have made Mr. Webster proud.

Her body, most assuredly. Her breasts were no longer slight, but plump and ripe, filling a man's hand completely. And he had large hands. Her body was soft, well-rounded. She responded to his touch with passion and eagerness, like a woman, and not the curious young girl she had once been.

Just thinking about her made his groin ache with need, his heart throb with yearning.

"Jesus!" he murmured as reality overcame him. *I've fallen in love with her all over again.*

"I've decided to put Rafe on the witness stand," Travis whispered to Hannah the following morning. The sleepless night he'd spent had taken its toll, making him appear ragged around the edges. "You were right. He needs to explain what happened. Tell his side of the story."

She clutched his arm. "Are you sure? McGrath is likely to tear him up on cross-examination. I want you to be prepared."

Instead of answering, he rose to his feet to address the court. "The defense calls Rafferty Bodine to the witness stand."

A murmur rose up from the gallery as Rafe, legs shackled, hands bound, was brought forward by Deputy Barnes to face his accusers. His father winked in encouragement as his son shuffled by, Emmaline blew him a kiss, and Ethan inclined his head, as if to say "Give 'em hell, little brother."

For almost an hour the accused gave compelling testimony as to what he had discovered the day of Ellie Bodine's murder, relating the sordid details of her condition when he found her, the effect the loss of his wife and child had upon him, and his belief that the Slaughters had taken their revenge, as they had once sworn to do.

Travis elicited the fact that Rafe had been consumed with sorrow and rage and in an emotional state when he had made the decision to go after the Slaughter gang on his own. With careful questioning he drew from Rafe the details of his years spent with the Texas Rangers, his remarkable record of valor, his reputation for honesty and integrity. And how in Rafe's opinion his position as a Texas Ranger had been the direct cause of the pain and suffering he'd endured at the hands of the Slaughters, how he blamed himself to this day for his first wife's death and the senseless murder of their unborn child.

Upon the completion of Rafe's testimony many of the men seated in the jury box had tears glistening in their eyes, though they did their best to hide them. Several spectators wept uncontrollably until the prosecutor, sensing that he was losing ground fast, requested a brief recess.

"It's going well," Hannah whispered to Travis once the judge had stepped down from the bench. "McGrath is worried."

"The bastard should be worried. Though I'm sure he's thinking up innumerable ways to discredit Rafe's testimony." Travis glanced at the prosecutor, who was scribbling notes fast and furiously, an intense look on his face.

"Of course. But your brother did a creditable job on the stand. He made a good witness, and he was very believable."

Travis squeezed her hand. "Thanks for convincing me to have Rafe testify. I don't think I would have had the guts to do it if it weren't for you."

Hannah wanted to wrap her arms about him, tell him not to worry, that he had made the right decision, that everything would work out all right. That sometimes good did triumph over evil and justice prevailed over all. But she couldn't. Instead, she swallowed the lump of fear in her throat, and said, "Don't thank me yet, Travis. We're only half-done."

Outside the courthouse Ben sought to comfort his daughter-in-law, who wept softly into her hands. "The boy's doing okay, Emma." Ben wrapped his arm about her shoulder and squeezed gently. "You mustn't fret. It's not good for the baby."

"I'm so worried about Rafe. Did you see how sad he looked on the stand? And scared? What if things don't turn out the way we hope they will?" She started blubbering again, which brought a soft rebuke from Lavinia.

"Hush now, Emmaline. You know Travis isn't going to let anything bad happen to his brother. You're not doing yourself or that baby a bit of good by carrying on so. Perhaps we should just take you home so you can rest."

She wiped tears from her eyes with a gloved hand. "I can't leave. Hannah said they plan to call me next to testify."

"Goddamn! You sure that woman knows what she's about? Women lawyers." Ben sneered. "I never heard of such a thing, calling a woman in your delicate condition to testify." He shook his head, clearly unconvinced of the Barkley woman's capabilities, despite everyone else's glowing opinions of her.

His wife snorted disdainfully. "You've never heard of older women having babies either, Mr. Bodine, but that doesn't mean it's wrong," Lavinia said, wondering why her husband was solicitous of others in the same condition, but not his own wife.

Ben hated it when Lavinia called him "Mr. Bodine" in that schoolteacher voice she had used on her former pupils. "Vin." He held out his hands beseechingly, but he was ignored.

"It's obvious that Hannah wants to bolster Rafe's testimony by having Emma back it up. I think it's very sound reasoning."

Emma nodded. "Travis admitted that Hannah has pretty much planned the whole strategy for the defense case. It was her idea to put Rafe on the stand."

"The boy was believable."

"High praise indeed coming from you, Mr. Bodine," Lavinia stated, before hooking her arm through Emma's and making her way back inside without so much as a word to her husband.

Ethan approached. Upon hearing the tail end of the conversation he felt almost sorry for his father. The man had a stunned look of disbelief on his face, like he couldn't quite figure out what had happened. In fact, Ben Bodine had been wearing that puzzled look quite a bit lately. "When are you going to learn, Pa, that it's useless to argue with a woman? If there's one thing I've learned since being married, it's that my wife's not going to be content till she has the last word."

"*Hmph!* Henpecked already, and it's only been a few months."

"Let's not forget who's sleeping alone these days."

A red flush danced over Ben's face. "What goes on in my home is nobody's business but mine."

"Well, tell that to Murph Rogers down at the livery or Enos Richards over at the tonsorial parlor. They seem to think your love life is fair game. Why, I wouldn't be at all surprised to read about it in Sid Barker's next editorial."

"What!"

"It's true. Most everyone in town is talking about how rude and uncaring you've been to Lavinia, and how she threw you out of your bedroom."

Indignation rode the proud man hard. "That's a lie! She's taken up sleeping in Travis's old room."

"That's just splitting hairs as far as everyone's concerned, Pa. You ain't sleeping in your wife's bed, and there ain't a soul who don't know it. I heard there was even a betting pool going on over at the saloon on how long you'd hold out."

"The hell you say!"

On that note, Ethan bit back a smile and headed into the courtroom, pleased by this morning's accomplishment. If there was one thing he enjoyed, it was getting the best of the old man. He slid into his seat just as Will McGrath approached Rafe on the witness stand.

"Isn't it true, Mr. Bodine, that you were sworn to uphold the law?"

Rafe nodded. "It is. I took my job quite seriously. Did it to the best of my abilities."

"Did your position as a Texas Ranger allow you to take the law into your own hands?"

"I did my duty as I saw fit. Never had any complaints. Up till now." There were a few chuckles at the remark, and Rafe eased back into his chair, looking a bit more relaxed.

"When your wife was murdered you were no longer wearing a Ranger badge. You had retired and were living life as a private citizen. Isn't that correct?"

"Yep. I'm surely retired. In fact, I'm about as retired as any lawman can be, I reckon."

More snickers resulted from Bodine's quip, making the prosecutor frown deeply. "So what gave you the right to take the law into your own hands and mete out vigilante justice? You had no proof that it was the Slaughters who had killed your family."

Rafe's eyes narrowed, hardened. "I knew. Here," he thumped his chest, "and here," he pointed to his gut. "I didn't stay alive all those years Rangering without having good instincts."

"That still didn't give you the right to ride out after those men."

"After reviewing the crime scene and studying the facts I decided to make a citizen's arrest. A Texas Ranger has certain discretionary powers."

A surprised, collective gasp went up, followed by

murmurs of approval. The jurors leaned forward in their seats, seemingly responsive to the answer. Hannah reached for Travis's hand and squeezed it gently.

"Did you murder Bobby Slaughter in cold blood, as the previous witness, Judy DeBerry, has testified?"

"I did not. Don't know how that whore could have witnessed much anyway. She was plying her wares at the time I walked into the room."

Hoots of laughter exploded. The judge was forced to bang his gavel for the umpteenth time and call for order in the court.

Red-faced, McGrath continued, "Do you consider the murder of three men to be amusing, Mr. Bodine?"

"Nope. And I didn't consider the butchering of my wife and child to be the least bit funny either, *Mr. McGrath*."

The prosecutor sneered, then went back to his legal pad to consult his notes, trying in vain to retain control of the witness. "One final question, Mr. Bodine. Do you have any remorse whatsoever for the taking of three lives, namely Bobby, Hank, and Luther Slaughter?"

"Those hombres were killed in self-defense."

"Just answer the question, Mr. Bodine."

Rafe chose his words carefully. "I've got as much remorse as the Slaughters did after they tortured my family."

Mrs. Fogarty gaped at the caller on her doorstep, her distaste clearly evident. "It's rather late to be calling, don't you think?"

It was only a little after eight o'clock, but the housekeeper made it sound as if it were well after midnight. Travis pasted on his most engaging smile, which he knew would probably have little effect on the older woman. Hell, it wasn't having much of an effect on the younger one. "Is Hannah Louise home, Mrs. Fogarty? I'd like to speak to her if she is."

After a few moment's hesitation, and much harrumphing on her part, she finally said, "Wait here." Travis took a seat on the porch swing. The scent of lilac filled the air, as did that of the wisteria that trellised the side of the porch. Crickets chirped noisily amid the sounds of approaching summer, surrounding him with a familiar cadence.

The front door opened and Travis turned to find Hannah. She was tying a red-plaid shawl around her shoulders as she came to sit next to him on the swing. It was such a familiar sight, and his heart lightened a bit at her smile. She appeared happy to see him.

He couldn't recall exactly the number of times they had sat on this very swing, making plans for their future, kissing, and sharing secrets in the dark, but they had been numerous.

"I hope it's not too late for a visit. I was at the office and lost track of time."

"Not at all. But you shouldn't be working so hard, Travis. Things are going well with the trial, and you'll do no one any good, least of all yourself, if you should fall ill before it ends."

"I'm fine. Lavinia sends Ethan into town to check

up on me, and he's always carrying what he calls 'care baskets' filled with cookies, sandwiches, and the like. I don't think she believes Mrs. Langley is feeding me properly."

"Lavinia's a kind woman. And except for her fried chicken, which is pretty tasty, your landlady isn't much of a cook."

Easing his arm over the back of the swing, he let it rest near Hannah's neck and shoulders, fighting the urge to toy with the golden strands of hair that brushed his hand. "I was wondering if you were planning to attend the Founder's Day Celebration this Saturday?"

She shrugged. "I hadn't given it much thought. Why?"

The swing creaked as it glided back and forth. Travis felt suddenly nervous and tongue-tied—not a good trait for an attorney. Or a suitor. Sticking his finger into the stiff collar of his shirt to loosen it, he replied, "I hear they're going to have some kind of bachelor's auction. I was wondering if you were planning to bid on anyone in particular?"

Travis looked so uncharacteristically distraught, Hannah swallowed her smile. She'd heard about the auction from Maude, who'd been incensed by the very idea of it, especially after she learned who had thought it up. One thing Maude and Fiona had in common was their dislike and disapproval of Olive and Margaret.

"*Hmmm.*" She tapped her chin, as if contemplating the possibilities. "I'm definitely not going to bid on Will McGrath, not after the way he went after Rafe this morning. And I doubt I'll bid on Tommy Noonan, though I hear his mother is planning to fix her fabulous chocolate raspberry cake, which I absolutely adore. She's going to put it into his luncheon basket to entice the eligible women to bid for him. I think that's unfair, don't you? The cake's far more appealing than Tommy."

Travis didn't even know he was supposed to have a basket. Olivia had neglected to tell him that part. "I . . . I was kinda hoping you might want to bid on me, Hannah."

Her eyes widened in disbelief. "You! Why on earth would I want to do that?" She laughed at the absurdity of his suggestion and shook her head. "Tongues would wag for sure if I was to bid on you. There's still the trial to consider. And I can't afford to have my reputation sullied more than it already has been." She could see that he was clearly disappointed by her decision.

"You're probably right. I hadn't thought about that."

"I wouldn't worry too much. I'm sure Olive and Margaret will bid on you. In fact, I have it on good authority that Olive has robbed her cookie jar of its life savings so that no one can outbid her." It was a lie, but an effective one. Travis blanched whiter than his shirt. "You won't be left standing on the podium all by yourself, counselor."

"That's what I'm afraid of." He gulped so hard she could see his Adam's apple bobbing.

"Perhaps I can talk Willy into bidding on you.

She's always up for a lark. And I doubt that Ethan would mind. He's not overly fond of the spinsters."

Despair etched his face. "Willy's married. The bidders have to be single."

"You are in a pinch." She pretended to consider his dilemma. "There's Mrs. Fogarty. She's been widowed so long that everyone just assumes she's single."

"That woman hates my guts!"

"Well, she's not too fond of my mother either, but they seem to be getting along better. I heard Maude ask Mama for her apple pie recipe the other day."

"That's nice," he said without a smidgen of enthusiasm.

"What about Dorcus Martin? She's pretty and available. Perhaps she'll bid on you."

He looked horrified. "She's practically in diapers! No thanks. I prefer a more mature woman."

His fingers brushed the nape of her neck and tingles traveled down her spine. Hannah swallowed. "Sometimes older women are set in their ways."

Taking her hand, he caressed it tenderly before bringing it to his lips for a kiss. "The older woman I have in mind is flexible, smart, and sweet. And she knows how to cook pretty well, too."

His compliments lifted her heart. "Really? She sounds wonderful. Do you think this paragon of virtue is likely to bid on you Saturday?"

"No. She's made it clear that she needs to keep her distance, which is probably wise. Because the next time I get her all alone I'm likely to have my way with her."

Her heart thumping louder than a bass drum in a marching band, Hannah swallowed with some difficulty. Finally, she flashed him a blinding, somewhat seductive, smile, and said, "You'd best be careful, Travis Bodine, or the woman in question might misconstrue your behavior as a sign of interest."

Kissing her hand, Travis deposited it back in her lap and stood. "Then she wouldn't be wrong. Good night, sweet Hannah. Pleasant dreams."

Hannah leaned back against the swing and watched as Travis became swallowed up by the night, then she released a deep sigh of longing.

Chapter Fourteen

THE SPONDELLA SISTERS—ALL FOUR HUNDRED pounds collectively—were threatening to collapse the makeshift stage with their overly abundant presence. Heads garbed in caps that had something resembling ram horns protruding from them, they wore yards and yards of yellow brocade that looked suspiciously like someone's old draperies wrapped around their massive bosoms. The entire effect looked like something straight out of a Greek tragedy.

As the enthusiastic twins hit a piercing high note, dogs began howling, and several of the horses grew restless and whinnied. Hannah fought the urge to cover her ears. The Italian aria they belted out with so much enthusiasm was certainly entertaining, if loud, and it fit in well with the festive mood of the Founder's Day Celebration.

Hannah liked Antoinette and Maria Spondella. Their toothy smiles were infectious, their personalities pleasant, and she never tired of hearing about their former escapades as circus performers.

Though not everyone in town was as generous in their opinions. Olive and Margaret had gone out of their way to be unkind to the twins, talking about them behind their backs, laughing at their spontaneous urges to perform whenever the spirit moved them. But then, Olive and Margaret, being as dour and straightlaced as any two spinsters could be, would never have been able to appreciate such unique individuals as the Spondellas.

Hannah'd had ample opportunity to observe the many free spirits of Greenwich Village while in New York. Nonconformists, many called them. They were artists, writers, people who walked to the beat of their own drums and held views often contrary to those of polite company. Society folks, she'd learned, often rebuked what they didn't understand.

There was no excuse for ignorance and prejudice, as far as Hannah Louise was concerned. And that extended to ridiculing overweight women who enjoyed performing operatic arias.

"Land sakes! I never would have asked them to perform if I'd known they were going to be so awful." Pulling a face, Olive made the cutting remark just as she crossed in front of Hannah. The attorney was unable to let it pass.

Grasping the spinster's arm, Hannah halted the startled woman in midstride. "I couldn't help overhearing what you said, Olive, and I must say that I totally disagree. I thought the twins were in rare form today. It was very gracious of the Spondellas to perform for all of us. When I think of all the time it must have taken them to fashion those exquisite costumes—" Her eyes widened in mock wonderment. "It was such a professional performance. I haven't seen one as good since leaving New York."

Brows raised nearly to their hairline, Olive and Margaret looked askance at each other, then Margaret said, "Well, how nice that you're enjoying yourself, Hannah Louise. Are you planning to attend the Bachelor's Auction later today?"

Hannah shrugged, noting the tenseness on their faces as they stood waiting for her answer. "I hadn't given it much thought. I've got some work to catch up on over at the office, so I may have to pass. Though it sounds like great fun."

They brightened instantly. "Oh well. Then we mustn't detain you from your work. I wouldn't dream of having our little auction distract you from what's important." Olive did her best to appear gracious and sympathetic at the same time, but she only succeeded in looking like someone who needed a large dose of castor oil.

"Yes, indeed," Margaret concurred. "Rafe's defense must be your number one concern, and not some silly auction."

"How generous of you to realize that." Hannah bit the inside of her cheek to keep from laughing aloud at the foolish women's transparent motives.

Poor Travis doesn't stand a chance.

"If you'll excuse me, I have the urge to taste some pies before I leave the festivities."

"By all means," they both said, stepping out of her way.

Stopping not a foot from where she'd been standing, Hannah turned to face them again. "Do you know if Travis will be participating in the auction today?"

Olive's face fell. "Well . . . uh . . . I think so."

"You've both made this auction sound like so much fun. I think I'll reconsider and attend. What time did you say it started?"

Margaret's lips pinched into a disapproving frown. "We didn't. But it begins promptly at noon."

"What about the trial?" Olive asked in a last-ditch effort to distract Hannah.

"I'm sure I'll have plenty of time to do both. Guess I'll see you there. And thanks for telling me about it. To think—I might actually have missed it if you hadn't been so kind as to mention it." With an airy wave, Hannah walked away, feeling lighthearted and just a teeny bit triumphant.

Diving through the throng of people, she stopped to chat with Dorcas Martin's mother, waved at Maude, who pitched horseshoes with the same intensity that she beat rugs, and made her way to the row of tables where the pie-eating exhibition was about to take place.

Feeling a soft tap on her shoulder, she turned to find her mother and father at her elbow, and her eyes widened in surprise. "Mama! Papa! I didn't expect to see you here today. Especially you, Papa." She kissed his grizzled cheek. "You must be feeling better." Noting that Fiona had her arm draped through her father's, Hannah felt a rush of pleasure that her parents were getting along so well.

She'd suspected as much, having noted over the past week the shy smiles they'd exchanged, the tentative stroking of hands when they thought no one was looking, and hearing the affection in their voices whenever they addressed each other. Of course, had she asked neither would have admitted a thing about their feelings to her.

"I told Thaddeus that staying cooped up in the house was just the worst thing in the world for him and that he needed to get outside in the fresh air and sunshine. He finally agreed." Patting his hand, Fiona beamed up at him with such devotion the judge actually blushed.

"Fiona can be persuasive when she puts her mind to it," he admitted. "And I haven't been to one of these celebrations in years. Heard about the auction and thought it might be a hoot to see grown men make fools of themselves." He chuckled at the possibility.

"Well, I'm very glad you've come. And I'm doubly delighted to see you both looking so content."

Exchanging a self-conscious look with her husband, Fiona cranked her head and looked about. "Where's your young man, Hannah Louise? I haven't seen a trace of Travis since we arrived."

Thaddeus harrumphed. "He's probably hiding out

from those two harridans. I heard they tried to rig the auction so they'd come out the winners."

"No!" Hannah covered her mouth and giggled, shaking her head. "They're persistent. I'll give them that."

Fiona wasn't nearly as kind. "They both need a good thrashing, the way they've been throwing themselves at that poor man. It's obvious Travis has eyes for no one but our Hannah, so why they even persist in pursuing him is beyond me."

"Mama!" Hannah's face flushed hot. She looked around to make sure no one had overheard. "You mustn't say such things. Especially in public where anyone can hear you."

"Oh posh! It's true. Why shouldn't I speak the truth?"

No one had time to point out the unflattering, prevailing public opinion about Travis and Hannah to Fiona, because Murph Rogers and a few of his friends had struck up a rendition of "*The Yellow Rose of Texas*," making further conversation impossible.

Hannah thought that was probably just as well. No one ever got the last word in with Fiona Barkley anyway.

Travis gazed down at the eager faces below the stage and felt like a side of beef hanging in Bull Danvers's meat market. Feeling his face redden with humiliation, he wished he'd never allowed Olive to talk him into participating in the stupid auction, good cause or not.

"Yoo-hoo . . . Travis . . ." Margaret was waving a bright yellow handkerchief at him from the crowd, licking her lips like a predator ready to devour her prey. He swallowed, praying hard that a gust of wind would come up and blow him into the next county.

Another wish denied.

Instead, he found himself staring into Olive's eager face. She was holding up a luncheon basket, pointing at it and winking, like they were sharing some great secret. He knew now why she hadn't mentioned his bringing a lunch.

Lyle "Boomer" Wilkins walked to the front of the stage and cleared his throat. The mayor of Misery had a loud, commanding voice and had earned his nickname because of it. "Welcome, ladies and gentlemen," he began.

Travis's stomach dropped to somewhere in the vicinity of his feet.

"Sweating again, huh, Bodine? Seems like you've been doing that in court a lot lately." Will McGrath chuckled. "I wouldn't worry about being picked though. Doubt you and I'll have any problem. Hear the ladies are quite taken with this auction idea." The prosecutor looked pleased by the notion.

Travis bit back a retort, for he knew the man was only goading him on, and Will always did relish being the center of attention. Well, he could have center stage all to himself, because Travis wanted no part of it.

"Wish I'd never agreed to do it," he admitted, wiping his perspiring neck with his bandanna against the burning rays of the sun. June was proving to be a torturous month temperature-wise.

"Guess you feel that same way about defending your brother, too. It's obvious you're getting your butt kicked in court."

"And it's obvious, McGrath, that you're going to get yours kicked from one end of the street to the other when this trial comes to an end. I'm looking forward to that as much as you're looking forward to getting auctioned off."

Will fell silent, and Travis turned his attention back to the crowd. He caught sight of Willy and Emmaline, then Ethan, who moved to stand next to them. He was grinning like the Cheshire cat, and Travis, who was in no mood for his brother's teasing, would have loved to stuff his fist into that wide-open crevice Ethan called a mouth.

"Hey, little brother," Ethan called out with a wave. "Hope you ain't the last one to be picked."

Travis spotted Hannah Louise standing near her parents, and hope blossomed anew. Perhaps she had changed her mind about bidding on him. He could only hope that she would take pity and bail him out of his predicament with the two spinsters. But her smile was one of apology, not encouragement, and that didn't bode well.

"What am I bid for Silas Warner?" the auctioneer shouted. "Silas tells me he's looking for a wife, ladies."

Whoops of joy abounded, along with nervous twitters. The bidding commenced with Dorcas Martin offering one dollar.

When Travis's turn came, he was dismayed to note that he and Will were the only ones left standing on stage. His ego took a bit of a hit at the fact that he hadn't been one of the first ones to go.

Even Tommy Noonan and his chocolate raspberry cake had been bought before him. It had been galling to hear Hannah Louise bid two dollars for the brawny bootmaker, even though Travis knew that the damn cake had been her only motive. Lucy Cummings's bid had been higher at two dollars and fifty cents, and Tommy had gone off with her. But it would have served Hannah right had she won, Travis thought uncharitably.

The bidding began in earnest. Waving their hands furiously, Margaret and Olive tried to outdo each other in both voice intensity and offer. But in the end the carrot-topped spinster won, and she couldn't have looked more delighted. Travis, on the other hand, felt physically ill and made plans for a cowardly retreat.

"Ma'am?"

Hannah turned to find Deputy Barnes standing behind her. She smiled, wiping the blueberry pie filling from her lips with a linen hankie. She liked the soft-spoken lawman, whose unfailing politeness and gentle ways seemed incongruous with his chosen profession. "Good afternoon, Deputy. What can I do for you?"

"It's the prisoner, ma'am. Rafe's requested to talk

to his brother, but I can't find him nowhere. It's like he just up and disappeared off the face of this earth."

She cocked a puzzled brow, wondering what could have happened to Travis. "Really? Well, I guess Mr. Bodine will have to settle for me then." With one last longing look at the delicious pie, she said, "Shall we go?"

At the jailhouse, Hannah waited while Billy Barnes unlocked Rafe's cell and let her in. The prisoner was staring forlornly out the small, iron-barred window at the festivities, and didn't bother to turn around until he heard the sound of her voice. "Hello, Rafe."

"Oh, I thought for a minute it was Emma." His look of disappointment touched her as he brushed back a lock of unruly black hair and gestured toward the bunk. "Have a seat. Where's Travis? I sent Bill out to find him."

"The deputy was unable to locate your brother, so I offered to come instead. I hope that's all right."

He shrugged. "Sure. Your company's just as good. And you're a sight prettier than Travis anyway." His grin was engaging, and Hannah found herself smiling, despite the awkwardness of the situation.

Though she was defending the man before her, she really had no personal knowledge of him, other than what Travis had related. Her brief conversations with the defendant had been confined to the courtroom. Travis had conducted all of the interviews concerning his brother, believing that Rafe would feel more comfortable talking to him rather than a woman. Hannah welcomed the opportunity to get to know Rafe Bodine better.

"Is there a problem I can help you with?" She smoothed the folds of her skirt, trying to appear businesslike, though her white-cotton gloves were horribly stained with blueberry juice.

Rafe straddled a wooden chair, gazing intently at her with eyes as vividly blue and disconcerting as his brother's. "I mostly wanted to get Travis's impressions about how he felt the case was going. Most of what's been said on the stand's been lies. I hope you realize that."

"I wouldn't have agreed to help with your case if I believed otherwise, Rafe. But since most of your dealings have been with your brother, I welcome the chance to hear your story firsthand. Other than what's been said in court, and what Travis and Emma have told me, I don't really know that much about you."

"There ain't much to tell. I didn't shoot Slaughter in cold blood. But I could have, after what he did to my family." He proceeded to relate the events of his first wife's murder in excruciating detail, confessing that his marriage to Ellie Masters Bodine had been based on friendship and their parents' expectations, rather than a deep-seated love. But despite that fact, it was undeniably clear that his first wife had meant a great deal to him and that he'd felt compelled to avenge her murder.

Hannah listened attentively, increasingly saddened for what this man had endured.

"You planning to put Emma on the stand?" he

asked after he'd finished recounting the tale. "I'm worried it might be too much for her. That bastard McGrath won't be as considerate of her condition as Travis. I don't want anything to jeopardize the welfare of the baby, or Emma's life, even if it means that I have to pay for the consequences with my own."

"I'd planned to put Emma on the stand the same day you testified, but Judge Hix recessed early that day because of the plans surrounding the Founder's Day Celebration. I still intend to have her testify on Monday, but I will request that Emma's testimony and the redirect examination by the prosecutor be brief and to the point. I wouldn't do anything to injure her health." It said a great deal to Hannah that Rafe was more than willing to exchange his life for that of his wife and unborn child. Those weren't the words and deeds of a murderer.

She stood, and Rafe followed her to the cell door. "I'm glad we had the opportunity to talk. I'm more convinced than ever that Madam DeBerry is lying, but I haven't figured out a way to prove it yet. But one way or another I'm going to see that you're acquitted of these murder charges."

"You sound pretty darn sure of yourself."

"I am."

"Travis was a damn fool for letting you go, if you don't mind me saying so, Hannah Louise. Me and Ethan gave him a bad time about getting engaged to you. We thought he was too young to get married. But I can see now that we were wrong."

"I appreciate your saying that, Rafe."

"I just hope my little brother comes to his senses soon and does right by you. There's nothing like the love of a good woman to set a man on the straight and narrow."

Blushing to the roots of her hair, Hannah didn't quite know what to say. Rafe Bodine's confession had come as a complete surprise, as did his unqualified support. Finally, she smiled. "Between you and me, Rafe, your brother might not be off the hook just yet."

With that in mind, Hannah left the courthouse eager to find Travis. She wanted to talk to him about the DeBerry woman's testimony, for she was convinced with a certainty that the madam had fabricated much of what she'd said.

For some reason known only to Judy DeBerry, the madam had lied on the stand. But why? Bobby Slaughter was dead. And though revenge was a possible reason, it just seemed too weak a motive. Madam DeBerry did not strike Hannah as the sentimental sort. She was avaricious and more concerned about herself than others. Why then?

Money was always a strong motivator. Perhaps she had been put up to it, paid off, even threatened.

McGrath. It always came back to him. He wasn't above such a thing. From what she'd learned from her father, the prosecutor had a history of underhanded dealings. It was entirely possible that he had coerced the witness to lie. He needed to win this case in order to secure his reelection. It was very possible.

Hannah was bound and determined to figure out a way to prove her suspicions. She was also determined to make Travis Bodine fall in love with her again, and she wasn't quite certain which of the two dilemmas she faced would be the more difficult.

"You're a coward, Travis Bodine," Travis told himself, hammering the last piece of lath to the wall frame, then stepping back to examine his handiwork. "But you're a damn good carpenter."

He was pleased with the steady progress he'd made on the house, despite the time constraints of the trial and his preoccupation with Hannah Louise. The interior walls were up and waiting for plaster, the stone fireplace set. The roofing shingles had been laid, and the exterior siding was waiting for a coat of paint. He still needed to complete the interior trim, install the new stove and icebox he'd purchased from the Montgomery Ward catalog, and lay the pine planks for the flooring. He figured another month, two tops, and he'd be moving in.

What would Hannah Louise think of the house? He took another critical look about. His house wasn't as fine or as fancy as her family's, certainly not as large as the Bodine homestead, but it was plenty big for a young lawyer, his wife, and maybe a couple of kids.

Walking toward the rear of the dwelling where the master bedroom was situated, he stood in the doorway and imagined a brass bedstead with a colorful quilt upon it, a walnut dresser with his and hers comb sets atop it. There might be an oak rocker in the far corner near the fireplace, where Hannah could sit and sing lullabies to their first child.

"Whoa, Bodine!" he said, taking a step back. "Let's not rush it. Hannah's given you no indication that she's interested in pursuing a marriage and family." Unless he counted those heated kisses they'd exchanged and the ardent way she'd responded to his touch.

With a rueful shake of his head, he picked up his hammer and went back to work. Keeping himself busy was about the only thing that was likely to keep his overactive imagination and glands in check.

As Travis continued to work, Hannah was making her way through the front gate and up the walk to his house. She'd pried out of a very intoxicated Ethan where his brother had run off to and smiled at the notion that Travis had chosen to run instead of facing Margaret like a man.

She doubted there was a cowardly bone in his body, but she also knew firsthand that the spinsters had the ability to make grown men weep and staid ladies turn into shrews.

The front door stood open, so she went in. "Travis? Are you here?" Her reply was the insistent pounding of a hammer.

Following the sound, which led her toward the back of the house, and being careful not to step on loose boards or protruding nails, she found Travis in one of the rear rooms, engrossed in a window frame that he was trying to straighten.

She opened her mouth to announce her presence, but then, taking in the sight of his naked back, the sweat trickling down his neck, the way the muscles in his buttocks bunched as he leaned toward his task, she thought better of it. Hannah'd never given much thought to a man's derriere before, but she concluded that Travis had a particularly attractive one. On that disquieting note, she cleared her throat.

Travis turned, wiped the sweat out of his eyes with the back of his hand, then smiled. "You found me out, I see. I suppose you think I'm a coward."

"Under normal circumstances I might. But seeing as how you were running away from Margaret Willoughby, I can't condemn you too harshly for your ungentlemanly behavior. Though the poor woman was terribly distraught to be left all alone with her luncheon basket and no eligible bachelor."

He heaved a contrite sigh. "I didn't want to hurt Margaret's feelings, but I just couldn't bring myself to stay and eat lunch with her."

"But she paid for the privilege, Travis."

"I intend to reimburse her the first chance I get. And the money she bid was for a good cause."

Digging into the canvas bag she held, she fished out a few sandwiches she had made. "I figured you might not have eaten, so I fixed you something."

"Thanks." A boom of thunder sounded in the distance. He gazed out the window to find that the sky had darkened considerably. "Looks like we might get a little rain."

Hannah followed him into the front room, where the door still stood ajar. She could see fat droplets of rain pelting the dirt. Soon, puddles would form to make the ground a muddy mess. "It's already here. You'd best shut the door or that sawdust on the floor is going to get drenched." The wind came up just then, saving Travis the trouble.

At the sound, Hannah jumped back, rubbing her arms against the chill. "A few minutes ago it was hotter than Hades, and now it's turning cold."

"I'll start a fire. It'll be a good test of whether or not I have any skill as a stonemason. I'll never be as good as the man who taught me, but I think I did a pretty good job of building it. Guess we'll soon see."

He tossed a few wood scraps into the fireplace and lit them. In a few minutes the fire burned brightly, the chimney drawing up the smoke as it should, and Travis couldn't have looked more pleased had he invented the blaze flaming within. "It works."

"You needn't sound so surprised. I never had any doubts." That wasn't quite true, but she figured he didn't need to know that. She was actually surprised and quite impressed to discover what a skilled builder Travis had become. As a young boy he'd always liked constructing little forts and bridges out of twigs and tree limbs, but she never dreamed he'd become so proficient with a hammer and saw.

He laid a blanket over the sawdust. "Sit down and join me. You've made plenty enough for two. And I brought some lemonade with me, just in case I was forced to remain here for the duration." He handed her a mason jar filled with the lemonade his landlady had made that morning.

She grinned. "You're terrible. But I'll take you up on the offer. Since I made the sandwiches I happen to know they're good."

"A woman who can cook is a rare treasure indeed."

"You're only saying that because you're hungry."

He stopped eating and stared at her intently, his eyes filling with desire. "I'm always hungry when I'm around you, Hannah Louise. But not for food. Would you like me to prove it?" He leaned toward her, and she swallowed.

Chapter Fifteen

HANNAH WAS VERY TEMPTED TO TAKE TRAVIS UP on his dare. Making love with him had been uppermost on her mind of late. She still remained a virgin. And at twenty-eight that was hardly cause for celebration. But she supposed that her heart had known all along, even when her mind denied it, that she belonged body and soul only to Travis and always would.

Despite the intensity of her feelings, Hannah had too much common sense to act rashly. Practicality and reason finally won out, and she changed the subject. "I visited your brother at the jail today. He's doing well."

That got Travis's immediate attention. "How come you went to see Rafe?"

She explained the details surrounding her visit, then added, "I told him we would somehow prove that Judy DeBerry is lying. Now all we've got to do is figure out how."

His expression softened. "You really love being a

lawyer, figuring out all the strategies involved in winning a case, don't you?"

She brought her knees to her chest, curling her arms around them, and stared into the flames of the fire. "I confess I do. I like being challenged, and the law certainly does that."

"I was wrong about you, Hannah. Wrong about a great many things." Travis had had a great deal of time to think lately, to brood, and he'd come to the realization that he'd been mistaken five years ago. He should never have acted so rashly, should never have broken their engagement. He'd been wrong to deny her the career choice that meant so much to her and for which she was obviously so well suited.

He realized now that he'd been jealous of her accomplishments and had felt threatened that they would eclipse his own. He'd wanted to impress his family, especially the old man, and knew that his ego had played a big part in his regrettable decision.

Of all people, he should have known better than to underestimate someone else's worth or their need to accomplish something important.

His father had underestimated his abilities many times over the years, never giving Travis the benefit of the doubt, or believing that he could successfully complete what he set out to do. He'd been forced into the shadows of his older brothers. As the baby of the family he'd been coddled, teased, loved, but not allowed to step out on his own into the sunlight and prove his worth.

That had come later, when he'd finally decided to defy his father and the odds and pursue a law career.

By not allowing Hannah to emerge from behind his shadow—a husband's shadow—and become equal in all things, he had done her the same disservice. In doing so, he had denied them both a lifetime of happiness together.

Hannah's eyes had widened at Travis's unexpected confession. "Travis, I—"

He shook his head to forestall her comments. "No, let me finish. This needs to be said. I should never have expected you to give up your law career for me, should never have put you in a position to choose. It was selfish of me.

"You're a wonderful attorney, Hannah. You're as competent and smart as any male lawyer, maybe more so, certainly more than me. You've a rare gift for memorization of details, and you're very astute when it comes to judging human nature. You deserve the same respect and admiration as a man in that position. You've earned it.

"I realize I'm five years late in saying it, Hannah Louise, but please accept my apology. I'm sorry for being so shortsighted and egotistical."

Hannah was deeply moved by words she'd long dreamed of hearing, and she swallowed the lump in her throat. For Travis to admit such a thing, to offer an apology . . . She loved him more in that moment than she ever thought possible.

"You're not the only one who should apologize,

Travis. I've always regretted leaving like I did. Perhaps if I'd stayed, been less stubborn and prideful, we would have worked things out between us. But I was hurt, and so took the coward's way out."

Travis drew her into his arms. "We've both made mistakes. Perhaps we were too immature to know what was really important."

She caressed his cheek gently. "I think we've both done a lot of growing up in the last five years."

"Sweet Hannah." He kissed the tip of her nose, then his lips found her mouth, and he was lost.

Wrapping her arms about him, Hannah matched him kiss for kiss, needing to express just how much his words meant to her, how his mouth on her own, his hands on her breasts, were what she wanted, had been dreaming of every night in her lonely bed. She wanted Travis with an intensity that frightened, but at the same time felt so right. "Make love to me, Travis," she murmured. "I need you so."

He pulled back and gazed into eyes filled with passion and longing. "Are you certain? I don't want to hurt you again, love. I never wanted to hurt you." He brushed golden strands of hair from her face. He'd waited what seemed like a lifetime to hear those words from her lips, but he had to be sure. There were other, more important, words he still yearned for, and he wouldn't allow a moment's passion to rob him of that declaration.

In answer her hands moved to the buttons of her gown, and she boldly began to undo them. He put out his hand to stop her. "Let me do it. I want to undress you."

She nodded, allowing him to remove her dress, her undergarments, until she was completely naked before him.

The firelight danced over Hannah, turning her skin to burnished copper, and Travis felt awed by the sight of her. Perfection was a rare thing, but here it was now, seated before him. "You're so beautiful. I can scarcely believe that God created such an exquisite woman."

She fought the blush creeping over her. Emboldened by the admiration and longing she saw in his eyes, she replied, "Now it's your turn to undress." Reaching up, she removed the last of her hairpins, allowing her blond tresses to cascade over her shoulders and breasts in a silken veil.

Travis made short work of his clothing. When he was as naked as she, and the evidence of his desire quite apparent, she began to explore slowly the differences between their bodies.

He was hard, where she was soft. The furring of his chest felt strangely erotic beneath her fingertips as she smoothed her palms over solid muscles. She kissed his nipples, and he drew a ragged breath. He sucked hers, and she nearly passed out from the sheer ecstasy of it.

Easing her onto the blanket, Travis moved his hand to the juncture of her thighs, separating the dewy petals of her womanhood to find the pulsing bud beneath.

"Oh!" Hannah's eyes flew open, and she sucked in her breath. "Oh my!"

He continued the exquisite torture until she was wet, ready, and writhing beneath him. Placing his maleness against her, he allowed her time to grow used to the idea of their joining, giving her one more chance to change her mind. He wanted her to be sure. As sure as he was of this moment and how right their coming together would be.

But Hannah had no intention of changing her mind. Opening her legs wider, she felt for his shaft. It was long, hard, and pulsed beneath her hand as she stroked it tentatively, inquisitively. Travis's moan of pleasure made her brazen, and she guided him to her, urging him to give her what she craved, what she needed.

It was all the invitation Travis needed.

He entered slowly, finding her virginal barrier still intact. Relief and love flowed through him at that moment. He would be her first, and that knowledge pleased him. He intended to make Hannah his forever.

"This may hurt a bit," he whispered.

"It'll hurt a lot more if you don't do it." Her innocent confession made him smile.

Plunging forward, he swallowed her pained gasp with his mouth, then began a slow rhythmic motion that soon had her bucking hard against him. "Slow down, love, slow down," he crooned. "We've got plenty of time. I want to savor this . . . you . . . for as long as possible."

They began a frenzied, passionate climb to the top. Hannah's nerve endings were on fire. She could hardly draw a breath, a coherent thought, as he continued to push her higher and higher toward the peak of fulfillment.

She knew he was holding back. She could see the sweat on his upper lip, feel him tense, as if every effort to delay his own release was torture. And she loved him even more for the sacrifice.

The tension built quickly. Hannah felt as though she were riding the tail end of a comet and would burst into flame at any moment. "Travis. Oh, dear God!" Suddenly without warning she reached her climax and felt as if she were shattering into a million glorious pieces. A moment later, he followed her to the top, releasing a deep sigh of satisfaction as his seed flowed into her and they were one. The smile that broadened his face made her heart sing.

The fire crackled and hissed. The rain pummeled the roof with big fat drops and splattered against the door. The howling wind banged determinedly for entrance. But snuggled tightly together, the lovers had thoughts only for each other. The world could have collapsed around them at that moment and neither would have noticed. Or cared.

Soon the flush of their lovemaking receded and reality returned. Hannah wanted to shout out her love for this man who had made her a woman—his woman. But she was uncertain of Travis's feelings and afraid of being hurt again. And so she said nothing.

Travis wanted desperately to confess his undying love for Hannah and ask for her hand in marriage, but he feared that she would not agree to marry him a second time. And so he said nothing.

Neither confessed what was in their hearts, for they knew that come Monday morning the trial would resume and they had to remain focused on Rafe's defense and nothing else.

But they also knew that the trial wouldn't last forever, and the time for decisions would soon be close at hand.

Monday morning came and, with it, the resumption of the murder trial. Emmaline Bodine was on the witness stand being cross-examined by the prosecutor, who was treating her with kid gloves—behavior totally uncharacteristic of McGrath.

"What's with McGrath?" Hannah whispered to Travis, doing her best to keep her mind on the trial and not on what had happened between them just two short days ago. Her heart hammered with longing whenever she thought of their being together, and she wondered, no hoped, that he felt the same way, too. He leaned toward her, and Hannah fought the urge to nibble his left ear.

"You mean because he's treating Emma with some civility?"

She nodded, unable to speak when his lips were so close to her mouth, unable to concentrate when all she could think about was lying naked in his arms once again.

"I had a little chat with Will this morning. Told him

if he so much as said one rude thing, or made any unflattering innuendoes about my sister-in-law, I would
personally take him out behind the courthouse and beat
the crap out of him. And when I was through I'd sic
Ethan on him."

Her romantic musings ended abruptly. Hannah sat
up straight, turning her attention back to Travis and the
proceedings. "If he says anything to the judge, you'll be
accused of tampering with the trial."

"Don't worry. He's not going to say anything. Mc-
Grath is scared to death of Ethan. Always has been. And
I couldn't risk his upsetting Emma. I owe Rafe that
much."

She glanced at the defendant out of the corner of
her eye and found that he looked much relieved by the
way his wife's testimony was being handled. Thinking
back to their recent conversation, and her own suspicions about McGrath—suspicions she had yet to reveal
to Travis—she was glad he had taken it upon himself to
halt the prosecutor in his tracks. "Your methods are
rather unorthodox, counselor, but I admire you for using
them just the same. I doubt I would have been inclined
to do something so bold."

He patted her hand beneath the table and tingles of
awareness darted up her arm. "You don't have a brother
like Ethan to use as intimidation," he reminded her with
a grin. "He can be very persuasive."

"So can you," she said. "When you put your mind
to it."

*   *   *

Hannah knocked softly on her mother's bedroom door then entered to find Fiona seated at the dressing table. The kerosene lantern on the dresser flickered softly, illuminating the serene expression she wore as she pulled the silver-handled hairbrush through her long tresses.

"I hope I'm not disturbing you, Mama." Fiona's smile was bemused as she turned to face her daughter, and Hannah wondered what her mother had been doing the past three hours since dinner. She wore the look of a woman who'd been recently made love to. That, coupled with the fact that she'd heard her father whistling like a lark as she passed by his door, seemed to indicate that the Barkleys' marriage was back on firm footing.

"Not at all, dear. I was just daydreaming. Did you need to speak to me about something? Perhaps you've had word from the warden in Wyoming?"

Hannah sighed deeply. "No, not yet." Surely she should have heard something by now, and wondered what was taking so long to get a response. "I've come about another matter, something equally as important."

Seating herself beside Hannah on the bed, Fiona clasped her daughter's hand. "Tell me what's troubling you, Hannah dear. You've got worry lines all across your forehead. Trust me when I say that you don't want to be furrowing your brow like that. It makes horrible wrinkles."

"Wrinkles are the least of my problems, Mama. I'm worried about the case.

"Every instinct I possess tells me that Judy De-

Berry is lying through her teeth, but I haven't found a way to discredit her. I think she may have been bribed or threatened to falsify her testimony. And I suspect that Will McGrath is somehow involved."

Her brow shot up. "What does Travis think?"

"He agrees that the woman is lying, but I haven't told him about what I suspect about McGrath."

"Why ever not? I should think he'd want to take the proper action."

"I went to Travis's new house to tell him, but—" Hannah's face reddened. "But we never got around to discussing the situation."

"I see." Fiona didn't have the nerve to ask what they'd been doing instead of talking. She thought she had a pretty good idea. And that worried her.

"I'm hesitant to accuse someone of tampering with a witness without sufficient proof, Mama. And I'm not certain I'll be able to find the proof we need."

Noting the frustration on her daughter's face, Fiona pondered the problem for a moment, then said, "Madam DeBerry is from Justiceburg, which isn't all that far from here. I could go there, see what I can find out."

Hannah's mouth fell open. "Mama! The woman's a prostitute. She runs a bordello. How will you be able to gather any information? You'll immediately arouse suspicion if you start asking a bunch of questions. You don't exactly look like a woman of the streets."

"Leave that to me." Fiona's face grew animated. "I'm a very resourceful woman. And don't breathe a word of this to your father. I'm sure he wouldn't approve of my going. We've had our difficulties over prostitutes before."

Eyes wide, Hannah gasped. "Mama!"

"Not in that way, Hannah Louise." Fiona shook her head. "How could you even think such a thing? Your father was always faithful to me when we were together."

"But you said—"

"It had to do with another trial, another prostitute."

"This other prostitute. Was she part of the reason you left?"

"She was the whole reason, ridiculous as that may sound." She explained fully the details, then heaved a sigh. "I was stupid to have let the young woman's death come between your father and me. Thaddeus did what he thought was right. But at the time I didn't see it that way. I thought he was too harsh, the punishment unjust.

"It took me a long time to realize that nothing is more important than being with the man you love."

Hannah wrapped her arms about her mother. "We've both learned that painful lesson the hard way, Mama. But perhaps we're both smart enough to rectify our mistakes."

"I know we are, child. So let's decide what I should pack for my adventurous foray into the world of prostitution."

"Mama! For shame," Hannah said, clearly shocked, and Fiona laughed uproariously.

As Travis made his way from the boardinghouse to his office the following morning, he could think of little else beside Hannah Louise. Court was in recess for the day—Judge Hix had come down with a cold—so he and Hannah had agreed to meet at the office to prepare questions for the examination of Ben Bodine, who they intended to call as a character witness later that week.

But try as he might it wasn't his father's testimony that was consuming Travis's mind. The image of Hannah Louise lying naked beneath him, the feel of her heat as he plunged deep within her, the sweet taste of her lips, came unbidden and unexpectedly, occupying his thoughts to such a degree that there was room for little else.

The thick bulge forming quickly between his legs made it obvious that he wouldn't be concentrating on legal matters today. Lowering his leather portfolio to hide his growing arousal, he looked about to make sure no one had noticed that he was giving Enos Richard's barber pole some serious competition.

Hannah had just crossed the street and was coming toward him when he reached the outside staircase. He waited for her, keeping the portfolio firmly in place.

"Good morning, Travis," she said, her smile far more blinding than the sun and certainly much warmer. He felt the jolt clear down to his toes. When she made to ascend the stairs, he stepped in front, blocking her way.

"Let's not work today," he suggested. "I was thinking that perhaps we should go on a picnic."

Eyes widening, her smile faltered a bit. "A picnic?

But what about your father's testimony? I thought you
wanted—"

He clasped her arm. "I want you, Hannah." He
cleared his throat at her stunned expression. "I mean—I
want to be with you, spend some time alone with you.
Let's rent a buggy and drive out to Cattail Creek. It's a
beautiful day. We can go swimming, have lunch." He
shrugged innocently. "Do whatever comes to mind."

Hannah was torn. She wanted nothing more than to
spend the day frolicking with Travis on the banks of
Cattail Creek—they'd gone there often in their youth—
but the obligations of Rafe's trial weighed heavily upon
her. And she was worried about her mother, who'd left
for Justiceburg at dawn, using the excuse of a shopping
expedition. Thankfully, the judge seemed to accept the
explanation without question.

"If we don't plan our questions, we won't be prepared when court resumes tomorrow," she pointed out.

He stroked her arm and gooseflesh erupted everywhere. "We can come back to the office later and examine each other."

Her mouth unhinged, even as her heart began
pounding at the possibilities. "Travis, I—"

"What I meant to say is that we can prepare questions and ask them of each other. A rehearsal of sorts.
I'll play the witness and you can be the attorney."

His boyish eagerness made her smile. "Does the attorney get to ask the witness whatever she wants?"

"Absolutely."

"And will he answer truthfully?"

"Well that depends on the questions. You can't expect the witness to incriminate himself. That would be a violation of the Fifth Amendment."

"But I was under the distinct impression that the witness wanted to be violated."

Before Travis could form a reply, Hannah walked off down the street toward the livery. Travis ran after her, holding the damn portfolio out in front of him as he did.

"I'm so glad I let you talk me into coming here, Travis. I haven't been to Cattail Creek in ages, and it's always been one of my favorite places." She leaned back against the trunk of a cottonwood and tossed a handful of pebbles into the water, watching concentric swirls form around them.

Travis had shed his coat and vest and was lying on a blanket, hands clasped behind his head, gazing up at the cloudless cerulean sky. The mockingbirds chattered, the wind howled incessantly, but both were such frequent occurrences that he paid them no mind. "It's so peaceful here."

"You've been working too hard. We both have. I guess it's good that we took a day to ourselves."

He held his hand out to her. "Come and lie down with me on the blanket."

"I thought you wanted to go swimming. The water looks awfully inviting." Sweat trickled between her breasts, and she relished the opportunity to cool off in the stream.

Sitting up, he grinned. "And what will you wear to swim in?"

She gazed down at the cotton dress she wore and shrugged. "Same thing I wore last time we did this, I guess."

"You were only fourteen, as I recall, and didn't look nearly as fetching in your underwear as you do now. Your breasts weren't nearly as—"

"It's hot, and I'm going swimming," she interrupted, not eager to be reminded of her adolescent flat-chested figure. She'd taken a great deal of teasing in school because of it. "You've already seen me in the altogether anyway, so what's the difference?"

Instantly aroused, Travis began to undress. "I'm not sure I'll be able to keep my mind on swimming once we get in that water, Hannah Louise."

She laughed. "That water's sure to be cold, and it's likely to shrink all of your nefarious intentions." Removing her stockings, she folded her dress neatly and placed it on the blanket, then headed for the water. Travis stripped down to his drawers and followed right behind her.

She screamed as her body hit the cold surface of the water. "Good Lord! It's freezing!"

He bobbed up next to her, grabbing her about the waist. "I'd be happy to warm you up, my sweet." He kissed her long and hard, then tossed her back into the water and began to swim laps about her. Travis had always been a strong swimmer, while Hannah, fearful of the water to a large degree, tended to move cautiously, like a turtle, little strokes at a time.

"Don't play too rough, Travis. You know I don't like it."

He came up beneath her again, and she yelped. "I could drag you out into the center of the creek, have my way with you, and you wouldn't be able to do a thing about it."

"Who says I want to do a thing about it?" she tossed back, before ducking under his arm and escaping.

With slow, ineffectual strokes, she swam determinedly for shore, eager to make a game of it, but Travis's strokes were stronger and quicker, and he caught up to her before she could reach it.

"I've never made love in a stream before," he said, nuzzling the skin right below her ear.

"That's because your equipment would freeze, turn blue, then fall off."

"A good point." Hauling her out of the water, he scooped her up in his arms. "But I'm warming up quickly now."

He laid her down on the blanket. Her breasts and nipples showed clearly through the wet cotton of her thin lawn undergarments, and Travis's eyes transfixed on them. "I wasn't sure it was possible, but you're even more appealing with your clothes on than without."

Instantaneous heat flushed Hannah's system, and she fought the urge to cover herself. "You'll embarrass me, if you keep that up."

Purposely misconstruing her meaning, he stared

down at his crotch. "That's likely to stay up, sweet." Gasping, she covered her mouth before her giggle could escape.

He dropped down quickly beside her. "Hannah, you drive me wild. I want to make love to you again."

"Then don't waste time talking about it, counselor. You lawyers talk entirely too much."

Without uttering another word, they disrobed completely and lay in each other's arms, kissing passionately.

Both became aroused quickly, but when Hannah insisted that Travis take her without hesitation, he shook his head. "I want to taste you first. Make you totally mine."

She was unsure of his meaning, until his mouth left her lips to suckle her nipples, then moved slowly down her stomach to settle at the juncture of her thighs. "Travis!"

He felt her body tense but ignored her protests, coaxing her legs apart. "I want to know all of you, Hannah. Let me." When his lips and tongue found the tiny bud of her femininity, Hannah was hopeless to do anything but comply. Soon her hands were in his damp hair as she bucked insistently against the onslaught of his mouth, allowing him the access he demanded.

"Oh, Travis," she whispered, wondering if something so glorious could be considered shameful.

He brought her to climax quickly, then swallowed her screams of pleasure with his mouth as he plunged to the very depths of her core and secured his own release.

When they were sated and relaxed once more, Hannah reached out to stroke the hair on his chest. "That was wonderful. I never realized that making love could be so . . . so fulfilling and glorious."

He smiled, bringing her hand to his mouth for a kiss. "There's more to life than what's inside a court-room, Hannah. You're only just starting to realize that now. We both are in fact."

She nodded, then began to giggle uncontrollably.

"What's so funny?"

"I was just thinking of Olive and Margaret's reaction should they happen upon us out here in the open, naked as the day we were born."

Travis snorted. "We're miles from town, and I sincerely doubt that either one of the spinsters has ever been naked."

"Surely when they bathe?"

He shook his head. "Women like that bathe with their drawers on. They like to preserve their modesty."

"How do you know that?"

He shrugged. "I know a thing or two about women."

"You know how to please them. I'll give you that. And you also know how to make them lose all of their inhibitions." Her smile disappeared, and her brows drew together. "If anyone finds out about us, I'll be ruined. Not to mention what the adverse publicity would do to our chances with the trial."

"No one will find out until we're ready to tell them."

Hannah's heart hitched. Travis made it sound as if

they might actually have a future together, but she was too unsure of his feelings to question him further about it. "My social, not to mention professional, reputation will be in tatters if anyone discovers what we've been doing. We really must be more discreet in the future."

His smile widened into a grin. "Then we're going to do this again?"

Her smile turned seductive as her hand moved down his belly provocatively, inching ever nearer to the source of her pleasure. "Didn't you say you wanted me to *examine* you later?"

A low growl emanating from his chest, Travis placed her hand on his hardened member and covered her naked body once more. "I'm ready and willing to begin your examination right now, love."

Chapter Sixteen

Travis PLOPPED DOWN IN HIS CHAIR AND SIFTED through the pile of mail on his desk. He had a difficult time losing the smile that seemed permanently etched on his face. Especially when the cause of that smile would be coming through the doorway at any moment.

Hannah. He sighed deeply. It was so good between them right now, he could scarce believe that they'd ever been apart for five years.

Like an eager schoolboy he kept glancing at the door, waiting for it to open, then his eyes focused on a dirt-stained envelope postmarked Wyoming and his attention became diverted. Opening it, his eyes darkened as he read the contents:

Dear Miss Barkley, Your letter has reached me regarding the interrogation of the prisoner, Roy Lee Slaughter. I'm sorry to inform you—

Travis reread the passage and the name "Roy Lee Slaughter" and his blood began to boil.

"I'm sorry to inform you that Roy Lee Slaughter

has been found dead in his cell, an apparent suicide. Sincerely, Bartholomew Pepper, Warden, Wyoming Territorial Prison.

Banging the desk with his fist, Travis shouted, "Damn your stubborn hide, Hannah Louise!" Rising to his feet, he paced back and forth across the room, waving the incriminating evidence in the air.

Just then, the front door banged closed and Hannah Louise entered. She was smiling, her face glowing with happiness. But her smile melted quickly under Travis's lethal gaze.

"Travis, what's wrong? Whatever is the—" She pulled up short at the sight of the letter, his accusing stare, and guilt replaced her glow. "I can explain."

"Can you now? I doubt that, Hannah Louise. I expressly forbade you to carry through with your ridiculous scheme to visit Roy Lee Slaughter in prison, yet you decided to go behind my back and do it anyway. With no thought to your safety or anything else.

"How were you planning to explain your absence from the trial? Or hadn't you thought that far ahead?"

She held out her hands beseechingly. "Travis, we needed Slaughter's testimony. I thought I was doing the right thing."

"By defying my wishes?" He ran agitated fingers through his hair. "Jesus, Hannah. It's like history is repeating itself. I had hoped we would learn from our past mistakes."

She flinched as if struck. "I admit that I shouldn't have gone behind your back, and I'm sorry for that. But as your cocounsel I felt interviewing Roy Lee Slaughter was a good defense move. I have to consider Rafe's welfare above all else. Even if it means making you mad at me.

"And I haven't changed my opinion. I still think we should go to Wyoming and talk to the prisoner."

He handed her the letter. "Don't bother. Slaughter is dead. Apparently he hung himself. Guess he didn't want to spend the rest of his life behind bars."

She scanned the contents, heaved a sigh, then said, "I doubt your brother will shed any tears over his death."

"Rafe will be happy to hear the man's dead, and I can't say I blame him. He only spared his life because Emma begged him to."

"Sometimes women are a lot smarter than men are willing to give them credit for."

He crossed the room and took Hannah's hands in his own. "You already know that I think you're smart, Hannah, and an excellent lawyer. But we've got to be able to trust each other, if we're going to"—her heart quickened and she held her breath—"work together effectively." She released her breath in disappointment.

Chewing her lower lip thoughtfully, Hannah wondered how Travis would react to the next bombshell she was going to drop on him. She wasn't eager to find out. "I have something else to tell you, Travis, and you may not approve of what I've done." That was probably an understatement, she thought, swallowing hard.

He arched a brow. "Why doesn't that surprise me?"

"I've been trying to figure out why Judy DeBerry has been lying on the witness stand."

"Go on."

"I believe that she may have been paid off or even threatened to give false testimony. I think—"

"McGrath is involved," he finished, her thoughts mirroring his own suspicions.

"Exactly. But I need proof."

"Jesus, Hannah! What have you done now?"

"I've sent my mother to Justiceburg to see if she can come up with anything we can use against Mc-Grath."

His eyes widened in disbelief. But rather than the harsh condemnation she was expecting, Travis tossed back his head and laughed. "You sent Fiona to Justiceburg?" He couldn't contain his amusement.

Annoyed that he thought her plan so stupid, she crossed her arms over her chest and waited for him to regain his composure. "Are you through howling like a coyote?"

He bit the inside of his cheek and nodded. "I think so."

"Mama will be home on the evening stage. She sent me a telegram this morning. Apparently my suspicions are correct. Mama didn't elaborate, but she believes she has found proof of McGrath's involvement."

Hope lit Travis's eyes as he weighed the information, but he remained noncommittal. "I'll come by your home this evening and talk to her about this so-called proof."

"Don't let on to Papa why Mama's been gone. He'd be furious if he knew that she went behind his back."

He lifted her chin with his forefinger and stared intently into her eyes. "It seems your father and I have quite a bit in common."

Thinking that her father was stubborn, intractable, and horribly opinionated, Hannah smiled innocently, then said, "Yes. Yes, you do."

Heat and humidity hung over the Bodines' backyard like a smothering wool blanket. Lavinia affixed the wooden pin to the clothesline, then wiped the perspiration from her brow with the back of her hand. Reaching into the wicker basket, she withdrew another wet sheet from the pile.

"Grandma, when are we going inside to have lemonade? I'm awful thirsty."

Lavinia smiled indulgently at Miriam, Emmaline's second youngest of the five children she'd adopted, then clasped the pole of the clothesline as a wave of dizziness overtook her. Taking a deep breath to steady herself, she waited for the light-headed feeling to pass. "I'm almost done, child. It shouldn't be much longer."

"Miranda said that we might get to bake cookies later, is that true? I like cookies." The young girl twisted the ends of her braids, a hopeful expression on her face.

"We'll have to see about that, honey. It's turned out much warmer than I thought, and I'm not sure I'm feeling up to baking just now. Lighting the woodstove on

such a warm day will make the kitchen unbearable."
Lavinia suddenly paled as white as the sheet in her
hand.

"Grandma?" The child tugged on her grand-
mother's skirt. "You're not sick, are you, Grandma?
Grandma! What's wrong, Grandma?"

Just then, Lavinia's ears started ringing, and the
child's insistent questions became harder and harder to
hear. Finally, she said, "Run, Miriam," sliding down the
length of pole to the ground. "Run, child, and fetch your
grandpa. Tell him Grandma's feeling poorly."

What seemed like an eternity in reality took only a
few moments as Ben suddenly appeared, kneeling on
the ground beside her. The look of alarm on his face
touched Lavinia as no words of sympathy could.

"Vin! Vin! Are you all right?" He reached into the
laundry basket and retrieved a wet dish towel, wiping it
over her ashen face and pressing it against the back of
her neck. She started to get up, but he motioned her back
down. "Good Lord, woman! You took ten years off my
life when I saw you lying there on the ground still as a
corpse, and Miriam screaming at the top of her lungs
that you was dying."

"I'm sorry. I guess the heat just got to me. I nearly
fainted."

After she assured him that she was going to be all
right, Ben helped her to her feet. "You've been overdoing lately, Vin. Willy was right to chastise you about it a
few weeks back. From here on out the kids and I will
take over your chores."

"Don't be silly. I'm perfectly all right."

Miriam's older brothers and sister arrived just then, looking terribly distraught by the afternoon's events. "Don't you worry, Grandma," David said, puffing up in self-importance as only a ten-and-a-half-year-old boy could. "Me and Danny can take over your chores. We know how to gather eggs and feed the chickens."

"And I can help with the dishes," Miranda offered, not about to be outdone by a boy. Everyone knew that doing dishes was women's work.

"I can help bake cookies," Miriam offered.

"We'll all help." Ben gathered the children to him. "Now, you run and play while I tend to your grandma. And don't be making any noise in the house. I want her to rest. And you'd best check on Pansy to make sure she's still napping."

"Yes, Grandpa," they shouted, running toward the house and dragging Miriam with them.

Ben helped Lavinia to the porch, seating her on the slat-backed rocker. Instead of the usual lecture she expected on the foolishness of older women getting pregnant, her husband surprised her by saying, "You just rest easy, darlin', while I fetch you a glass of cold lemonade."

Her eyes widened, then she smiled gratefully. "I'd appreciate that very much, Benjamin."

"No trouble at all, darlin'. No trouble at all."

After Ben disappeared into the house, Lavinia released a sigh. Her husband hadn't been this solicitous of her welfare since before the announcement of her pregnancy, and she didn't know quite what to make of it.

"*Make the most of it*," the small voice inside her head urged.

Patting her mound contentedly, Lavinia thought that perhaps she would. It was about time Ben Bodine started acting like a husband and an expectant father, she decided with a smile.

Will McGrath adjusted the flame on his desk lamp and read the telegram he'd just received from his contact at the prison. Roy Lee Slaughter was dead. He leaned back in his oak swivel chair, ignoring the squeak, and smiled, pleased with his handiwork.

Money was such an effective tool when used smartly, he thought. It bought Judy DeBerry's testimony against Rafe, and it got Roy Lee Slaughter executed, albeit a bit prematurely.

Retrieving a whiskey bottle from the bottom drawer of his desk, he poured himself a healthy swig. "To victory," he toasted. There was no way in hell that Bodine or Hannah Louise could defeat him now. He had the eyewitness, he'd eliminated the only possible other witness, and there was no way any of it could be laid at his doorstep.

Will was nothing if not careful. He'd learned over the years that paying attention to the minutest details was often the saving grace of any situation. That belief was especially important when applied to illegal maneuvers.

Winning wasn't everything, it was the only thing. Nobody paid any attention to losers. "To the victor go the spoils," he proclaimed, drinking down the whiskey.

Hannah Louise would make quite a reward for this most recent victory, he decided, feeling himself harden. She would be the ultimate win, the most satisfying compensation for a job well-done.

She and Bodine had grown close. He'd seen them together in court, heads bowed, whispering like lovers. He'd observed the gentle touches, the furtive looks. Well, she might have screwed Bodine, but she was still a prime piece as far as Will was concerned.

He'd wanted to get between Hannah Louise Barkley's milky white thighs since they were teenagers. He thought he could win and woo her, but she'd picked Travis over him.

Now he was tired of waiting. If Hannah Louise wouldn't come to him willingly, then he might just have to take her by force.

Travis had just related to his brother the fact that Roy Lee Slaughter was dead. But rather than the elation he expected to see, there was only resignation on Rafe's face.

"So it's finally over." Rafe dropped to his bunk and shook his head. "I expected to feel differently—happy, excited. But all I feel is disgust that another human being is dead. I'm tired of all the killing and bloodshed, Travis. I just want to get on with my life."

Travis squeezed Rafe's shoulder, then sat beside

him on the narrow bunk. "Don't give up just yet, Rafe. We're making headway in the courtroom. I can feel it. You've got to hang on a little while longer."

"When I stare at those twelve men in that jury box all I can think about is that rope being tightened around my neck. About Emma being left alone with six children to care for, and no husband to provide for them."

"Hannah and I are doing everything possible to see that you are acquitted."

Rafe glanced up, a glimmer of hope in his eyes. "Has Hannah come up with anything that can prove the whore's lying?" Rafe asked. "She told me she was going to try."

Travis hesitated to mention the wild scheme Hannah had concocted with her mother, but he thought perhaps that knowing the lengths she had gone to discredit Judy DeBerry might make Rafe feel better. "She's working on it right now. Hannah sent her mother to Justiceburg to see if she could find out anything about the DeBerry woman and our esteemed prosecutor. She thinks they may be in cahoots."

Rafe's eyebrow arched. "McGrath. Now that doesn't surprise me. The little bastard has always hated us for some reason."

"We were lucky, Rafe. I never gave it much thought until now, but we three had each other. And our parents loved us and provided a good home. I guess Will just resented that about our family. He grew up poorer than most, and it couldn't have been easy for him not to feel some resentment. In some ways I feel sorry for him."

Rafe snorted disdainfully. "Yeah. Well, we'll see how sorry you feel when I'm swinging at the end of a rope in the hot Texas breeze. If the bastard's gone to the trouble of messing with a witness, then he really wants to see me dead."

Just then, Ethan entered the cell, took one look at his brothers' faces, and uttered a few colorful epithets. "Is this a funeral convention, or what? You two look like you've just made a pact with the devil."

Travis filled Ethan in on Hannah's suspicions about McGrath. To which Ethan replied, "Why don't I just take the little son of a bitch for a ride and put him out of his misery. Then we won't have to worry about him tampering with witnesses or anyone else."

There was something awfully appealing about Ethan's simplistic solution, and there was a small part of Travis that wished he could allow his brother to carry out his threat. It would save everyone a lot of time, trouble, and heartache.

But in the end it wouldn't really solve anything. Rafe would still be on trial for murder. And the three of them would be no better than McGrath. And in Travis's opinion, that would be worse than death.

Chapter Seventeen

In the parlor of the Barkley home that evening, Travis sipped on his sherry and studied the women before him, wondering how such small, innocent-looking creatures could concoct such large, nefarious schemes.

It was obvious Hannah had taken after her mother in many ways. She might have gained her love of the law from her father, but it was from Fiona that she had inherited her zest for life and fearless sense of adventure.

Life would never be boring with Hannah Louise around, he decided.

Still smarting over Hannah's earlier indiscretion and trying to keep his temper in check, he asked, "Now, which one of you is going to enlighten me about this trip to Justiceburg?"

"Hannah, dear," Fiona said, "please see if your father has retired for the evening."

Puzzled and somewhat suspicious of her mother's

request, for Hannah knew that Fiona knew exactly when the judge had retired, she nevertheless did as instructed and disappeared from the room, leaving Fiona and Travis sequestered together. Which was exactly what Fiona had intended all along.

"I know you're upset about this little scheme of mine and Hannah's, Travis, but I'd like you to know that it was as much my idea as Hannah's to go to Justiceburg, and you shouldn't be too angry with her. If I hadn't consented to go . . . Well, that is all water under the bridge now, I suppose."

"Hannah's impulsiveness is nothing new, Mrs. Barkley. Yours, however, comes as a bit of a shock."

Fiona smiled, genuinely liking this young man before her. She hadn't been quite certain when Travis and Hannah had gotten engaged five years ago that she approved of the match. Travis had been so small-town minded, while Hannah was eager to experience life to its fullest. But she could see now that the boy she'd left ten years before had become quite a decent man, one whom she'd be proud to call son.

"I doubt you'd change a hair on my daughter's head if you had the chance, young man. The girl you were once attracted to has evolved into so much more than a mere woman. She's smart, independent, and courageous. I'll grant you that she's a bit impulsive, but I'd rather that than have her be a mealymouthed lamb with no mind of her own.

"And she thinks a great deal of you, Travis. She's forever telling me what a wonderful lawyer you've become. I must say, Hannah isn't usually so effusive about the men in her life, except perhaps for her father."

Hannah entered, and Travis was unable to respond, which was probably Mrs. Barkley's intention, knowing how she liked to have the last word and all.

"Papa's in bed, Mama. Your arrival must have tired him out."

Remembering her and Thaddeus's most recent activity, Fiona blushed to the roots of her hair and shifted uncomfortably in her seat. "Yes, well—Shall, we get down to the business at hand?"

Travis didn't wait for a second invitation. "Hannah tells me that you have proof that Will McGrath is behind Judy DeBerry's false testimony. Would you care to elaborate, Mrs. Barkley?"

"My dear boy, I think you're now old enough to address me as Fiona. And I'd be happy to tell you what I think. I've never been the shy, retiring type, as you well know."

Travis and Hannah exchanged amused looks.

"As you are aware, Madam DeBerry runs a bordello. It's not much to look at, or at least it wasn't before Rafe was put on trial for murder. Rumor has it that the woman came into a great deal of money shortly after the trial began. She's been refurbishing her house of ill repute, and she's even begun construction on a fancy new home at the far end of town. Our madam is branching out, so to speak."

"Tell him about what those prostitutes told you, Mama," Hannah urged.

Travis smiled inwardly at the animation on both women's faces. For respectable women, they were quite caught up in the seamier aspects of life in Justiceburg. "Yes, do tell, Fiona. And don't leave out any of the sordid details. I think Hannah's looking forward to hearing those."

Her cheeks flushing deep pink, Hannah shot him an aggravated look before her mother continued with her narrative.

"Passing myself off as a seamstress, I was able to speak to a couple of Madam DeBerry's working girls. They were far less proficient with a needle than I, so I was able to get away with the ruse. And I used to be able to sew a fairly neat stitch in—"

"Mama! Just give us the details or we'll be here all night."

Fiona flashed Travis an apologetic smile. "The prostitutes told me that the madam had been spending great sums of money on the new house, buying all sorts of furniture and 'gewgaws,' I believe was how they put it. They confided that the prosecutor from Misery had been a frequent visitor at the bordello, and that Judy didn't charge him one red cent for—" Fiona blushed becomingly. "—for services rendered."

Travis gazed at Hannah's hopeful expression and shook his head. Though he wasn't surprised to hear that McGrath had been a frequent visitor in Justiceburg, that just wasn't enough to accuse a man of impropriety.

"Granted the man's a snake, but there's nothing that connects him to a bribe. McGrath might fancy whores. And he certainly had ample reason to visit Judy DeBerry, since she is his star witness. But there's just not enough concrete evidence to support our belief that he paid off Judy DeBerry. McGrath is smart. He wouldn't have left a trail."

"But that's where you're wrong, Travis." Fiona reached into her dress pocket and fished out an envelope. "One of the young women I spoke to, a Miss Ruby Boujoulais—"

"Ruby Boujoulais! Sounds like the name of a wine, for God sake," Travis said.

"Yes, well, if you were whoring for money, Travis, would you be using your real name?"

"Mama! Where on earth did you learn such a—"

Ignoring her daughter's dismay, Fiona continued. "According to Ruby, she used to be McGrath's paramour until he threw her over for Madam DeBerry. Ruby's embittered and wants revenge.

"She stole a letter from Judy's room written by McGrath to Judy, which implicates him in coercing the witness to lie."

"It's the proof we needed, Travis!" Hannah said. "The proof we've been waiting for."

Travis read over the letter and was not at all convinced. McGrath had carefully avoided placing his signature on the letter. And it had been stolen. It was very doubtful it would be admissible as evidence, under the circumstances.

"Hannah, the letter is useless. There's no signature. And it was gained in an unlawful manner. You know better than I that it won't be admissible. You're the expert on criminal procedure."

Hannah's face fell as she realized the truth of his words. Even though they had the proof that McGrath was involved, they wouldn't be able to use it. They would never be able to prove in a court of law that McGrath had bribed a witness. "I guess you went on a wild-goose chase, Mama. But I appreciate your efforts."

"Don't think for a minute that I didn't enjoy it. I found doing undercover work exhilarating. I wish I'd taken it up years ago and joined the Pinkertons, or some other detective agency. I would have been a great asset.

"At any rate, I've got some wonderful new hats and shoes to add to my wardrobe, so the trip wasn't a complete waste of time.

"Now, if you two young people will excuse me, I'm off to bed. Good night." She bussed Hannah's cheek then disappeared out the door, leaving Travis and Hannah alone on the horsehair sofa—the one Hannah's father claimed was as lumpy as Maude's oatmeal.

"I'm sorry things didn't work out as you'd planned, Hannah." Travis took her hand and squeezed it comfortingly. "I don't approve of your methods, but I have to give you points for trying."

"Are you still mad at me about the warden's letter?" She chewed her lower lip, waiting for his answer. She'd never forgive herself if she had ruined things between them. Again.

He pulled her onto his lap. "I may forgive you, if you kiss me to show me how sorry you are."

Wrapping her arms about his neck, Hannah proceeded to show him that she was indeed very sorry. Starting at his ear, she placed feathery kisses on his lobe, delighting in the halting way he sucked in his breath. Then working her way down his stubbled jaw, she trailed kisses to his mouth, pressing her lips against his and insinuating her tongue into his mouth.

Immediately aroused, Travis pulled back, his voice sounding hoarse, even to his own ears. "God, Hannah! You'd better stop that, or I'll—"

"You'll what? Ravish me?" Ignoring him, she began to unbutton his shirt.

Before he had a chance to shout, "Yes, dammit!" the parlor door flew open with a bang, startling them both, and Maude entered the room, a disapproving frown etched deeply on her face.

"Here now. We'll have none of that in this house, young man." She flung an arm out in Travis's direction. "Shame on you, Hannah Louise. Carrying on with the Bodine boy right under your parents' noses."

Maude pointed an accusing finger at Travis. "Make yourself presentable and get out. I'll not have you ravishing this girl right in her mother's very own parlor. For shame."

Travis's face turned a guilty shade of beet red as he pushed Hannah off his lap and leapt to his feet in one swift movement. Clutching his shirtfront, which was gaping open thanks to Hannah's enthusiastic seduction, he swallowed with some difficulty, mumbled his apologies, and quit the room in a matter of a heartbeat, feeling exactly as mortified as he had when he'd been ten and Mrs. Fogarty had caught him and Hannah Louise playing doctor under the elm tree in the backyard.

Hannah watched Travis's reaction with something akin to amazement, and thought it quite apparent that Travis had not yet lost his fear or respect for Maude. Leaning back against the sofa, she started to laugh.

"What are you laughing about, missy? I warned you that getting involved with Travis Bodine was going to be your ruination."

At the look of indignation on the housekeeper's face, Hannah began to giggle again. And once she started, she just couldn't stop, no matter how hard she tried. Clasping her middle, she howled until tears ran down her face, then ran out of the room and up the stairs before Maude could take her to task over it.

Staring at Hannah's retreating back, Maude threw up her hands in disgust. "Well, I never—" The young woman was either touched in the head or in love. Maude couldn't decide which was worse. She opted for the latter.

Late the following morning, Hannah reclined in her bathtub, soaking in hot, rose-scented water and reflecting upon her relationship with Travis.

They were lovers now, but he had made no avowals of love, had made no commitments of a life together. She could hardly blame him after what had happened between them the last time, but she'd hoped that they had put all of that aside and could begin again.

A soft knock sounded on the bathroom door, interrupting her disquieting thoughts, and her mother's voice floated in soon afterward. "Hannah, it's Mama. May I come in?"

Sinking lower into the soapy water to preserve her modesty, Hannah called out for her mother to enter. Fiona seated herself on the short wooden stool near the tub.

The scene was a familiar one. They'd had many talks like this in the New York brownstone Fiona owned, usually after Hannah had won a difficult law case. She always enjoyed discussing legal issues with her mother. Fiona's grasp of the law was remarkable and had always impressed her. Hannah felt that Fiona would have made a very capable attorney had she ever pursued that course.

Now, however, Hannah feared her mother had something else entirely on her mind. She looked agitated about something, and Fiona had never been one to mince words. This time proved no exception.

"I understand that you and Travis—" She paused, searching for the right words. Fiona wanted very much to be supportive of her daughter, not condemning. If she hadn't been so permissive a mother, perhaps this wouldn't have happened. "How shall I say this—that your relationship may have gone beyond mere friends or business associates. Is that correct, Hannah Louise?"

Hannah felt her face flush hot, and it had nothing to do with the steam rising off the water. "I assume you've been listening to town gossip, Mama." She swallowed with some difficulty. Apparently word of her affair with Travis had leaked out.

"Your father and I were absolutely livid when we heard from Maude that you and Travis have been—" She shook her head, unable to voice her concerns. "I can't believe my normally levelheaded daughter would behave so foolishly."

Damn Maude and her interfering ways! Hannah thought, trying to brazen it out as best she could. "I'm twenty-eight years old, Mama. I'm no longer a child, but a grown woman. If I decide to pursue a relationship with Travis, that's nobody's business but mine, and Travis's. It's my life, my happiness, at stake."

"Hannah," her mother's voice gentled, "think of the years of hard work you've put in to achieve what you have. Think of your reputation. And I'm speaking of your legal reputation, not your social one. A reputation that you've worked very long and hard to establish. Do you really want to throw it all away?

"Your scandalous conduct could have far-reaching consequences. It's obvious that everyone in Misery knows you and Travis are sleeping together. It'll probably make front-page news before long."

"Mama!" Hannah's face crimsoned an even deeper hue, and she slipped lower into the tub. "That's an appalling thing to say." Appalling, but most likely true.

Fiona's voice softened. "I'm not condemning you for it, honey. I want you to be happy. And if Travis makes you happy, then by all means sleep with him. However, I really think you should consider marrying him first. A woman often suffers the consequences of her actions."

"You mean the gossipmongers? I don't really think—"

Fiona grew exasperated. "That's part of the problem, Hannah Louise. You aren't thinking clearly. What I mean is," she took a fortifying breath, "that you could end up getting pregnant. Bearing a child out of wedlock would be unthinkable, as you well know. Even I'm not that liberal-minded. And God knows your father would likely expire right on the spot if he ever had to deal with such a consequence." Fiona shivered at the idea.

Thaddeus doted on Hannah Louise, believed she could do no wrong. She'd always be his little girl, no matter her age. But even he would draw the line at his daughter ever bearing an illegitimate child. Perish the thought!

Travis's child. Beneath the water Hannah's hands moved to cover her abdomen, and she patted it thoughtfully. *I'd never even considered the possibility.* Her heartbeat tripled; her pulse raced at the thought. "It hadn't occurred to me that I could get pregnant." She suddenly felt very stupid and childish.

Her mother gave Hannah an "I don't know what I'm going to do with you" look, then said, "That's because your heart and head are forever stuffed into law books and things of a legal nature, dear. You're neglectful at times of the more practical aspects of life.

"When Maude brought your conduct of last evening to my attention—"

"Maude again." Hannah sighed and shook her head. The housekeeper hadn't wasted any time relating what she had observed. The whole situation was becoming more humiliating by the minute.

"Maude loves you and worries over you. And I don't blame her one little bit. I should have counseled you myself. But I took it for granted that after all these years—I mean, I just assumed at your age you would take the proper precautions and—"

"I was a virgin, Mama. I'd never been with a man like that before Travis, and I—"

Fiona hid her surprise with sarcasm. "Well, how nice for Travis. But that doesn't alter the fact that you could bear his child. And, unless I'm very much mistaken, he hasn't asked you to marry him again. Has he?"

Tears slipped down Hannah's face. Frustrated, she slapped the water with the palm of her hand, nearly wetting her mother, who leaned back to avoid becoming drenched. "No. And I'm not sure he ever will. He's made no avowals of love, Mama, if that's what you're asking. But I know deep in my heart that he still cares for me."

"And what of your professional relationship, Hannah? Has Travis reconciled himself to your career, or are you willing to give it up for him?"

"I don't know. I've made mistakes regarding the trial. I shouldn't have gone behind his back like I did about the letter to Wyoming and your trip to Justiceburg."

"We must always face the consequences of our actions, dear. I should never have encouraged you to pursue that trip to Wyoming. Though I did so enjoy the one to Justiceburg."

"But I only wanted to do what was best for Rafe, and I wanted so much for Travis to win this case."

"You didn't want it for yourself?" Fiona arched a disbelieving brow. "I know how competitive you are, Hannah Louise."

"Maybe I did, just a little. But I wanted it more for Travis. He's brilliant and a wonderful attorney. I want him to receive the recognition he deserves. And I can't stand seeing him so miserable over his brother. The prospect of losing this case is not something Travis can bear. He'll blame himself forever if Rafe is convicted."

"You truly love him, don't you, Hannah? I guess you always have." Hannah and Travis had been playmates—soul mates—since childhood. Some things were just destined to be.

Hannah heaved a dispirited sigh. "Yes. I love him very much. But I don't know how he feels about me."

Fiona stood, handing her daughter a fluffy white towel. "Your skin's starting to shrivel, dear, and your bathwater is turning cold. I suggest you get dressed and join your father in the study. He wants to speak to you."

"Papa wants to speak to me about Travis?" Horrified by the prospect, Hannah swallowed with some difficulty, then said, "I can't speak to Papa. I can't bear to see the disappointment on his face." Of all people, his respect was the one she wanted most and couldn't bear to lose.

"There are times when Thaddeus can be hard as nails and uncaring, but not when they relate to his only daughter. You don't give the men in your life much credit, Hannah Louise."

Hannah noted the serenity on her mother's face that hadn't been there a few weeks ago, and said, "You and Papa are working things out, aren't you, Mama? I've noticed the way his health has improved dramatically since your return. It's like he was never sick at all."

Fiona smiled softly. "How neatly you've turned the tables on me."

"It's a trick I learned from Papa."

"I love Thaddeus every bit as much as you love Travis, Hannah Louise. And I intend to win back his love and be part of his life again. No one has made more mistakes than I have, but I'm determined to rectify my errors and live happily ever after, like a heroine from a fairy tale.

"I suggest you do the same, dear," she said, patting her daughter's cheek. "Happy endings are hard to come by. Sometimes we have to write our own."

Hannah's hand sweated profusely as she turned the brass knob to her father's study. Wiping it on her pink-striped day dress, she felt suddenly like a child about to be taken out to the woodshed and beaten soundly for misbehaving. The fact that her father had never laid a hand on her in the twenty-eight years she'd been alive hadn't lessened the threat of facing him one bit.

Taking a deep breath, she entered to find him

seated behind the massive desk. His expression was troubled when he looked up from his book to greet her. "Hello, Papa. Mama said that you wished to see me."

"Come in and sit down, daughter. I think we need to have a little chat about your recent activities."

She swallowed the lump of dread in her throat and decided to take an offensive posture. "I realize that you know about Travis and me, so there's no need to lecture me. Perhaps what I did was wrong, but I'm a grown woman now and must do what I deem best." Sliding into the leather chair, she folded her hands primly on her lap, hoping to disguise her nervousness.

Thaddeus James Barkley was a formidable opponent. She couldn't afford to give him the upper hand in a verbal duel by allowing him to smell weakness or apprehension. He'd grind her into mincemeat if she did.

It was one of the first lessons her father had taught her about being a lawyer and facing an adversary. And as much as she loved him, at this moment he was an adversary.

His lips thinned. "I think I should decide if a lecture is required, Hannah Louise. I'm the judge. I happen to be a lot older and more experienced than you. And, in case you've forgotten, I'm still your father."

"Yes, Papa. I realize that. But I'm a grown woman now, and you have to allow me to make my own mistakes."

"Well, it appears to me that you've made a whopper of one this time, Hannah Louise. To have an illicit affair without the benefit of marriage is one thing—and something I totally disapprove of—but to have that affair with your law partner during a murder trial is without question the most asinine, the most irresponsible thing I've ever heard of. The consequences of your actions could be devastating not only to you, but to your client."

"Papa—"

He shook his head. "Don't interrupt until I'm finished. I've just gathered a good head of steam, and I intend to run with it until it peters out.

"How could you and Travis jeopardize Rafe Bodine's life like this? You are playing right into Will McGrath's hands, child. The man is scum. He looks for every weakness, every opportunity to win.

"And don't think I don't know about that ridiculous trip to Justiceburg that your mother made on your behalf. Or the letter that you wrote to the warden of that prison in Wyoming." Hannah's eyes widened at that. "Are you purposely trying to get Rafe convicted, or does it just look that way?"

Hannah's face paled at the question. "I've already discussed both of those issues with Travis. You'll be pleased to know that he's been every bit as hard on me as you and has already given me a blistering setdown for my actions."

The judge leaned back in his chair, steepling his fingers in front of his face as he studied her. Despite her ability to disguise emotion, Hannah looked very upset. "It's never been my intention to sit in judgment on you, Hannah Louise. I realize that you're in love with Travis, and that people in love often forget themselves in a moment of passion. But in your position as legal counsel to a man on trial for murder, what you do affects others.

"Not to mention the fact that having a relationship out of wedlock is just asking for trouble, Hannah Louise. I'm sure you know what I'm talking about."

She did, and her hand went unconsciously to her belly. "Are you terribly disappointed with me, Papa? I don't want to lose your love and respect."

"Hannah." The judge released a sigh. "I'm your father and will always love you, no matter what. But Travis is your law partner, the person depending on you to help him make the right decisions, to help get his brother acquitted of murder. Having a love affair with him is not going to accomplish much except to make him distracted when he needs to be concentrating on this case.

"You took on a tremendous responsibility when you agreed to assist with Rafe Bodine's murder trial, not only to Rafe but to Travis as well. I'm not excusing Travis in any of this. He's as much, or more, to blame as you are for forgetting where his attention should be directed.

"Men are oftentimes distracted by a pretty woman."

Tears trickled down Hannah's cheeks. "I love him, Papa. And I want to be with him, always."

"Come, child. Sit here on my lap like you used to when you were a little girl. I think you need a hug. I know I do."

"Oh, Papa," she said, dropping into his lap and throwing her arms about his neck. "I love you so much. I'll never be as wise or as competent an attorney as you."

He patted her cheek, wiping away her tears with his thumb, wishing he could protect her. But life was a difficult teacher, and Hannah was fast becoming an apt pupil. And though she would always be his little girl, she was all grown-up now.

"Wisdom comes with years, my dear. You're not nearly old enough to be wise.

"I'm very proud of what you've accomplished, Hannah Louise. Very proud of the woman you've become. Everyone makes mistakes. It's how we rectify them that sets us apart and provides understanding."

"Thank you, Papa. I will try to live up to your expectations."

He hugged her close. "You already have, child. More than you'll ever know."

Chapter Eighteen

Travis and Ethan faced each other across the desk in Travis's office. It was Saturday night and both men were falling-down-on-their-ass drunk.

Willy had thrown a baby shower for Emma and had invited many of the town's womenfolk to attend, including Hannah. Travis and Ethan had spent the last few hours sharing two bottles of sour mash whiskey and commiserating about the trial, women, and the injustices of life in general.

"I'm in love with Hannah, Ethan, but I'm just not sure she's worth the heartache or the pain I'm likely to feel because of it." Travis shook his fist in the air, then banged it on the desktop, nearly toppling the whiskey bottle and himself. "I loved her once, and she left me. Who's to say that she won't leave me again once this trial is over with.

"I've had it with women. They're just more trouble than they're worth."

"Me too," Ethan agreed. "I've had it, too."

Travis stared bleary-eyed at his brother. "You can't have had it. You're married. And Willy's gonna have a baby."

Ethan teetered, almost tipping the chair over backward, then slammed forward, his boots hitting the floor with a thud. "Shit! I forgot. Guess I'll have to go home to her eventually then." His grin was decidedly lopsided, and Travis angled his head just to make sure his eyes weren't playing tricks on him.

"How come I still love her, Ethan, after everything that's happened?" He'd asked himself that question a thousand times over, but the answer had never satisfied him. He was scared—scared of making another mistake.

"That's just the trick nature plays on us poor unsuspecting males, little brother. You love Hannah." Ethan shrugged. "Never could figure out why, but you do, and that's that. You'll be miserable, just like you've been heartbroken these past five years, if you don't marry up with the woman.

"Anyway, she's helping to get Rafe outta jail. You need her, and so does Rafe."

Travis downed another shot of whiskey and wiped his mouth on his shirtsleeve, not caring that he'd just had it laundered last week. "No one ever thought I could do much on my own, Ethan. No one except Hannah Louise. Pa always compared me to you and Rafe, and I came up short, and even Emma didn't have enough confidence that I could get Rafe aquitted.

"Someday you're all going to see that I'm good enough to handle things on my own."

Ethan was drunk, but not enough not to hear the pain in his brother's voice. He was saddened by it, felt guilty as hell that he'd been partly the cause of it.

Had they slighted Travis, never allowing him the chance to prove himself because he was the youngest? They'd been well meaning in their effort to protect. But had they wounded the man by treating him like a boy? "Shit, Travis. I'm sorry. Guess I'm guilty as the rest for making you feel unappreciated and worthless."

Travis wiped his hand over his face in an attempt to mask his hurt. "It doesn't matter."

"Hell it doesn't! But know this: we're all very proud of you, proud of the man you've become. Even Pa has bragged on what a great job you've been doing with the trial. And his compliments are few and far between, as you well know."

"I might not have done such a good job if Hannah hadn't been there to help me," Travis admitted. "She's smart. And she knows a hell of a lot about criminal law. I'd be lost without her."

"Well, shit, little brother! Ain't that what I've been saying all along? You would be lost without Hannah Louise. About time you realized that fact."

Ethan clutched his brother's shoulder and squeezed. "Women are surely a pain in the butt, but we can't live without them and find any happiness. God knows I tried. Never thought I'd marry and settle down, but when you meet the right woman you've got no choice in the matter. She's like a burr under your saddle.

Until you do something about it, you're just plain miserable."

"I'm miserable now," Travis insisted. "I love Hannah Louise, always have. Can't think of my life without her in it. But God she makes me crazy sometimes. Did you know that she was actually going to go to Wyoming and talk to a vicious murderer all by herself?" He shuddered whenever he thought about it.

Ethan nodded sagely. "You're too far gone to fight it, little brother. So, why bother? Just marry the woman and put yourself out of your misery. That's what I did. And I ain't regretted it for a moment."

Travis digested his brother's advice, and the more he thought about it, the easier it went down. "I must really be drunk if what you're telling me makes sense, Ethan."

His brother grinned, wondering when the wedding was going to take place.

Since talking with her father and attending Emma's baby shower, which had made her realize just how much she wanted a child of her own, Hannah had been doing a great deal of thinking about Travis, marriage, and her future.

She decided that there was really only one way to find out what Travis's intentions were toward her and that was to ask him. If he didn't desire marriage, then she would return to New York and resume her law career there. It would be too painful to remain in Misery and watch Travis's affections settle on another.

Judge Hix had taken the bench and was calling for the defense to present their next witness, so there wasn't time to talk to him now. But she would, and soon. Hannah caught Travis's eye and smiled her encouragement, then turned her attention back to the proceedings.

Travis fought hard to keep his face perfectly impassive and his feelings hidden. Hannah's smile was like sunshine on a gloomy day. But he couldn't allow his love for her to interfere with the trial, which was easier said than done. The scent of her cologne wafted toward him, conjuring up some very special memories. With a sigh of longing, he rose to his feet to question his brother, who had just taken the witness stand.

Ethan looked as if he'd just crawled on his hands and knees from the depths of hell. He resembled a horse who'd been ridden hard and put away wet. His brother's usually tanned complexion was pale, and he weaved a bit when he walked, which might have been due to the large kettledrum banging loudly and insistently inside his head—the same drum that thundered inside his own. If he never imbibed another shot of whiskey, it would be too soon, Travis decided.

"Ranger Bodine—" Travis cast his brother a pitying look and began to question Ethan on the various skills it took to become a Texas Ranger. Then he said, "Please tell the jury what Rangers are taught from the moment they enter the militia."

"Well now—" Ethan leaned back, and the chair squeaked loudly, making him wince painfully. "A Ranger's best defense to protect himself is to attack, dominate, and subdue the enemy. Kill him before he kills you."

"And this rather unorthodox-sounding procedure is considered standard among the Texas Rangers?"

"Kill or be killed. I much prefer the former," Ethan added to a chorus of snickers.

"What is the motto of the Texas Rangers, Captain Bodine?"

Like a naughty schoolboy the Ranger grinned. "One riot, one Ranger." The room burst out in laughter, and the judge banged his gavel and ordered quiet. "That means it don't take a whole lot of us to get the job done," he explained, his blue eyes twinkling as the prosecutor jumped to his feet.

"Objection, Your Honor!" Will McGrath stated. "I fail to see how a lesson on the Texas Rangers is going to help the jury decide whether or not Rafe Bodine is guilty of murder."

"My client's background plays a great part in who he is, Your Honor," Travis insisted. "And it may explain why Rafe Bodine acted as he did. The question goes to his ability as a lawman and his state of mind at the time of Bobby Slaughter's death.

"A man trained to act a certain way in any given situation is not likely to deviate from that behavior when faced with similar circumstances."

The judge pondered the explanation, nodded, then said, "I'll allow this form of questioning, Mr. Bodine. We must remember"—he shot McGrath, who was about to object again, a warning look—"that a man's life is at stake here. We must explore all the possibilities."

Wearing his chastisement like a hair shirt, Will took his seat, cursing softly under his breath.

Olive, too, was upset that Will had been silenced. Since the bachelor auction the two had grown close, and she'd decided to realign her sympathies with the one man who truly appreciated her.

Margaret still pined over Travis. She refused to believe that the handsome attorney was in love with someone other than herself and had not changed her loyalties. They now sat apart, Olive on the prosecution's side, Margaret on the defense's.

Travis turned his attention back to his brother. "Isn't it true, Captain Bodine, that a Texas Ranger has three maxims he lives by?"

"Maxims?" Ethan wrinkled his forehead in confusion. "My wife's fond of using those ten-dollar words, but I confess I'm not as learned as she is." He turned toward the men seated in the jury box and added, "Willy's a horticulturist. Knows all about plants and such."

Travis's face reddened as the court burst out in laughter once again. Hannah smiled inwardly at Ethan's antics. The jury had warmed to the Ranger's offbeat, folksy sense of humor, and she was glad Travis had chosen to use him as a witness, despite her earlier objections. His gut instincts had proven correct once again, which made her feel even more shame for doubting his abilities.

"A maxim is a principle, a rule of conduct," the

judge explained to the witness. Then in an angry tone he addressed the court: "If there are any more outbursts of this nature, I will clear this courtroom. This is not a sideshow or a three-ring circus. Though there are those of you who are trying to turn it into such." The room quieted immediately. "Please answer the question, Ranger Bodine," he directed.

"A Ranger is taught never to wear a gun unless he knows how to use it, never to draw that gun unless he intends to use it, and never to shoot except to kill."

"I've got one more question, Captain. When you stop your Rangering duties for the day and go home to your lovely wife, do you cease being a Ranger?"

"Hell no! I'll be a Ranger till the day I die. Even if I'm not riding with the Rangers, I'll abide by those maxims"—he grinned—"and rules of conduct that I was taught. Rangering's in my blood, same as Rafe's. It ain't an easy thing to lose or to forget."

Will McGrath stood, took one look at Ethan Bodine's menacing visage, and opted not to question the Ranger. That left one last defense witness: Benjamin Bodine.

Once the courtroom had cleared during a brief fifteen-minute recess, Hannah said to Travis, "Your father wears a hard shell, Travis, and does not display much emotion. It'll be up to you to reduce him to tears if possible. The jury needs to see his reaction to your brother's arrest and possible conviction. They need to be made to feel everything he and the rest of your family feel."

Travis paled. "He'll hate me for it. You know Pa doesn't like to appear weak, especially in public."

She clutched his arm. "He'll hate you more if you don't do everything in your power to get Rafe acquitted."

He knew Hannah was right. But that didn't make what he had to do any easier.

"Mr. Bodine," Travis began, finding it a tad awkward to address his father in such a formal manner. "Please tell us how you felt when you first learned about the death of your daughter-in-law, Ellie Bodine."

Ben glanced at his son warily, then at his wife, who nodded her encouragement. "Ellie was a lovely young woman. Always had a smile on her face and a kind word for everyone. She loved my son, Rafe, with all her heart and had from the time they were toddlers.

"I found it hard to believe that anyone would kill such a sweet, young thing. It was so senseless, such a waste of a human life. That woman would never have hurt a fly."

"Did you know that your son's wife was pregnant?"

Ben shook his head, and his eyes grew moist. "No. She hadn't told anyone except her husband, I guess. Even her ma and pa didn't know. They were devastated, we all were, when we found out the baby had been killed, too."

"You've always wanted grandchildren, haven't you, Mr. Bodine?"

McGrath jumped to his feet. "Objection, Your Honor! This line of questioning has nothing to do with the trial."

"Shut up, McGrath," someone in the back yelled. "We want to hear what Ben's got to say."

"Yeah," another spectator shouted. "Shut yer trap."

"Your objection is overruled, Mr. McGrath. And this is the last warning I will issue about these outbursts."

"But, Your Honor—"

"Please continue, Mr. Bodine."

"I've always been after my boys to settle down and get married. Never thought any of them would. They were what you called free spirits. Then Rafe decided to quit the Texas Rangers and marry Ellie Masters. It was the happiest day of my life, 'cause I figured that I'd soon be having grandbabies." A small smile touched his lips.

"Why was it so important to have grandchildren, Mr. Bodine?"

Ben studied the earnest expression on his son's face, looked at Rafe, then at Ethan, and said, "I've always been hard on all three of my boys. I didn't spoil them enough when they were young'ns, always expected too much, I guess. Their ma always said that I was pushing them away, but I didn't listen.

"I guess I felt that I could make amends, sort of start over and correct my earlier mistakes, if I had some grandchildren to spoil.

"Children are the best reflection of what a man's

life has amounted to. Judging from the three sons I have, I guess I've accomplished a lot in my sixty-two years."

Rafe was visibly moved by his father's words and stared down at his hands. Ethan coughed discreetly into his to conceal how choked up he'd become. Travis smiled warmly at his father, as if to say, "I'm proud to be your son."

Clearing his throat, he asked, "Mr. Bodine, do you feel that your son had just cause to avenge his wife's death?"

Ben looked at Rafe and couldn't conceal the love and pride he felt. Removing a handkerchief from his back pocket, he blew his nose and dabbed at his eyes. "My son put his life on the line many times for the state of Texas. Both my sons did. I never understood what prompted them to do it. I thought they were foolish to risk their lives for no good reason. But I see now that I was wrong. Rafe lived his life honorably. Did what he thought best and never gave a thought to the risks or the consequences.

"If my son went after the Slaughters, it was because there was too much Ranger still left in him not to right a wrong or see that justice was carried out.

"I'm a peaceable man, as most people in this room know, but I'd have done the same if someone had come after one of mine. A man's got a right to defend his property, his life, and that of his family's. My son was just doing what he'd been raised to do: love, honor, and protect his wife, his family, and his home, whether that be Texas or a small piece of it."

Chapter Nineteen

THERE HADN'T BEEN A DRY EYE LEFT IN THE HUSHED courtroom by the time Ben Bodine finished his testimony and rushed, visibly shaken, from the proceedings. Hannah had felt inordinately proud of Travis at that moment and desperately wanted to tell him so. But he'd been surrounded by his family and a host of well-wishers, and she'd never gotten the chance.

First thing this morning, the closing statements had been presented by both the defense and the prosecution. Both sides had tried to present their positions as best they could based on the evidence and testimony of witnesses.

The trial was finally over, and Rafe Bodine's life was now in the hands of the twelve men presently sequestered in the sparsely furnished jury room located at the back of the courthouse. It was their task to decide the facts, apply the law as contained in the judge's instructions, and reach a unanimous verdict.

No one knew how long it would take them to bring

back a verdict. She'd seen guilty decisions brought back within an hour and innocent ones done in the same length of time. There was no way to tell how a jury was going to react once they got together to deliberate a case. Sometimes they became deadlocked over a point of law and were unable to reach a verdict, and the judge had to declare a mistrial.

That wasn't likely to happen in Rafe's trial. Judge Hix was a firm believer in due process and wasn't likely to accept anything but a unanimous decision from the jury. He considered anything less to be a shirking of one's civic responsibility.

It would take time to reach that verdict. And the waiting always proved to be the hardest part.

"Not doing you or that oriental carpet a lick of good to be pacing across it like you are," Maude declared. "Why don't you sit yourself down at the table and join your mama and me in some milk and peach pie? It's mighty tasty, if I do say so myself." Maude was turning into a pretty respectable cook, thanks to Fiona's patient tutelage. The two women had actually grown tolerant, if not somewhat fond, of each other.

Hannah shook her head. "I couldn't eat a thing. I'm too nervous." And she was also worried about Travis during such a difficult time. She'd wanted to go to him at the conclusion of the proceedings to offer her support and tell him how proud she was of him, but he had left hurriedly to accompany Rafe back to his cell.

Travis's brother and sister-in-law would need comforting and a strong shoulder to lean on at such a time, and she, not being a member of their family, felt she would only be in the way.

"Please sit down, Hannah Louise," her mother insisted. "Watching you walk back and forth is making my head spin." Acceding to her mother's wishes, Hannah ground to a halt. The despair on her face was heart-wrenching to Fiona. "Why don't you go to him, Hannah? Travis needs you, and it's as obvious as the misery on your face that you need him, too."

"I'm sure he wants to be alone with his family right now. I wouldn't want to intrude. This is a difficult time for all of them."

Maude's expression was resigned as she gazed at the young woman. She wanted Hannah Louise to be happy and prayed with all her heart and soul that she soon would be. "Travis isn't with his family at the moment. I saw him head off down the street not fifteen minutes ago toward that new house he's almost got finished.

"It'd be a mighty fine house for a pair of newly-weds, I'm thinking."

Hannah couldn't believe what she was hearing. "Why, Maude Fogarty! I thought you didn't want me to get back together with Travis."

Maude and Fiona exchanged meaningful looks, then Maude said, "Best to have you marry that boy rather than have you carrying on a scandalous relationship." Her lips pursed in disapproval. "Your mother and I didn't bring you up to be a loose woman, Hannah Louise."

Hannah almost choked on the woman's words. "Loose, am I? Funny you should talk of such things. I've heard from several people that you and Mr. Boyette, the blacksmith, have been keeping some pretty late hours, Maude, and I doubt you've been discussing the finer points of horseshoes."

The housekeeper's face turned bright red, and Fiona threw back her head and laughed. "Really, Maude? You and the blacksmith?"

"And what are you laughing about, Mrs. Barkley? I've seen you sneaking from the judge's room in the wee hours of the morning when you thought no one was lookin'. And you in your nightwear."

"Mama! You and Papa? You're back together?" Hannah couldn't contain her smile. She had suspected as much, but to actually have it confirmed—She felt almost giddy.

"If they got any closer they'd be like flies on paper," Maude declared, taking a huge bite of pie. "Why do you think the judge has been looking so full of himself lately? The man's recovery has been nothing short of miraculous."

Fiona's cheeks blossomed a becoming shade of pink. "Thaddeus and I have reached an understanding," she finally confessed. "I'll be moving back to Misery permanently."

Hannah threw her arms about her mother's trim waist. "Oh, Mama! I'm so happy for you, and for Papa, too." She looked about, expecting to see her father walking through the doorway at any moment to yell

"Surprise!" like he used to when she was small. "Where is Papa, by the way? I haven't seen him since court ended this morning."

"Your father's at the tailor shop. He decided that since he was feeling so much improved, he would buy himself a new suit."

Maude's mouth unhinged at the revelation. "The judge is buying himself a new suit? Well, don't that beat all? The man hasn't had new duds in fifteen years. I expected to bury him in that old black superfine he'd been saving for the occasion."

"Thaddeus now has another far more joyous occasion to wear a new suit. We've decided to renew our wedding vows. We're making a fresh start after all these years apart, so we decided it only appropriate that we begin at the very beginning."

Maude nodded matter-of-factly. "Been expecting that announcement for a good while now. And I'm pleased as all get-out to hear it." The judge and his wife belonged together. Any fool could see that, and Maude Fogarty was no fool.

Eyes wide with wonder, Hannah squealed in delight, clapping her hands excitedly. "Mama! This is such wonderful news. It's not often a daughter has the privilege of watching her parents get married. When is this blessed event to take place? Am I to be maid of honor? And what are you going to wear?"

As her daughter reeled off question after question, Fiona smiled fondly, patting the exuberant young woman's cheek. Only Hannah would think of clothing at a time like this. She was her mother's daughter after all. "We haven't picked a date yet, dear, but you'll be the first to know when we do.

"Now why don't you go find your young man, so you can start planning your own wedding? Travis loves you, Hannah Louise. You love him. So quit wasting time and go tell him."

So happy she could burst, Hannah's smile widened into a grin. "I will. But first I must go upstairs and bathe, change my dress—" She would tell Travis she loved him. But in her own time. And in her own very special way.

Dressed in a blue-and-white-striped taffeta gown with matching straw bonnet, Hannah felt confident as she strode quickly down the street toward Travis's new home.

Though the sun was just starting to dip into the horizon, the temperature remained blistering hot, but she was determined that nothing or no one was going to mar her good mood. She felt jubilant about her parents' reconciliation and had come to some serious decisions concerning her own happiness.

Nothing, not her career or her pride, would ever come between her and Travis again. That was a promise Hannah had made to herself and one she intended to keep.

Her determination to remain jubilant was suddenly put to the test when she found Olive Fasbinder and Will McGrath coming toward her. They were strolling arm in arm, looking very much like a couple, and Hannah's eyes widened at the odd pairing of the two.

Pasting on an affable smile, she greeted them. "Good afternoon, Olive . . . Will." The spinster looked almost pretty in the rust-and-gold print gown she wore. The smile she so rarely displayed as she gazed adoringly at her companion had transformed her appearance from dour to radiant.

"Will's taking me to dinner this evening," Olive announced in a gloating fashion.

Will smiled down at the spinster, but his smile never quite reached his eyes, making Hannah wonder what kind of cruel game he was playing. It was obvious that Olive was smitten. And despite all of their differences, she hated to think that Olive might get hurt. "How nice for you both."

The spinster's bright smile suddenly slid into a smirk. "I wouldn't worry overly much, Hannah Louise." She clutched Will's arm tighter. "I'm sure you'll meet someone when you return to New York.

"Now that the trial's over, you will be leaving soon, won't you?" The eagerness in her voice was unmistakable. Hannah thought it sad that Olive still felt threatened by her. She needn't be. Hannah's heart was firmly attached to another.

Her leaving Misery depended on a great many things, not the least of which was Travis. And none that were any of Olive's business.

With every ounce of willpower she possessed, Hannah resisted the rude comment teetering on the tip of her tongue. "One never knows what the future will hold. You're living proof of that, Olive." She forced a smile. "Now, if you'll both excuse me, I'm in a bit of a hurry." Sweeping her skirts aside before the spinster could respond, she continued down the street, repeating silently over and over again that she wouldn't let anything or anyone spoil her good mood.

Will watched Hannah walk away and was more determined than ever to possess her. Olive was but a pleasant diversion; the scrawny spinster a pale imitation of the woman he really craved.

There was only one way to get even with the Bodines, and he intended to take it. Then Hannah Louise would be his once and for all.

Travis had just arrived home from visiting Rafe at the jailhouse for the second time that day. For some reason known only to Rafe, his brother had requested his company again. And imagining how anxious Rafe must feel as he awaited the verdict, Travis had put everything aside, including the new sink he had bought for the kitchen, and had hurried back down to the jail to offer what comfort he could.

But upon his arrival, Rafe hadn't seemed nervous or morose, as Travis had expected. In fact, he'd seemed like his old self, joking with Emma, trading quips with Ethan, and devouring the steak dinner that their father had ordered sent over from the restaurant.

Very strange behavior for a man in his precarious position, Travis thought, seating himself on the front porch stoop. Shaking his head, he decided that a man who had just stood trial for murder had the right to act a little strange if he wanted to.

It was a beautiful time of day. The sun was nestling into the horizon and turning the evening sky brilliant shades of orange and pink. The cicadas chimed their distinctive patter, while tree frogs croaked out an accompaniment.

Travis inhaled deeply the scent of jasmine, popping a couple of gumdrops into his mouth, and wondered again what kind of verdict the jury would render against his brother.

He'd done all he could to get Rafe acquitted. Hannah, too, had given her all, and he would always be indebted to her for that. Now it was up to twelve just men and God to decide if his brother would hang for murder.

Engrossed in thought, he stared down at a trail of ants marching along like a military column and didn't hear the creak of the front gate or notice that a visitor had entered. It wasn't until the scent of rose perfume reached him, and he heard the clearing of a feminine voice, that Travis looked up to find Hannah Louise standing before him.

"Hannah!" The sight of her took his breath away, and he choked on the candy he had just swallowed.

Alarmed at the strangled sounds, Hannah stepped toward him. "Are you all right?"

Nodding, he jumped to his feet, embarrassed by his reaction. "Yes. I was just eating some gumdrops, and one—" The reason for his anxiousness seemed lame even to him, so he halted the explanation in midsentence. "Did you come to talk about the trial? I'm sorry I had to leave so quickly today, but—"

She shook her head, making the blue-silk flower atop her bonnet bob every which way. "I didn't come to talk about the trial, or Rafe, or anything having to do with business. I came to talk about us."

Hannah's bluntness surprised Travis. They were still standing outside in front of the porch, so he opened the door and ushered her inside.

"You look very pretty this evening. Are you going somewhere special?"

"Just here," she said, removing her bonnet and setting it on a workbench.

A quick glance around the room told Hannah that the house was nearly completed. The interior trim had been installed and partially painted a lovely forest green color. The pine floors had been sanded and stained a rich honey color. "The house looks wonderful. You must be very proud."

"It's almost done. Another week should do it. Would you like to sit down? I don't have much furniture, but there's a bench I can clear off."

"No thank you. I prefer to stand to say what I have to say." Then, if it didn't go well, she could make a quick escape out the front door.

He crossed his arms over his chest, waiting expectantly for her to continue. She swallowed nervously, finally saying, "I've been doing a lot of thinking lately, Travis, and—"

"Uh-oh. That could mean trouble."

"I guess that depends on how you look at it. I'm hoping you'll be pleased by what I'm about to say."

Fear knotted his belly. *Please, don't let it be good-bye.* He couldn't stand the thought of never seeing Hannah again, holding her in his arms, making love to her—

She smiled softly. "I love you, Travis. I've loved you all my life. I'm sorry that I put my law career before our relationship once before, but—"

Astonishment had him rocking back on his boot heels. "Whoa! Back up. What did you say?" Travis wasn't sure he had heard her correctly, but his heart was hammering in triple time anyway.

"I said: I love you, Travis Bodine. But if you don't feel the same way, then I've decided that the best thing for me to do is go back to New York and—"

A smile lighting his face, Travis stepped forward, drawing her into his arms. "I've loved you from the time you were in diapers, Hannah Louise Barkley. Even when you broke my heart into little pieces I continued to love you. And I love you now. If you think that I'd allow you to ever leave me again—Well, I won't." He crushed her to him. "God, Hannah! I thought you had come to say good-bye."

"Oh, Travis." Tears filled her eyes, and she wrapped her arms about his waist. "I love you so much. I would never leave you. In fact, I've come to propose. Would you do me the honor of marrying me?"

His eyes widened, then he grinned. "You're proposing marriage to me?"

She nodded. "Turnabout is fair play. You proposed the first time, so I thought it only fair that I do so the second and, I hope, final time."

"Hannah Louise Barkley, you've made me the happiest man on the face of this earth. I love you. Hell yes, I want to marry you. I want to make love to you. And not necessarily in that order." He kissed her then, passionately, thoroughly, until her toes curled heavenward.

"This is the best birthday present you could have ever given me," he said.

She looked momentarily stricken. "It's your birthday? And I forgot. Oh, Travis, I'm so sorry."

"That's okay. You can give me my present now." He grinned erotically. "I think you know what I want."

Just then, two of the bedroom doors burst open and the entire Bodine clan poured forward, except for Rafe and Emma, who remained at the jail, sharing some private moments together. They'd been instrumental in throwing Travis off the track about his surprise party and delaying his arrival home.

"Surprise! Happy Birthday!" everyone shouted.

Travis's mouth dropped open. He looked so totally flabbergasted that Hannah knew immediately that he had no idea that his family had been hiding from him, or that they had overheard their entire conversation.

Hannah didn't know whether to feel humiliated or exhilarated. She opted for the latter.

"'Bout time you two decided to get hitched." Ben came forward to engulf his future daughter-in-law in a bear hug. "Welcome to the family, Hannah Louise. It's where you've belonged all along."

"Thank . . . thank you, Mr. Bodine."

"None of that mister stuff now. You call me Pa, just like the rest of my kids. Ain't that right, boy?" he said to Travis, before wrapping his arms about him, too.

"I'm proud of you, boy. Just wanted you to know that."

Something suspiciously like tears welled in Travis's eyes, and he swallowed the lump in his throat. "Thanks, Pa. That means a lot coming from you."

"Of course it does. And I meant every word. You're as fine a son and lawyer as any man could hope for."

Ethan's shrill whistle filled the air. "A birthday and marriage proposal all on the same day. Ain't you the lucky one, little brother?" He grabbed hold of Travis's hand and pumped it, then swung Hannah around in the air and kissed her soundly on the cheek. "Welcome to the family, Hannah darlin'."

Willy strode—some would say waddled—forward and kissed Hannah's cheek. "Now we'll truly be sisters. I'm so happy for both of you."

Hannah was so astounded by everything she could barely utter a word. Just then, she spotted Lavinia coming toward her with arms outstretched, beaming from ear to ear. Finally giving into her emotion, she burst into tears. "I'm so happy, Lavinia," she declared, nestling against the woman's soft breasts.

"I know, honey. And you deserve to be. I'm so proud of you for proposing to Travis like you did. Appears to me that all my boys have found women with as much strength of character, guts, and determination as they themselves have got. It takes a special woman to hold on to a Bodine."

"You're damn right it does, Vin." Ben stepped forward to wrap his arm about his wife's waist. "Bodine men are thickheaded fools most of the time. Thank God we've got women like you to straighten us out." He kissed her cheek, then strolled away, leaving the pregnant woman speechless.

"If Travis loves me half as much as that man loves you, Lavinia, I'll consider myself a lucky woman," Hannah said, kissing her future mother-in-law's cheek, now wet with tears.

Travis stepped forward as Lavinia drifted to the other side of the room to where her husband stood with Willy knee-deep in conversation about the beneficial properties of alfalfa. "You can rest assured that I do love you that much and more." Nuzzling her ear, he whispered, "I'll be showing you a bit later, love. I'd do it right now, but we might shock the old folks."

Hannah giggled like a schoolgirl. "I dare say the 'old folks' know a thing or two about making love. Lavinia didn't get that swollen belly from overeating, you know. And my parents have been indulging in some pretty shocking behavior." He grinned, then kissed her ear again, and gooseflesh erupted over her arms and neck.

"I hate being bested by those two old men on my

birthday. Guess I'll just have to do my damnedest to get you with child as quickly as possible."

It wasn't just Hannah's heart that swelled with joy. Other parts of her body were starting to feel mighty uncomfortable as well, and that need was reflected in her eyes and in Travis's. Caressing his cheek, she replied breathlessly, "Do you think you can make short work of the birthday cake Lavinia brought? I find I'm hungry for something else entirely."

"This birthday cake is delicious. I just never imagined eating it off of your stomach, love."

Travis licked frosting from Hannah's belly button and she giggled, her laughter turning into a moan of desire when his tongue trailed down her belly to tease the aching bud of her femininity.

"Oh, Travis," she murmured when she finally found her voice. "Let's turn this into a yearly tradition."

He looked up and arched a brow, fighting back a grin. "I was hoping to enjoy this delectable pastime more than once a year."

Her face blushed to match the rosy hue of her naked flesh. "I meant eating the birthday cake in bed."

His look turned wildly erotic as he reached for a dollop of frosting and smeared it on her most private part. "I didn't."

"Oh God!" She clutched the edges of the blanket Travis had spread out on the floor and reveled in the sweet torture his mouth and tongue inflicted upon her. When she didn't think she could stand one more second of it, he rose up and over her to take her hardened nipples into his mouth.

"You're so very sweet, Hannah."

"That's just the frosting," she couldn't resist saying, a naughty smile hovering about her lips.

"Making fun of my love words, are you? We'll see about that." He positioned his maleness between her thighs. "I think I know just the right form of punishment for a saucy wench like you." He wiggled his brows in what was supposed to look threatening, but she laughed. That laughter was short-lived as Travis buried himself deep within her, filling her with his love and passion and making her cry out.

Palming her buttocks, he lifted her off the floor, moving deeper inside her, stroking in and out, until he had her begging for mercy.

"Stop! I can't stand any more, Travis. Please!"

He plied her pulsing bud with his fingertip as they rocked in the age-old rhythm of the love dance. "Had enough punishment?" he asked. Driving in to the hilt, he took them both over the precipice of their desire as Hannah cried out her love for him and he for her.

When they were once again able to breathe normally, their heartbeats slowing to a more regular beat, Travis propped himself up on his elbow and smiled down at Hannah, basking in her contented expression. She was positively glowing.

"If you ever wear that look out in public, love, everyone in town, including your father, is going to know what we've been doing."

Her lashes flew up, and she smiled seductively, caressing his cheek. "Mama tells me that everyone in town already knows, including Papa. Careful he doesn't come after you with a shotgun."

"There's no need. I intend to make an honest woman out of you."

"Being a bit disreputable certainly has its charms," she replied. "But do you think we could make love in a bed once in a while? We've never done this in a bed. It might be a novelty."

He kissed the tip of her nose. "I'm going to buy the biggest bed I can find to furnish our bedroom, Hannah Louise. Then I'm going to keep you in it twenty-four hours a day."

Her eyes widened in mock alarm. "But won't we get hungry, Travis? I mean: twenty-four hours seems like an awfully long time to go without eating."

"Who says we're going to go without eating?" At her shocked gasp, he arched a brow, then added, looking quite pleased with himself, "In the immortal words of Marie Antoinette: 'Let 'em eat cake.'"

Chapter Twenty

T HE JURY HAD REACHED A VERDICT. THE TWELVE men sat stone-faced in the jury box, giving no indication as to what that verdict might be.

In their seats beside the defendant, Hannah and Travis waited restlessly for Judge Hix to take the bench and render the decision to the interested spectators in the courtroom.

"Looks like this is it." Rafe did his best not to appear as frightened as he felt. "Just want you both to know that no matter what happens from here on out, I think you did one hell of a job defending me. Thanks."

"If there's any justice in this world," Hannah said, her voice shaking with emotion, "you'll be going home to your wife and family this evening." She reached out to take his hand and gave it a comforting squeeze, praying with all her heart and soul that her and Travis's efforts had been enough.

Travis's face showed the strain of the past few weeks and the prospect of an unfavorable verdict. "I appreciate you saying that, Rafe. But Hannah and I want you to know that if things don't go our way today, we have no intention of giving up. We intend to appeal the decision all the way to the Supreme Court if necessary." He would never let his brother hang. Never!

"Well let's just hope it won't come to that. I'd hate to be the cause of delaying your honeymoon." Rafe smiled and held out his hand to Travis.

"Congratulations, by the way, little brother. Guess I missed out on all the festivities last night. Ethan told me that when everyone dashed into the room and shouted surprise your mouth dropped open so wide you could have driven a herd of wild mustangs into it." Rafe chuckled and shook his head. "Wish I could've been there."

"Glad they arrived then and not an hour later." Travis shared a meaningful look with his fiancée, who blushed in embarrassment at the thought of what had transpired between them the previous evening. Birthday cake would never taste quite the same again.

"My little brother is a fortunate man, Hannah Louise. Though I'm not sure he deserves you."

Used to the camaraderie and teasing that went on between the three brothers, Rafe's comment didn't faze Hannah one bit. "I intend to remind him of that every single day of our lives together."

Just then, Judge Hix entered the room, looking terribly officious. The clerk of the court ordered everyone to rise, halting their conversation. Travis leaned over and whispered to Hannah, "Remember that I love you.

No matter what happens I'll always be grateful for everything you did to help get Rafe acquitted."

She took great comfort in that as the judge asked the foreman if they had reached a verdict. Butterfly wings were beating hard inside her stomach, and her heart was pounding so hard she could feel it in her throat. She could only imagine what Rafe must be feeling. And Emma.

Please, God! she prayed. *Let Rafe be acquitted.*

Chester Garnett, part-time druggist, part-time dentist, rose to his feet and wiped his forehead with his handkerchief, trying not to sweat all over the paper he held unsteadily in his hands. His voice was shaky when he spoke. "We have, Your Honor."

"Will the defendant please rise and face the jury?"

The entire room held a collective breath as Rafe stood and confronted the jury of his peers. Hannah and Travis stood right alongside him, and she crossed her fingers in the folds of her skirt and whispered another silent prayer.

The judge reached out for the written decision, read it, then handed it back to the clerk, his impassive face giving no clue as to what the jury had decided as he instructed the nervous foreman, "Please tell the court how you find the defendant, Rafferty Bodine?"

"In the charge of first degree murder in the death of Bobby Slaughter"—Chester cleared his throat loudly—"we, the jury, find the defendant, Rafferty Bodine, not guilty."

"Praise God!" Lavinia's voice floated above the jubilant roar of the courtroom. "Thank you! Thank you, Lord!"

Just then, a defiant, wild-eyed Will McGrath jumped up from his seat, shouting obscenities. Before anyone knew what he was about, he pulled a derringer from inside his suit jacket and yanked Hannah to him, using her as a shield.

"You're not going to win again, Bodine. I'm here to see that you all pay for what you've done. Hannah Louise is mine. She always has been. And if I can't have her nobody can." The implication that he would kill her was obvious.

Hannah stood wide-eyed and terrified as Will held his arm firmly about her midsection, pointing his weapon at Rafe and Travis. "Please, Will! Don't do this," she pleaded.

"McGrath!" Travis shouted, attempting to take a step forward, but Rafe held him back. "Let her go."

"You Bodines think you're so smart, so superior to everyone else. Well, who's the brilliant attorney now? Who's the real hero?"

At the man's insane comments, Emma screamed. "Somebody stop him!"

Judge Hix bolted from his seat. "Mr. McGrath, put that gun away this instant."

Ethan used the chaos in the courtroom to sneak up behind McGrath. Knocking the derringer from his hand, he pushed Hannah out of the way, and tackled him to the ground.

"It's all right, Judge. I got the little bastard covered." Pulling McGrath to his feet amid a chorus of cheers and applause, Ethan winked at both his brothers, then dragged the screaming prosecutor from the courtroom.

Hannah wept softly into Travis's chest. "I can't believe he did such a thing."

"*Ssh.* It's all right. You're safe now." Travis shook his head, unable to believe how obsessed and desperate McGrath had become.

Hannah sniffed a few times, then said, "Let's not let McGrath spoil Rafe's victory." She gave her client a blinding smile. "Congratulations, Rafe. You're free."

With tears in his eyes, Rafe wrapped his arms about Hannah and Travis, thanking them profusely for saving his life. Then he spun toward his wife, who was standing right behind him weeping softly into her hands, and hugged her to his chest, saying, "It's over, Emma. We can go home now." She nodded, then threw her arms about his neck, clinging to him tightly.

Travis drew Hannah into his arms and mimicked his brother's action, kissing her passionately on the lips. "Thank you for everything you did, Hannah. I couldn't have done this without you."

Tears of joy and relief glistened in her eyes as she smiled up at him. "Yes, you could. But I'm glad I was able to help. We make a good team, counselor, and I wouldn't have missed this day for anything."

The courtroom became a mass of frenzied excitement. No one paid Judge Hix, who was banging his gavel frantically and shouting for order in the courtroom, the least bit of attention. No one saw him shrug his shoulders, toss the gavel up in the air, and say to the clerk, "Get me a ticket back to Dallas. This isn't a courthouse; it's a nuthouse."

Olive appeared suddenly at Hannah and Travis's side, snorting her disdain at them. "You've damaged Will emotionally, I'll have you know. I hope you're both pleased with your handiwork." She hurried out of the courtroom toward the jail without a backward glance.

The couple exchanged startled looks. "I'm not sure which one of them is more deranged," Hannah said, shaking her head in disbelief. "I can't believe Olive is actually defending McGrath's actions. The man could have killed someone."

Hannah thought it tragic that Olive couldn't see that Will had only been using her to further his own goals. Despite everything, she felt sorry for the woman, who was an innocent pawn in Will's deranged machinations.

Travis had died a thousand deaths when McGrath had tried to take Hannah hostage. No amount of punishment would be too severe for the bastard. "I intend to do everything in my power to see that McGrath is put away for good. With charges of attempted kidnapping and murder against him, it shouldn't be difficult to get a conviction and to have him permanently disbarred. The man is scum."

Hannah kissed him on the cheek. "I don't want to worry about Olive or Will one moment longer. I just want to concentrate on us."

Travis's eyes warmed. "Me too," he replied, kissing her again. "Shall we go home?"

She nodded. "But first I need to speak to my parents. I'll only be a few minutes."

Hannah had no sooner walked away when Margaret Willoughby sidled up next to him, looking as devastated as Olive had just moments ago. "I understand you and Hannah Louise Barkley will soon be announcing your engagement, Travis." Her lips puckered in distaste, and she looked like she was sucking a tart lemon dry. "I must say that I am quite surprised to hear that. I assumed after the last time Miss Barkley broke your heart, you would have had more sense than to allow her to trifle with your emotions again."

"I love her. We love each other. What else can I say, Margaret?" He spotted Hannah across the room discussing the verdict with her father, and his heart swelled with pride and love. "She's an extraordinary woman. A man would wait five lifetimes, let alone five years, to be married to a woman like that."

Disappointment etched deep lines into the spinster's face. "Then I guess we have nothing further to say. I did so hope that things would work out differently between us, but I can understand a man like yourself falling prey to artifice and womanly wiles." With as much bravado as she could muster, she spun on her heel and departed.

Travis felt sorry for Margaret. She was an unhappy woman who had apparently read something into their relationship that just wasn't there, had never been there. But he wished her well nonetheless and hoped that she found someone with whom she could share her life.

He could afford to be generous. Everything he'd prayed for, dreamed about, had come true: Rafe had been acquitted of murder, and he'd been instrumental in helping to achieve that, the woman he loved more than life itself had agreed to marry him, and he'd finally won the respect of his father and brothers. Maybe he'd always had the latter, but today he felt validated by what had occurred.

Lost in thought, he didn't hear Hannah approach until she was standing right next to him. She looked ebullient but exhausted. "Are you ready to go, Travis? I believe there's to be a celebration of sorts at your parents' ranch later today."

He wrapped his arm about her shoulders. "I'd much rather be alone with you, love. But knowing Pa, it's going to be a humdinger of a party and one we shouldn't miss."

"I wouldn't dream of missing it. You're sure to be given a hero's welcome upon our arrival," she said, patting his cheek. "And you deserve the recognition."

"Rafe's the hero, in my opinion. He might not have gone about things the right way, but he accomplished what needed to be done."

"Your family's lucky to have you, and so am I." She rose up on tiptoes and kissed his cheek. "I can't wait to become Mrs. Travis Bodine."

"Talk like that is going to get you ravished, Miss Barkley." The smile he flashed held unspoken promises.

"I was counting on that, Mr. Bodine."

At the party later that evening, Emmaline's youngest daughter, Pansy, rushed forward to wrap her arms about her father's legs, shouting, "Papa! Papa!" and Hannah Louise choked back tears at the joyous expression on Rafe's face as she observed them together.

"Oh, Travis," she said, heaving a sigh. "I'm so happy everything worked out as it did. Rafe and Emmaline seem so happy. And the children are ecstatic to have their father home again. Just seeing them together like this makes me believe all the more that truth and justice do prevail."

"I know exactly how you feel, love, for I feel the same way. Rafe is a wonderful husband and father. I only hope I can be half as good when the time comes." And he hoped that time would be soon. He was counting the days until he and Hannah could be married and start their life together. He'd waited five long years, he didn't want to wait five more minutes to make her his wife.

"I know something you're twice as good at now, counselor." The glow of their recent lovemaking still blushed her cheeks pink and shone in her eyes, and Travis grinned.

"Keep that kind of talk up, Hannah Louise, and I won't care that there's a roomful of people here. I'm going to—"

"Oh look!" Hannah interrupted with a smile. "There's Willy and Ethan." She waved at the couple, who began to weave their way through the crowd toward them.

"Pa must have invited half the county," Ethan said as he approached. "I can't recall ever having this many people in the house. In fact, I didn't know we knew this many people."

The turnout had been greater than expected. The noise level in the house certainly indicated as much. Travis raised his voice to be heard above the din. "I think Rafe would have preferred being alone with his wife and kids this evening, but Pa was determined to share the celebration with his friends and family."

"Well I'm glad he invited us," Willy said. "I could use some good food for a change."

"Your cooking's not that bad, Willy darlin'," Ethan teased. His wife leveled an aggravated look at him before spinning on her heel and heading off toward the refreshment table.

"Whoops! Guess I'd better go after her. She's been real moody lately. Lavinia says it's because of the baby."

Travis watched Ethan hurry after his wife, and he smiled, shaking his head in disbelief. It was still hard to believe that hard-as-nails Ethan, the feared Texas Ranger, had been tamed by a flower-planting horticulturist. "My brother's a changed man, Hannah."

"Well he's not the only one." She glanced at Ben, who had his arm wrapped around his middle son's shoulders, looking happier and more at peace than she'd seen him in a very long time. The trial had been hard on all of them, but it had been especially difficult for Ben, a man who kept his emotions hidden and his burdens to himself.

"I think your father's mellowed a bit. I guess the trial, and the fact that Lavinia's expecting their first child, may have soothed the savage beast, so to speak."

Travis laughed at her absurd conclusion. "I think it's the whiskey that's mellowed Pa. He's still as cantankerous as ever. I'd wager a bag of gumdrops on that."

Ben was staring down at his wife, and the look of adoration on his face said that Travis was very much mistaken. People changed. Travis had. Rafe and Ethan had. She certainly had grown for the better. So why not Ben? "I'll take that wager, counselor."

His brow shot up. "And if you lose?"

"I won't. But on the off chance that you're right and I'm wrong, I'll buy you a steak dinner."

Travis had no more shaken Hannah's hand to seal the agreement when his father ordered the fiddler to quit playing and called for quiet in the room. "Pa hates speeches. So this must be real important," he whispered, clearly puzzled by the older man's behavior.

"I daresay it is," Hannah replied, a secretive smile touching her lips.

"First off, I'd like to thank everyone for coming to share in our joy about Rafe getting out of jail. We owe a debt of gratitude to our son Travis and his new fiancée, Hannah Louise Barkley." Ben introduced the happy

couple, who smiled gratefully amid boisterous cheers
and shouts of "Congratulations!"

"Thank you." Travis held Hannah close to his side.
"I'm the luckiest man in Misery, though I think my
brothers and father might argue that point."

"Damn right we would, boy!" Ben slapped his
youngest son's back, then said, "As most of you know,
my wife Lavinia is expecting our first child in a few
months. You probably also know that I've been acting
like a horse's ass since hearing the news."

"You've always been a horse's ass, Ben," shouted
his best friend and neighbor, Will Masters, and everyone
roared again.

Lavinia's hands flew to her crimsoned cheeks, and
she smiled almost shyly at her husband.

"Bring it in, boys," Ben directed his eldest sons,
then said to Will: "Shut up! I'm trying to make amends
to the little woman here." Everyone laughed again, then
the patriarch of the Bodine clan cleared his throat. "As I
was saying, I've been a fool lately about this baby
Lavinia's carrying. I want to set the record straight and
let everyone know that I'm real proud and happy that
I'm going to be a father again." He held out his arms to
his wife who rushed into them.

"Vin, I hope you'll forgive a foolish old man?" She
nodded, too emotional to speak, and he kissed her on the
lips. "In that case—" He signaled to Ethan and Rafe,
who brought forward a beautiful maple cradle that had
been fashioned by his own hand as a surprise for his
wife. Ben had intended to give it to her at the birth of the

baby, but decided that this would be a far more appropriate time.

"This is for our new baby, Vin. I hope you like it. I made it myself."

Spying the cradle, Lavinia gasped, then burst into tears. "Oh, Benjamin! It's just beautiful. I can't believe you made this for me." She ran her hand reverently over the smooth wood. "Thank you for this and for everything else," she whispered, kissing his cheek. "I love it and you."

Hannah witnessed the entire exchange with tears falling down her cheeks. "That's the most beautiful thing I've ever heard or seen," she said, sniffling several times.

The three brothers exchanged grins, then Travis said, "I hope you're not expecting me to build a cradle when our first baby's born, because I'm not *that* good with my hands."

Wilhemina giggled. "That's not what I've been hearing, Travis," and Hannah Louise turned three shades of purple.

Emmaline cast her sister-in-law a stunned look. "I think your husband's been a bad influence on you, Wilhemina."

Laughing, the two couples wandered over to the other side of the room to get some refreshment, leaving Travis and Hannah alone.

"I feel so blessed, Travis. Mama and Papa are back together, we're going to be married, and I finally get to be part of this crazy, wonderful family of yours. I couldn't ask for anything more."

Drawing her to a secluded corner of the parlor, he kissed her passionately on the lips. "I love you, Hannah. Always have and always will. The only thing that'll make me even happier is when we have our first child."

She caressed his cheek. "I can't wait to bear your child. You're going to make a wonderful father, Travis. I hope your son looks just like you."

"You're not pregnant now, are you?"

His look was so hopeful, it went right to her heart. At that moment, she wished she could tell him what he longed to hear. "No," she said softly. "But I'm going to work very hard to get pregnant just as soon as we're married."

"Then let's get married. Now. Tonight. I don't want to wait a moment longer."

Her eyes widened. "Tonight? Who would marry us on such short notice?"

"Your father," he answered without hesitation, indicating that he'd given the matter a great deal of thought. "He'd be the perfect choice."

"My mother would have an absolute fit. She's been dreaming about our wedding for years. I couldn't deprive her of it. Why, she's already compiling her guest list. Even Maude is getting excited about it."

He sighed in defeat. He might have been able to argue with one woman, but three was impossible. "All right. I'll give you one month. Not a moment longer."

"It's a deal. As long as both Emma and Willy can

be bridesmaids. And I think Miriam and Miranda will make the most adorable flower girls. And Pansy can be the ring bearer—" Daniel and David could be ushers. She tapped her chin, considering all the possibilities.

"Are you always going to be this hard a negotiator, Miss Barkley?"

"Indeed. Which reminds me: you owe me a bag of gumdrops. I believe I proved beyond a reasonable doubt that your father has mellowed. And I expect you to pay up on your wager, counselor."

Pulling her into his chest once again, he kissed her passionately, then said, "It's going to be difficult being married to a lawyer. I can see it now. I'm going to have to keep my wits sharpened at all times. I won't ever get my way without an argument. And you'll no doubt make wagers that I'll continue to lose."

"Maybe," she said, her smile seductive as her hand drifted down his thigh to find him hard with need—a need as powerful and demanding as her own. "But I'll let you make love to me whenever you want."

He didn't waste any time accepting the offer. "It's a deal."

"Shall we seal our negotiation with a kiss then?"

She puckered up and was startled when he shook his head and said, "No, love," then swept her up into his arms and headed for the stairs, not caring that they were surrounded by a multitude of people. "What I have in mind is nonnegotiable."

"But what will people say if we leave the party like

this?" Anticipation made her voice breathless, her heart hammer.

"That I love you. That I want to make love to my fiancée."

She nuzzled her face in his neck and kissed him. "I want to make love to you, too."

After a great deal of oral debate, a meeting of minds and two rapidly beating hearts, some soft kisses and tender caresses, and a hard—very hard—won encounter, the negotiation was successfully merged, as were the two parties involved.

Epilogue

Misery, Texas, Christmas Eve 1880

"I CAN'T BELIEVE HOW BEAUTIFUL EVERYTHING looks and how wonderful it all smells." The tall evergreen had been decorated with red-velvet bows and strings of popcorn, and stood proudly in the corner. Beneath it rested gaily wrapped packages of all shapes and sizes that Hannah couldn't wait to unwrap. Fresh mistletoe hung overhead in each doorway, and the spiced cider simmering on the stove filled the room with a tantalizing aroma.

"This is going to be the best Christmas ever." Hannah Louise's bright smile lit the room as she stared out the parlor window at the falling snow and hugged herself tightly. "I prayed for snow, but I never expected any."

She hadn't expected to find herself pregnant with her first child either, but she was, and she couldn't wait to tell Travis the news. It would be her Christmas present to him. The one thing he'd been wanting for months. The one gift only she was capable of giving him.

"You've obviously got connections with the man upstairs, love." Travis tossed another log onto the fire. The pine caught immediately and burst into flame, crackling and hissing and adding to the warm, cheery ambience of the room. "Besides, it's supposed to snow on Christmas Eve. It's tradition. And you know how I like tradition. I can't wait to share my next birthday cake with you. I'm going to make sure it has lots of frosting on it."

She grinned at his teasing, then said, "I hope this snow doesn't slow down your family. The wind's starting to blow pretty hard out there." Wiping the condensation from the glass with the heel of her hand, she peered out and frowned. It was too dark outside to see much of anything, except the frozen flakes painting the glass white, and she worried that travel would soon be impossible.

"With Mama and Papa still second honeymooning in Europe, I'd be terribly disappointed not to have Lavinia and Ben here." They'd become like second parents to her, and she wanted to share her and Travis's first Christmas with them.

"Have you heard from Fiona and the judge again?" Travis asked. "I still can't imagine the two of them traipsing all over Europe together."

Hannah's smile was ebullient and she nodded. "I had a letter just before you arrived home. They're in

France, having what Mama calls 'a romantic resurgence.' They've seen some wonderful sights, and Mama sounds deliriously happy. I can't wait for them to get home so I can hear all about their adventures."

"Well, if she's dragging your father all over creation, I don't know how deliriously happy he is at the moment," Travis replied, crossing to the window and wrapping his arms about her. "But if the judge is half as contented as I am, then he is indeed a happy man." He nestled her backside to him, resting his chin on her head.

The clock on the mantel chimed six, and Hannah's sigh was audible. "It's getting late, Travis. I expected Lavinia and Ben an hour ago."

"My family will be here, love. I promise. My brothers told me only this morning that they were planning to surprise all seven of the children by bringing everyone over in a sleigh."

"A sleigh?" Hannah squealed with delight. "How wonderful. You must promise to take me for a ride in it. I know little Luke and Benjamin Thomas are just going to love riding in it, as will the older children."

Travis smiled at her enthusiasm and promised to take her for a ride first chance he got. Then he said, "Imagine Ethan naming his son after Pa." He'd been totally but pleasantly surprised by Ethan's decision. "Guess my big brother's always had a soft spot for the old man and just never showed it."

"Both Emma's and Willy's babies are just adorable. I can't wait to hold them again." Emma's baby, Lucas, named after her deceased brother, was nearly three months old. Willy's baby was over two months, and both women were finding new motherhood much to their liking.

Lavinia had been a great help to both women during their respective confinements and had been lending a hand with the children when she could. Her own child would be arriving shortly after the start of the new year, and Ben had curtailed most of her activities. He had grown positively protective, and Hannah had no doubt that Travis would be of a similar state of mind when he discovered the news of her pregnancy. No doubt, he would insist that she retire from practicing law.

Since the success of Rafe's trial, the law practice she and Travis shared had grown considerably and was thriving beyond their expectations. And though she intended to be sensible during the latter months of her confinement, and after the child was born, she had no intention of quitting altogether. But she would perform most of her work at home, while Travis continued to use the office.

She had this wonderful idea about adding an office on to the rear of the house, but she wasn't quite ready to spring that on Travis yet. First things first.

"Travis." She turned in his arms and nuzzled his chin. "Do you mind if I give you my present before everyone arrives? It's special, and I'd like to present it to you in private."

"Something you made?" Hannah was always surprising him with love notes attached to bags of gumdrops, which he usually found in his briefcase, or flowers pressed into his law books.

She kissed his lips softly. "More like something we made together."

His brow wrinkled in confusion, then as her words became clear, his face lit with unabashed joy. "You're pregnant! You're going to have a baby! When did you find out?"

Her face mirroring his own excitement, she wrapped her arms about his waist and hugged him tightly. "I couldn't wait to tell you. Doc Leahy confirmed it when I went to visit him yesterday."

"And you kept it a secret for a whole day?" He seemed more astonished by that than the fact that she was pregnant. Hannah wanted to laugh.

"Merry Christmas, Travis."

He kissed her with passion and tenderness, then patted her still flat stomach, his face reflecting the awe he felt. "My son. You're carrying my son."

"It's my son, too, in case you've forgotten. And it just might turn out to be a girl."

"Not if I have anything to say about it."

"You don't."

"Is this discussion open for negotiation?" He kissed her nose, then her lips again, and she melted against him.

"I believe this baby is a result of one of our previous negotiations," she pointed out.

"As lawyers I feel that negotiating is probably the best way to settle things between us, don't you?" He pressed against her, the terms of her surrender clearly evident.

She reached down to touch him. "You drive a very hard bargain, counselor."

"I love you, Hannah."

"I love you more, Travis."

"Is that open for negotiation?"

"No. It's not."

"Then I guess I'd better just shut up and kiss you."

"I guess you'd better."

He did, most thoroughly, and when he was finished, she admitted, "I hear bells ringing." The Bodines' sleigh had arrived.

He grinned. "Damn, but I'm good."

"Yes, you are."

"Merry Christmas, love."

"Merry Christmas—"

"Are you ever going to let me have the last word?"

She shook her head and grinned. "I don't think so."

*A Special Note
from
Millie Criswell
to You*

Dear Reader:

From the time I was able to holler giddy-yap, I've been a sucker for Westerns, As a child, John Wayne fueled my imagination of what a real Western hero was like, then Clint Eastwood took over in my formative years.

Now that I've—ahem—matured, I write my own Western heroes—men like Rafe Bodine in DESPERATE (July 1997), who's been compared to "John Wayne at his most gallant," by *Publisher's Weekly*. Well, let me tell you that to have one of my heroes compared to John Wayne, everybody's ultimate Western hero, was quite an honor and a thrill . Then there's Ethan Bodine, the woman-hating Texas Ranger from DANGEROUS (February 1998), whose flinty-eyed stare could melt snow in mid-winter. I sure as heck wouldn't have minded trading places with heroine Wilhemina Granville and riding the trail with him! Last, but certainly by no means least, is lawyer Travis Bodine, whom you've just met in DEFIANT. A quiet hero, like many of the men who won the west, but a hero just the same. (And my mother always told me to watch out for the quiet ones).

1

Readers are always curious to know where authors get their ideas from. Well, you may be interested to learn that I conceived the idea for the three Bodine brothers after watching an episode of the REAL WEST on the Arts & Entertainment Channel. Kenny Rogers was relating the story of the notorious Clanton brothers when suddenly that little spark of inspiration went off that compelled me to write a series of books about brothers on different sides of the law. Hence: the "Lawmen" trilogy was born.

Readers often find series books frustrating, complaining that the story leaves them hanging, or they can't find the other books in the series. Keeping that in mind, I took special care to make sure that each book in the "Lawmen" trilogy stands on its own, with each story line resolved at the end. You won't ever be left dangling at the end of one of my books. That's happened to me a few times, and I agree that it's awfully frustrating.

All the books of the "Lawmen" trilogy, or my previous "Flowers of the West" trilogy, WILD HEATHER, SWEET LAUREL, and PRIM ROSE are still available and can be ordered from your local bookstore or directly from Warner Books.

You can read an excerpt from these books or learn about upcoming titles by accessing my web site at http://www.1q.com/romance/millie.

Now that I've completed two successful trilogies, I've decided to turn my hand once more to writing books with an individual flavor. TRUE LOVE, scheduled for release in the spring of 1999, is a heartwarming Western romance featuring a dime novelist named Emily Jean Bartlett and former Wild West performer, Jess Murdock, a legend in his own time, and the reluctant subject of Emily's next book.

As an author, you can imagine what fun I had with Emily's character as she sets out to turn the publishing world on its ear and drive Jess Murdock crazy in the process. It was fascinating to delve into the world of publishing as it was in the late 1800's, and to discover the similarities that exist with the publishing business as it is today.

I was quite surprised to learn that bestseller lists actually existed as early as 1895 and that the list encompassed over 16 bookstores nationwide. Quite a feat, considering the lack of computers and fax machines at that time! Editors acquired manuscripts much the same way they do today, and authors still faced the daunting prospect of making deadlines.

I hope you'll find the publishing history aspect of TRUE LOVE every bit as interesting as I did. By the way, TRUE LOVE derives its title from the fictitious Montana town where the book is set, and you'll learn how and why the town got such an unusual name when you read the book.

Since I write historical romance, I thought you might be interested to learn a little bit about my own history, romance included! I've been happily married for twenty-nine years to my hero/husband Larry, who fancies himself the subject of all of my books. (I think it was rather smart of me to let him thank that, don't you?) We have two grown children and one neurotic, but lovable, Boston Terrier named Jesse James. (See, I told you I was a sucker for Western heroes, or rogues, as in this case). Our oldest child is a practicing attorney and my son is presently enrolled in law school. Neither child is married, so we have no grandchildren to spoil as yet, but we're ever hopeful.

As I stated earlier, for those of you with Internet access, you can read all about my upcoming and existing books on my web site at http://www.lq.com/romance/millie. Or you can write to me directly in care of Warner Books and request a copy of my newsletter.

I'm very grateful for all of your cards, E-mails, and letters! I devour each and every one when they arrive, and I do my best to answer them in a timely fashion. I'm as fascinated to learn all about you, my reader, as you are to learn all about me. So keep them coming!

Thanks for allowing me and my characters to come into your life and spend a few hours with you. I hope you thought it was time well spent.

Until next time, I bid you Happy Reading!

Millie Criswell

FALL IN LOVE WITH AWARD-WINNING AUTHOR MILLIE CRISWELL

Flowers of the West Trilogy

- *WILD HEATHER*
  (0-446-60-171-3, $5.99 USA) ($6.99 CAN)
- *SWEET LAUREL*
  (0-446-60-172-1, $5.99 USA) ($6.99 CAN)
- *PRIM ROSE*
  (0-446-60-323-6, $5.99 USA) ($6.99 CAN)

The Lawmen Trilogy

- *DESPERATE*
  (0-446-60-415-1, $5.99 USA) ($6.99 CAN)
- *DANGEROUS*
  (0-446-60-497-6, $5.99 USA) ($6.99 CAN)
- *DEFIANT*
  (0-446-60-498-4, $5.99 USA) ($6.99 CAN)

AVAILABLE AT A BOOKSTORE NEAR YOU FROM

WARNER BOOKS

Fall in love with Joan Wolf

❦

"Romance writing at its best."
—*Publishers Weekly*

○ **THE DECEPTION**
(0-446-60-275-2, $5.99 USA) ($6.99 Can.)

○ **THE GUARDIAN**
(0-446-60-276-0, $5.99 USA) ($6.99 Can.)

○ **THE ARRANGEMENT**
(0-446-60-479-8 $6.50 USA) ($8.50 Can.)

○ **THE GAMBLE**
(0-446-60-534-4 $6.50 USA) ($8.50 Can.)

AVAILABLE AT BOOKSTORES EVERYWHERE
FROM
WARNER BOOKS

907-C

DOROTHY GARLOCK
TOUCHES YOUR HEART AND SOUL

Award-winning, bestselling author Dorothy Garlock brings romance and passion alive as no other author can! You'll love Dorothy Garlock's breathtaking romantic adventures.

"A gifted storyteller." —*Chicago Sun-Times*

- *ALMOST EDEN* (0-446-36-372-3, $5.99 USA) ($6.99 CAN)
- *ANNIE LASH* (0-446-60-303-1, $5.99 USA) ($6.99 CAN)
- *DREAM RIVER* (0-445-20-676-4, $5.99 USA) ($6.99 CAN)
- *FOREVER VICTORIA* (0-446-36-183-6, $5.99 USA) ($6.99 CAN)
- *A GENTLE GIVING* (0-446-35-990-4, $6.50 USA) ($7.99 CAN)
- *GLORIOUS DAWN* (0-446-36-182-8, $5.99 USA) ($6.99 CAN)
- *HOMEPLACE* (0-446-35-988-2, $5.99 USA) ($6.99 CAN)
- *LARKSPUR* (0-446-60-253-1, $6.50 USA) ($8.50 CAN)
- *THE LISTENING SKY* (0-446-60-252-3, $5.99 USA) ($6.99 CAN)
- *LONESOME RIVER* (0-445-20-362-5, $4.99 USA) ($5.99 CAN)
- *LOVE AND CHERISH* (0-446-36-524-6, $5.99 USA) ($6.99 CAN)
- *THIS LOVING LAND* (0-446-36-525-4, $5.99 USA) ($6.99 CAN)
- *MIDNIGHT BLUE* (0-446-35-522-4, $5.99 USA) ($6.99 CAN)
- *NIGHTROSE* (0-446-35-607-7, $5.50 USA) ($6.99 CAN)
- *RESTLESS WIND* (0-445-20-932-1, $5.99 USA) ($6.99 CAN)
- *RIBBON IN THE SKY* (0-446-35-989-0, $5.99 USA) ($6.99 CAN)
- *RIVER OF TOMORROW* (0-445-20-366-8, $5.99 USA) ($6.99 CAN)
- *THE SEARCHING HEARTS* (0-446-36-526-2, $5.99 USA) ($6.99 CAN)
- *SINS OF SUMMER* (0-446-36-414-2, $5.99 USA) ($6.99 CAN)
- *SWEETWATER* (0-446-60-255-8, $6.50 USA) ($8.50 CAN)
- *TENDERNESS* (0-446-36-370-7, $5.99 USA) ($6.99 CAN)
- *WAYWARD WIND* (0-445-20-214-9, $5.99 USA) ($6.99 CAN)
- *WILD SWEET WILDERNESS* (0-445-20-678-0, $5.99 USA) ($6.99 CAN)
- *WIND OF PROMISE* (0-445-20-368-4 $5.99 USA) ($6.99 CAN)
- *YESTERYEAR* (0-446-36-371-5, $5.99 USA) ($6.99 CAN)

AVAILABLE AT A BOOKSTORE NEAR YOU FROM
WARNER BOOKS